Over
Shadowed

Over Shadowed

K.W. Benton

Printed in the United States of America

First Printing, 2016

ISBN 978-0-9915662-4-2
Benton Books L.L.C.
Leesburg, Virginia, U.S.A.
www.kwbenton.com

Edited by Heather Capewell
Cover Art and Interior Design by Raven Tree Design
www.raventreedesign.com

To Ryan, Tucker and Zoë,
I adore you beyond mere words.

Acknowledgements

Thank you to my family and friends who have given their encouragement. A special thank you to the readers who pushed me through my internal debates helping me move forward. This book is for you.

Acknowledgments

Contents

Chapter One

Waking up in the middle of the night is disorienting, but finding the mother of one of your classmates sitting at the end of the bed can make you bolt upright. If that mother is known to be crazy, it might make you jump out of bed. If that insane mother sitting at the end of the bed in the middle of the night is dead, it might make you need rubber sheets.

"Good, you are awake," Mrs. Ackers says, in my head, as if she has been patiently waiting for a while.

"This isn't happening," I groan to myself.

"Nat, you need to help me communicate with Sara. That stupid girl does not recognize when I try to speak to her. This is very important," Mrs. Ackers insists. *"I need her to prepare for my return."*

"Mrs. Ackers, I'm not going to help you out for a few reasons. The first being, I'm desperately hoping you're a figment of my imagination. The second being, I don't help people who attempt killing my friends. The third and final reason being, I didn't like you when you were alive and definitely want nothing to do with you now you're dead. Particularly if it means you're coming back on a permanent basis. So, go ghosty somewhere else." I roll over and put a pillow over my head.

She stays for a while, trying to give me the heebee-geebees by knocking things off my nightstand and creaking open my closet door. Her attempts to persuade me, into helping her, go ignored. I am learning how to dismiss the dead. I hate that I have to admit this, but I see them. The dead I mean. Not all the dead; that would be excessive. Just the few who come find me for one reason or another. This is rather new, for me, so I am not clear on all the rules, but yeah, I can converse with the dead. That I meet. Don't ask me to have a chat with great Aunt Sally, to see if she will tell me where she hid the family silver. I won't get involved in all that. But I can see a few people who are no longer among the living. And some of them talk to me.

If you think I am okay with this, you are mistaken.

I would feel bad for Sara that this is her mother, but Sara was such a snot to my best friend. I can't summon a single pity for the girl. G.J., my best friend, had just moved here in January. She is a Witch. A real Witch is rare; I mean a black-haired-albino kind of rare. The attempt at murder was in an effort to use G.J. like a Duracell for Mrs. Ackers' own magic. See, Mrs. Ackers is or, I guess was, a Wiccan. Wiccans can only control the elements, fire, water, etc. But G.J. can pull any power to her and conduct it into magic. After G.J. moved here, the Wiccans in Mrs. Ackers' coven tried to attack her in retaliation—long story. But G.J. naturally absorbed whatever energy they'd tried to push at her. When G.J. tried to work power for something she was attempting to do, it would over cast. She did some hilarious stuff with only a thought. That chick cracks me up.

It all culminated in Mrs. Ackers trying to kill G.J.. So, you can see why, I am completely uninterested in doing anything for that nasty woman.

Our sophomore year is about to begin. Things should be smoother for G.J. this year. This is part of that long story. G.J.

is not just smart, but she is tall and absolutely gorgeous. She has no idea how people see her, which is part of her charm. She sees herself as an awkward geek. I let her roll with it. If she knew what half the boys in this town thought about her, it would make things more than a little uncomfortable. That is one of the ickier things about reading minds; you get to know way too much about people's secret thoughts. Sometimes, I really wish I did not know what kind of perverts I have to interact with on a daily basis. But since I am a psychic, such is life.

Why can I read minds? It is a family trait. My mom is a mind reader too. She keeps it on the down low, but everybody knows she can knock them out at the knees if she wanted to. Mom is very ethical about it. Me? Not so much. While I am not admitting to anything, if you could read minds, and people around you were taking a test, for instance, would you feel the need to study for an exam or would you possibly sit near the smartest kid and borrow some knowledge. Sadly, G.J.'s brain works way too fast for me to use her head. Before you try to pluck the first answer from her head, she is done with the test. Not that *I* would do such a thing. Insert evil grin here.

G.J. and I have trouble with boys. I guarantee you do not want to know what the nice boy in history class thinks every seven seconds. And heaven help you if you are in gym class with him. Let one girl forget her sports bra and the mental focus of the males in the room turns to steamy scenes and stripper poles, regardless of whether or not they normally think the girl is cute. My knowledge of people's innermost thoughts tends to put the kybosh on the romance department.

G.J.'s got her own issues. Most of our male friends have something extra going on in the paranormal department. Our town, Nine Mile Lake, is full of all kinds of people with extraordinary bloodlines. I've known most of my life, but it was a shock to G.J. and her Aunt Celia who is now her guardian.

Being in high school, I'm not above blackmail. You use what you've got to get by. I can be discrete. For the most part the powers that be in this town trust me, or my living status might be in question. Jack is my friend Adam's dad and Celia's husband; I know a whole bunch about him. The "Whoa!" kind of knowledge that would make anyone a bit edgy about being around that person. But one of the good things about reading someone's mind is I get all of it. The thoughts, the process of mind, and the emotions, Jack is a stand-up guy, even if some of the things he has done fall under … questionable.

Most guys who meet G.J. can't help thinking she is the bee's knees, so to speak. Smart, witty, compassionate, strong, womanly, and breathtakingly attractive, you can't really blame them. Adam and my other friend Hamilton are constantly vying for her attention. Not to mention Gus. Her suitor list is long and dubiously distinguished. They have no idea romance isn't on G.J.'s radar. If I ever get bored, I can go tune in to that group for a good laugh.

As far as I can tell, Celia is not anything special. She is pretty cool, don't get me wrong, but she has no unique abilities. Beyond G.J., Celia had no idea about this world until she married into it. That was quite the bombshell. I was not around for the great unveiling, but G.J. said it would have gone smoother had Celia not been pregnant. G.J. feels responsible since she had done some fertility rights while her powers were wonky, but I think that it was what Jack and Celia got up to than G.J.'s potential paranormal contributions.

G.J. is the only person who is okay with my perusal of her mind, because most of her thoughts are going to come out of her mouth. There is only one person I cannot read and he makes me crazy. Drake Aldrich! Please note, anytime I say his name, it sounds like an epitaph. He always rubs it in my face that I can't see into his head. G.J. and he are friends, so Drake is *always* around.

Have you ever been stuck in a friendship with someone you couldn't stand because they were in your circle? My frustration can be measured on the Richter scale. What is worse is he seems to be able to read me, and since that is my shtick, it makes me want to ball my fists and scream "Bwahhh!" every time he is around.

I like to know where I stand with people, and, since that is my normal, I do not cope well with being on unknown ground. G.J. has been practicing keeping her thoughts from me. I find the whole exercise amusing since she verbally erupts with everything that crosses her mind.

Drake has been there a couple of times when I was confronted with the no-longer-living. He was actually there when I had my first paranormal encounter. *That was awkward.* It had been during a field trip at the end of last year. Our ninth grade history classes visited the site of the 1974 World's Fair. It used to be the old rail yard in Spokane. Spokane was the outfitting post for most of the miners, loggers, and salmon fishers in the area. The town supplied people all the way up to Canada and into Idaho.

When they held the World's Fair, the city cleaned up a bunch of the old rail yards. It is kind of a cool place to visit, and I wouldn't mind going again, next time without the need to wear matching shirts with 200 of my peers. Why do schools insist on that? I guess it is better than having to hold on to one long rope so we don't wander off or get lost.

The trouble started because of Hamilton, but then again it usually does. G.J. and I were going to sit together on the bus, but he was trying to maneuver himself into the seat with her before I could get there. Sara grabbed his arm, which stopped Hamilton long enough that I almost squeezed past him to slide into the seat with G.J.. Adam, however, had a different plan and climbed over the seat and plopped next to her with a victorious grin. I took the seat across from them, and wouldn't you know it, already in that seat was Drake Aldrich.

"Nat, so good of you to join me," Drake said with that stupid smile I have grown to despise. Hamilton was towering over Adam and growling, completely blocking my escape.

"I'll leave in a sec. I JUST NEED HAMILTON TO GET OUT OF MY WAY!" this last I shouted at Hamilton rather than in reply to Drake.

"No need, this will give us a chance to talk," Drake said.

"Talk?" I repeated, squinting my eyes. "Why do you want to talk?"

"That is how people communicate," Drake said back with his smart aleck smile.

One of the teachers used the speaker system to direct Hamilton to take a seat. He sat in front of G.J., completely annoyed. I would have joined him, but Sara slid into the seat. Sara has a thing for Hamilton, if I failed to mention it before. The worst thing ever then happened. The teacher informed us our seat partners were our "safety buddies" all day long, and we should take that seriously, due to a recent uptick in disappearances of a number of people in the area. Meaning I was stuck with Drake all day. G.J. gave me a wince to tell me she was sorry. I groaned, Hamilton growled, and the only one of us that I could read who was truly happy about the imposed buddy system was Adam, who then put his arm around G.J.. This of course prompted Hamilton to want to remove said arm from Adam's body. Listening to the three of them was always worth a giggle.

"Something funny?" Drake asked, pulling my attention away from the soap opera beside us.

Losing my smile, I rolled my eyes sideways to glare at Drake. He was smiling still, but this time it was in a way that made me feel like he wanted to know what the joke was. Maybe? But how could I really know since I couldn't read his mind. Totally annoying.

It doesn't help that Drake is a handsome dude. He has dark hair and crystalline grey-green eyes, rimmed with thick, brown lashes. I try hard not to notice. He also has been student body president since before he was born. No one ever ran against him. The boy is just suave. He is the personification of that Dos Equis beer commercial guy.

I gave Drake my best scowl and focused on the people around us.

"I like where we are going today," Drake continued, as if I was paying any attention to him. "I have been down there a few times. Have you ever been?"

"What?" I asked in my why-are-you-talking-to-me tone.

"To that part of Spokane, have you ever been?" Drake re-asked.

"No." I said, and turned away.

"There are some cool things to see and do," he continued.

"Maybe that is why we're going there," I said in my singsong you-are-stupid-voice.

He laughed a little and said smiling again, "Maybe." He waited a few beats and said, "Did you pack a lunch?"

I held up the paper sack in my hand.

"Is that your favorite food in the world?" Drake eyed the mangled paper.

"It's a PBJ," I replied, raising my eyebrow in a silent are-you-an-idiot-question I have perfected.

"Well, I didn't bring a lunch. I was planning on going to Santé. So, since you are my buddy, you will have to join me," he dictated, like I had no say.

I glared at him from the corner of my eye. "I think we're supposed to stay with the group and I didn't bring enough money for that."

"It will be my treat. I'm sure I can persuade the chaperone of our need to eat," he said, smirking.

I rattled my paper sack. "I'm fine with what I brought. Wouldn't want it to go to waste."

He grabbed the paper sack and handed it to Adam, by leaning over my body. "Adam, Nat has this extra sandwich, you want it?"

In the blink of an eye, Adam had the bag open and had taken a bite out of my lunch so large half of it was gone. Through his mouthful, he mumbled, "Mmmanks."

G.J. smacked him on the back of the head and said in her drawl, "I swear, boy, there is no need for a disposal with you around. You ate half a farm for breakfast this mornin' as it is."

I left her to defend my now almost fully eaten lunch and turned on Drake. "You do know theft is a crime?"

"I promise to replace it," Drake said. "And I doubt you would press charges over a couple slices of bread held together by sticky condiments."

"Some things are about the principle," I shot back.

"Forgive me. Now I am obligated to pay for your lunch, though, so it's a win-win," he said.

"You mean you got your way and now I'm stuck doing what you want?" I grumbled.

"I like to think of it as an opportunity that both of us can benefit from," he said, and changed the subject, "You look nice today."

I glanced at his shirt, then down at the matching one I had on. I surveyed all of the other kids on the bus wearing the same thing. Feeling my one eyebrow raise, I turned back to him. "We are all in the same outfit. We look like a fertility treatment gone wrong."

Drake laughed. "You always have your own sense of style."

"What is that supposed to mean?"

"Exactly what I said, Nat, you are unique—"

"You mean, you think I'm strange." I narrowed my eyes in accusation.

"I didn't say that." Drake let out a sigh. "Let me try this again. You have your own way of dressing normally and throwing a tee shirt over top of you doesn't change the fact that you have your own style. A style I appreciate as being yours."

I skeptically eyed him. "Is that an insult?"

"I believed it to be a compliment. You work at dressing a certain way and I like it. The way you put colors together is distinctive. How can you possibly find that insulting?" Drake asked sounding slightly incensed.

"You didn't say you liked it previously, so how am I supposed to know," I said with a bit more hostility than was warranted.

"Why don't you change your assumption about how I'm going to treat you?"

"What?" I snapped at him.

"Have I ever been rude to you?"

I shrugged and looked away. "You did just take my lunch."

"I don't know what I've done to make you so angry with me all the time. Please tell me so I can stop whatever it is."

Drake almost sounded like he was pleading, but since I had no idea what he was really thinking I couldn't be sure. "I can never tell what you are thinking. It makes me crazy."

"Does it really bother you that much? I'm a pretty upfront guy, can't you just ask me if you need to know what I'm thinking?" Drake said, concern on his handsome face.

"No. People never say what they're really thinking. Except of course G.J. and believe it or not, even she holds back sometimes. So I will never be able to trust what you say or do," I explained.

"Never?"

"Ok, sometimes people say what they mean, but it's rarer than you might think," I defended my statement.

"No," Drake said, shaking his head, "I mean you will never trust me?"

Now I looked at him, as if he had not been listening. "How can I if I don't know what you're thinking?"

"You could just believe I'm starting from a good place, rather than assume I'm just a jerk all the time," Drake made the statement seeming nonchalant.

"See, that just proves my point. If you knew what people were thinking most of the time, you would never make that assumption. I'm not saying everyone is evil. But there are a lot of very selfish motives. There's a plan that somehow benefits the person. I'm not even touching on the truly vain or totally self-involved. Some people have simple motives or really enjoy helping others. You'd be saddened to know how rare they are. What I find amazing is those people don't have even the slightest notion they are so special." I was getting a little too melancholy, so I changed tack. "You also have to admit it's somewhat comforting to actually know what people really want when you have a conversation."

Drake stuck out his lower lip and nodded, as he scanned the passing scenery out the bus window, squinting his eyes against the sun. "I could be one of the 'Rare' ones." His gaze swung back. "Why don't you give me the benefit of the doubt?"

"Why do you care?" I turned toward G.J. and crew to escape conversing with Drake. G.J. was mentally running through her most recent Wicca lessons, Adam was running through a thorough anatomy of G.J.'s legs, and Hamilton was thinking about all the ways he would hurt Adam when we were off the bus and out of a chaperone's view. I was just about to move to Sara, when I caught the end of what Drake was saying.

"… know more." Drake looked at me in an expectant way.

"Pardon." I had no interest in this little chitchat.

Drake let out a deep sigh, his hot breath smelled of cinnamon and exotic spices as it warmed my face.

"Why don't we just pretend for today that I am a nice guy? You're stuck with me, might as well make the best out of it."

****

At the history museum, a uniformed woman raised her normal speaking voice to the breaking point so everyone could hear her. "Spokane was the great trading post in the northwest. Logging and mining companies used to make people pay to get a job, then fire all the workers and make them re-pay to get hired again. This and several other corrupt practices left the door open for the IWW, the International Workers of the World, or 'Wobblies,' to gain a strong foothold in Spokane. In 1909, it became such a problem the local government banned public speaking to crush the movement of Unions. Five hundred people were arrested. The Wobblies called for hundreds more to come to Spokane to overfill the jails. While unions were probably needed, the Wobblies took the idea of them to an extreme and wanted to overthrow capitalism entirely. This battle lasted for roughly eight years. In 1917, the Federal Government declared Martial Law."

This was somewhat interesting and allowed me to focus on the guide and not my safety buddy who liked to stand too close.

"Dude, could you not hover?" It was irritating that no matter how I fluctuated between trying to stay up with the group and dropping back, Drake was right by my side.

"We're buddies, it's my job." Again with that smirk.

"When did you become my helicopter parent?"

"I'm pro safety. What can I say?"

In one of my drop back moments, a man in old timey clothes asked me if I knew where the rally was and caught me off guard. The man asked the question mind-to-mind. While most people I know, know I can read minds in Nine Mile Lake. I do not run around with a palmistry hand and a 1-900 number on my shirt, so how did this guy know we could have a tête-à-tête mind-to-mind. I responded out loud, "I don't know about any rally."

Drake looked down at me. "Rally?"

The man mentally connected, his eyes full of bewildered confusion and more questions than he asked: *"Why are so many of you wearing the same clothes?"*

"It's a school trip," I answered.

"What school is so large?" the old timey man asked.

"Nat?" Drake asked.

"Like the shirt says, Lakeside," I answered.

"Nat?" Drake asked again, and grabbed my elbow to get my attention. "Who are you talking to?"

"This guy." I gestured to the man, but when I looked back, he was gone. I searched the street by swiveling my head first one way and then the other.

"Who?" Drake asked.

I shook my head and again searched for the man in the old timey clothes. Panic fluttered in my chest. You know, that moment when you actually question your own sanity.

"Nat, keep up, you slow poke," G.J. twanged from up ahead.

I walked briskly to catch up with the group. Drake, apparently, could saunter at any speed because he glided right beside me.

"What's wrong? You look like someone walked over your grave," G.J. asked.

"Can I talk to you a minute *alone*?" I had to tell her what just happened.

"Sure." As she pulled me away from the group, she leaned down a little so we could talk quietly. This of course prompted Hamilton to follow. She glared at him. He didn't even twitch an eyebrow and stayed where he was.

"Hamilton, I am five feet away, and I'm completely capable of defending myself, as you are intimately aware. Leave us be. Sheesh, it's a wonder you can leave me alone long enough for my daily ablutions."

"Who says that?" Hamilton half-snarled, more because she was making him stay away than caring what she'd said.

"People who read more than comic books," she shot at him with her sweet smile.

Adam laughed, which made Hamilton walk over and smack him on the back of the head. The two of them began an impromptu wrestling match.

"What's wrong, honey?" G.J. asked, her concern back on me.

"I think I'm going crazy. I just had a conversation with someone who was *not* there."

"Shoot, is that all? I do that all the time. I talk whether or not there's a person around." G.J. patted my arm trying to make me feel better.

"No, I mean, there was a guy, in old time looking clothes, he spoke to me mind-to-mind, then vanished. Poof. Gone. And Drake never saw him."

"She's right. There was nobody there," Drake sounded from right behind us.

G.J. and I jumped.

"Drake, honey, I don't think you being here qualifies for us speaking 'alone,'" G.J. said to his loitering.

"I'm her safety buddy. I have to stay with her all day." Drake had his arm halfway around me.

I squinted my eyes and looked up at him telegraphing, touch-me-and-die. Drake lowered his arm, but still stood close enough I felt heat collect between us. I shivered and moved to the other side of G.J.. One corner of Drake's mouth pulled up in that half smile. *I told you totally infuriating.*

G.J. said, "Don't worry about this now. I'm sure it was nothing a'tall. Stay with us and if it should happen again, let me know." She laced my arm though hers. "Drake, you and Adam are now safety buddies. Nat is mine. No arguments."

I love G.J..

"I owe Nat lunch," Drake launched his protest.

"Adam packed our lunches this mornin', I'm sure I have enough to share." G.J. marched forward, me in tow, to catch up with the group.

"A body your size needs a lot of food," Hamilton put in, Sara giggling at his side.

"Hamilton, you should really use a fork and knife to cut up that foot before you stick it in your mouth. I'd just hate it if you choked one of these days," G.J. dropped on Hamilton, as if giving him an etiquette lesson.

Smiling, I shook my head as we passed Hamilton. Some things never change.

I did not see the strange man for the rest of the day. G.J. convinced me there was a different explanation than my marbles were rolling under the nearest sofa. Turns out, as usual, she was right.

Over the summer, it happened a few more times. The first couple had me convinced I was missing the straw in my Slurpee. Mrs. Ackers first appeared trying to get my attention. She is actually the one who explained she was a ghost, along with her idea she would come back from the dead. After that, I took the rest of them in stride. My usual method is to ignore them, except when someone is speaking in your head, you can't just plug your ears.

Chapter Two

G.J. used to live on my bus route two stops closer to school. Since she moved in with Adam, the bus ride to school has been incredibly boring. I mean, there are only so many times I can mentally invade the frustrations of the bus driver to distract myself from the daily chaos. I am surprised there are not more bus drivers who go wacko. What is it about riding around in a big, yellow tin can, with multiple teens, that makes some kids think it's time to throw paper balls and scream? It is not novel; we do this five days a week, people. My school system transportation familiarity has taught me when I have kids, there will not be a Griswold experience in our future.

G.J. and I have the same homeroom, which is our English class, and lunch again this year. But that is about it. G.J. is in every advanced scholastic program she can get her hands on. With all the things she has to learn, my brain would be full by the end of week one, but not my BFF. Overachiever is a minimalist's way of describing her. I, on the other hand, think cleaning the hair out of my tub drain is more interesting than homework.

Ms. Brilliant Pants gives me a wave, as I work my way to the seat next to her, but I wait to chat with her since her back is to me. She is talking to someone I don't know on her other side.

Ms. Stontz hands out this year's student handbook as the announcements play on a large screen at the front of the room. After a moment of silence, the announcers talk about upcoming events. "Good morning and welcome back, we hope you all had a great summer…"

The announcer loses me after the first sentence, and I skim the minds of my classmates, which is equally as boring. Everyone has a touch of anxiety about the normal school stuff. Some are exhausted from trying to wake before noon for the first time in several weeks. Others focus on what the announcer is saying, so I tune back in.

"Tryouts for jazz band will take place this Friday. The guidance department is launching a new initiative to help prevent runaways. Safe Zone is a web-based social media site through the school's connection portal. Students can discuss personal situations with the counselors using an anonymous ID. The staff hopes to help with the missing student issue that has grown in this area. If you know of a friend who is having trouble, speak up for their safety. Today's lunch specials are…"

Yeah, they lose me again.

"Who on earth believes they can get on a computer and have anything they communicate with the school remain personal?" G.J. asks in a hushed tone.

"About half the people in here, but they're the same kids who think only their friends can see their pictures on Facebook or their Snapchat pics actually disappear," I inform her.

"Honestly? There should be a class held on social media dangers. Naivety will crush you now-a-days." G.J. mentally prepares a syllabus for such a class.

Shaking my head, I turn my attention back to Ms. Stontz as she begins class.

"For attendance, please pass this around, and write your name on the position your desk is mapped out on this paper." Ms. Stontz waves the sheet, like a flag, before handing it out to the first student in the right front seat.

"This semester we'll be discovering American Poets, starting with the likes of Emerson and his influence on the compositions of Thoreau. We'll look at a vast spectrum of works from Frost to Poe, touch on Walt Whitman and Sylvia Plath, and hopefully will end with our more modern greats like Maya Angelou. I expect you to discover things you like about each work, and I hold no illusions there won't be some things you are not fond of in this section.

"Your job will be to explain why you don't like any work or why you do. We will explore the meaning in each poem. Some poems have taken on a life beyond what the author had originally intended. These fascinating specters of thoughts have lived far beyond the years' most of these poets walked the Earth. They have inspired paintings, sculptures, movies, and other modern literature. Poetry is a true *art* form. Many times the work becomes greater after the death of the author. Much like with paintings."

G.J.'s pen scratching is the harmony to Ms. Stontz melody of monologue as she furiously writes notes. It's day one and she already does more work than I plan on for the whole year. In her head, she's quoting poems about a lake, two paths, and a creepy heartbeat. Blech. Bored, I peruse the room to my other side: a disheveled boy slumps in his seat. When my eyes meet his, he mentally says, "*Hey,*" in rather a surprised tone.

"Hey," I reply out loud, letting him know I don't like the nonverbal communique.

G.J. asks, "Did you say something?"

Responding to her, I say, "I just said, 'Hey.'"

G.J. leans toward me, as if she is about to ask a question, but Ms. Stontz says something, compelling G.J. to add to her already full page of notes.

I focus back on the kid next to me. His hair is matted on one side and sticks up, like his last comb was a pillow, and food stains dribble down the front of his shirt. If he cleaned up, he would be a decent looking guy. I am glad he doesn't smell. Nothing worse than being stuck next to the stinky guy in class.

"Hugo," once again, he's taking advantage of my mental mojo.

"If you don't stop, I'm going to take it as an invitation to tiptoe through your mental tulips," I hiss in an angry whisper.

"Nat, don't be rude. I'm trying to pay attention," G.J. admonishes me.

"It's not supposed to hurt, but it does." Hugo taps my brain again.

That is it. If this kid thinks I am going to play nice, and not figure out what he is thinking, he's nuts. I fully dive into his mind. As soon as I enter his head, violence hits me unlike any I've ever felt. Crashing panic, pain, euphoria, and confusion all swirl so I can't hold on to one thought. Terrorized, I pull out of this messed up kid's head. What in the world is wrong with him? I want to go back in and make sure there isn't a plan including firearms, explosives, and a map of the school, but I'm not brave enough to attempt connecting back with that vortex of awfulness. I will have to ask Principal Decker to keep an eye on him.

G.J. marks her name on the sheet and hands it to me. I write my name and hand it to Hugo the scary. He just looks at it. The paper crackles as I wave it for him to take. Again, he just moves his gaze from the paper to my face. I slap the paper down on his desk and ignore him for the rest of class. What a weirdo!

Just before the bell, I look over and Hugo is gone, the paper still untouched, sitting where I had left it. On the way out of class, I grab G.J. as she heads to her locker. "Dude, that guy next to me is a freak."

"What guy?" G.J. asks, as she spins the combination working to open her locker.

"Hugo the Unclean who was sitting on my other side from you," I explain.

G.J. stops putting her books away, facing me. "Nat? Are you feeling alright?"

"I'm fine, but I think Hugo could use a Twinkie-sized Prozac. I have never felt anything like that before." I shiver remembering. "He is truly disturbed."

"Hugo?" asks an all too familiar voice from behind me.

Ugh! "Private conversation happening here," motioning my hand back and forth between G.J. and me, I glare at Drake.

"I didn't mean to interrupt your gossiping, but I do need my books for my next class." Drake indicates I'm in front of his locker.

I tell G.J., "I'll catch you at lunch," as my way to exit.

"Sounds good," G.J. says, closing her locker and eyeing down the hall toward her next class. Her brain is always moving on to the next thing. "See you later, Drake." She waves to him absently over her shoulder. A swarm of letter jackets moves in around her and the masses scurrying to their ensuing period swallow her up.

As I walk away, Drake says, "See you at lunch, Nat. Have a good morning."

Why am I stuck with this guy?

Chapter Three

By the time lunch rolls around, I am less unsettled about the whole Hugo situation. Still think I should mention it to a guidance counselor, but what should I say? I think the guy is a nut bag just because? I'll ask G.J..

G.J. is already at the table, when I walk into the cafeteria. Since last year's discovery of food prep cleanliness issues, our group pretty much all pack lunches. She lights up her gorgeous smile and greets me, "Hey, Nat, how are your teachers so far?"

"They seem able to communicate." I shrug my response.

"Well that's a plus. I have a copy of *Nature* if you want to read it to get yourself familiar with Emerson," G.J. throws out, as if I have any idea what she is talking about.

"G.J., I think you should know something about me. If it isn't assigned, I'm not going to do it. I feel the need to point this out now so there is no confusion in the future about me joining a book club." She can be as academic as she wants; I enjoy a little down time.

Shaking her head, she asks, "So what were you saying about some guy in class?"

"What guy?" Hamilton asks, as he takes a seat next to G.J..

Rolling her eyes G.J. sighs and instructs, "If you would be so kind as to not interrupt, I would know what guy."

Hamilton puts his hands up in mock surrender.

"Lunch bag not even opened and you are giving up?" Adam joins the group and taunts Hamilton.

"Hey Adam," G.J. welcomes him. "I think I have your sandwich." She hands him what looks like a four-inch thick ball of meat stuffed between two slices of bread.

Adam, who has already opened his lunch, hands G.J. what is left of her partially eaten sandwich. "Sorry," he mumbles into the back of his hand, swallowing the half-chewed bite.

"Boy, your mouth collects more food than a black hole does matter." G.J. shakes her head as the rest of us piece together what she means.

Hamilton, annoyed, puts his massive sandwich in front of G.J.

"Hamilton, honey, I appreciate the gesture, but I can't fit all that in my stomach."

"You have plenty of room in there for that and more," Hamilton replies. Sadly, he's completely serious.

"Hamilton, you are truly an idiot," I chime in, while G.J. sits blinking unable to respond. Hamilton and his offensive comments are one of the few things that will make G.J. lose the ability to speak. What is worse is he has no idea what he says is a problem until he sees her reaction.

G.J. mentally shakes herself. Attempting to change the subject, she turns her back to Hamilton, sliding his sandwich in his direction, and focuses on me. "So what guy were you talking about?"

"The one who was sitting next to me. He said his name was Hugo," I explain, as Drake takes a seat next to Adam across from me.

"Hugo Garet?" Drake asks with a concerned tone.

"He didn't give his last name," I begrudgingly respond.

"I didn't see him." G.J.'s forehead begins to crinkle, her

gaze moving from one of our lunch partners to another indicating they should all pay attention.

"He was right next to me. Anyway, that kid's head is a scary place to be. All I got were terrorized emotions. I couldn't track a thought pattern. I am worried about what he will do." I am speaking to G.J., but all the boys at the table have switched on their wannabe-special ops team faces.

"Don't go in his head again," Drake commands, as if he has any say in what I do or do not do.

"Butt out," I shoot back.

G.J. grabs my arm to get my attention. "Nat, sweetie, I didn't *see* him."

"Nat, Hugo Garet is dead. He was one of the kids that went missing this summer." Drake drops that bombshell, like a cartoon anvil. "They found his body over the weekend."

My mind flashes to the boy in class. "Oh, God that wasn't food on his shirt." My few bites of lunch look to retrace their path out, and I put my hand over my mouth.

"Wow, you saw a dead guy in class. Awesome," Adam says.

Both G.J. and I give him our "Are you crazy?" look. G.J. grabs my hand and the back in a soothing way.

"Nat? Are you alright?" Drake asks, leaning across the table, reaching for me.

"I'm fine." I lean backward out of his reach.

"Sugar, you are nowhere near fine. Stop with the 'I'm too cool to freak out' nonsense," G.J. scolds me, giving me a half-hug at the same time. "Tell you what, come home with us today and we will work through this."

"She won't fit in the car," Hamilton says in his ever-helpful way.

"Then you will just have to walk." G.J. whips her head in his direction, her hair smacking his face with force as she glares at the huge boy.

"G. Don't worry about it, I need to talk to my mom first. If I feel up to it, I will come by later." As fun as it is to hear the two of them bicker, I'm not in the mood.

"Did Hugo say anything to you?" Drake asks.

I scowl at him. "'Hey.' 'Hugo,' and 'It's not supposed to hurt but it does.'"

"Well my creep-o-meter just hit eleven." G.J. wrinkles one side of her nose, pulling her lip up, her brow mimicking the action widening one eye.

"Have you seen him before?" Drake asks.

"I know his face from around, but I don't know the kid." My jaw is clenching and tightening my voice.

"No, I mean have you seen *this* version of him?" Drake persists.

"Leave it alone, Drake. G.J., I'm out of here. I'll call you later." I stand to leave.

Hamilton states flatly, "If you aren't going to eat your lunch give it to G.J."

It is G.J's turn to let Hamilton know he is a moron.

Chapter Four

Instinctively dodging my peers on my way to the gym for PE, I concentrate on examining my mental images of Hugo from English this morning. Now that I have some perspective, I know his shirt was covered in blood. I never saw the other side of his body. Maybe there was some kind of damage to explain what had happened to him. Mrs. Ackers' specter looked like she was heading out for lunch with the Rotary Club ladies. I don't think I have ever seen that woman without pumps and pearls. So why was Hugo such a mess? I am sure a wolf mauling would leave a mark.

I should have realized he was a ghost. This auto-mind speech thing should tip me off by now. I just wasn't expecting it, but really, I never expect to talk to the dead. They seem so life-like. Ugh! Even I have to shake my head at that. My whole body spins with the impact of hitting a very solid body. "Watch it." I shoot a sharp glare up, projecting perturbed at our collision, when I realize those bright blue eyes giving me just as much attitude as he was getting belong to my longtime friend.

"Oh, Gus, What's up?" I say by way of greeting, my annoyance forgotten.

"Nat..." Gus shuffles his feet and won't meet my eyes after our first glance. His black hair is mussed for the first time I can recall, and his milk pale skin appears kind of translucent. Grey veins visibly creep, like ivy, under the surface. Gus has been my friend for years. He has his own oddities, but he's a good guy, so I let his issues slide.

Finally focusing on me, he says with concern, "Hey, are you alright?"

"Well, if you consider seeing dead guys in English alright, then I'm cool." The tenor of my voice belies my unease.

"Are you talking about the authors?" Gus asks, confused.

"No, I saw Hugo Garet, the dead kid they found this weekend," I explain in faux nonchalance.

Gus' beautiful blue eyes grow so wide I am unsure if I will have to catch them as they fall out of his head. I instinctively reach for his thoughts. "*So hungry. Nat reads minds. She can't know. G.J. Danger. Get away!*"

Poof. Gus is no longer in front of me. Oh no! Is Gus a ghost too? Wait, no, part of the conversation was verbal. What just happened?

****

Between Gus' freak out and my newest poltergeist encounter, I simply go through the motions of the rest of my day. For the first day of school, the teachers seem to want to make you pay for having had summer vacation with the amount of homework they pile on. If this is indicative of the rest of the year, I should plan on zero social life. How many hours do they think are in a day?

Still in my own thoughts, I don't hear my name called until someone grabbing my arm stops my momentum.

"Are you all right?" Drake asks, worry in his eyes when they meet mine.

I shrug.

"Seriously, I am worried about you. This has to be disturbing you. Please, Nat…" Drake stops and lets go of my arm. "Just…" He starts and stops again, adjusting his backpack on his shoulder. "Just know, if you need to talk to someone… I'm here."

"I'm gonna miss my bus." I walk away. Like if I needed to chat he would be the one I would go to.

On the bus ride home, my cell vibrates in my pocket. I wriggle it out. Why are girls' pockets so stinking small? "Hey, Gus, what happened earlier? Where did you go?" I jump in with no preamble.

"Sorry about that, I remembered I had to be somewhere." Gus' voice sounds like he is hedging.

"Huh, like anywhere but near me?" I push. I have known Gus for a long time, he is one of my best friends, and it hurts to think he wouldn't want to be near me.

"Nat," Gus lets out a deep sighing noise, "Sometimes you shouldn't poke around in other people's heads, and I can't trust that you won't."

Well, I am totally busted there, might as well own up. "You're right. I try to give you space because I know you aren't a big fan of me perusing your mind. And I wouldn't have if you had not looked so scared when I mentioned what I had seen."

Gus aggressively fires, "What did you see?"

"I told you, I saw that Hugo Garet kid. And he was a mess." I try to remain calm, but I can almost feel Gus' tension through the wireless connection.

"No, Nat. In my thoughts, what did you see?" Gus' tone is quiet and scary. I have never been afraid of Gus, but there is a first for everything.

"Not much." Now I am the one hedging.

"Natalia." Gus uses my full first name, which has the opposite effect of what he wants.

"Augustine," I smart mouth back. "You aren't my teacher, or my Dad, so don't try to get all superior with me. But just so we are clear, I will be having a chitchat with G—"

Before I can even get out the second letter of my BFF's name Gus goes bananas. I hear this loud smashing noise, as he screams, "You will say NOTHING to her."

"Gus, what the hell? Are you threatening me?" I am truly stunned.

"Nat—" I hear him inhale deeply in an effort to calm down. Changing his tone to a pleading note, he says, "Don't discuss anything with her. She is too—" Gus releases another big sigh. "—Just don't."

"Gus, what is going on?"

"Things are difficult right now. I'll be in touch." And with that big ball of cryptic vagueness, Gus cuts the connection.

The bus slows and, glancing around, I realize we are at my stop. I slide my phone back into my pocket, when I stand, and head home. Well when life starts to go wonky, it really goes. I have to wonder if M. Night Shyamalan is secretly filming my life in order to regain his former glory. As I near my house, I sense people in my way, and with my head down, move to go around them.

"Stop." I hear in my head. Crap. I look up into the face of Hugo the Messy. He is not alone and he, nor his new cohorts, is as solid as he had been at school. They are all flickering, like a bad projector image.

"What?" I say a bit too loudly.

Across the street, other kids who got off the bus turn and look at me. Great, nothing like being the crazy person at your high school. I look back at the three images in front of me.

"You can see." All three of them connect to my brain at the same time, creating this odd chorus in my head.

I shake it to lose the sensation. In a much quieter tone, and trying not to move my lips overly much, so it doesn't look like I am completely bonkers I implore my newfound friends, I ask, "What is it you want?"

"See," is the only response.

I look carefully at the other two people with Hugo. One is an old man who looks homeless, and the other... well, let's just say I am certain she made her money in a horizontal position. *Wow, where would you even buy a getup like that? Really, Nat,* I ask myself, *critiquing the outfits of the dead?* That has to be a new low. "I see you. Now what?"

The trio says again, in my head, but louder this time, *"SEE!"*

A wave of energy rushes toward me in a gust of wind. My senses hit overload, and I lose my connection to my physical surroundings. I feel the sidewalk tear skin from my knees, as I collapse. My brain is bombarded with fear, terror, panic, and pain; it's dark. It is unclear who the emotions belong to. Are they theirs or mine? Someone is invading my personal space. I am being torn apart. Violence. Overwhelmed, my mind shuts down.

****

The phone is ringing, and, in a murmuring voice, my mom answers, "Let me see if she is up." As she comes close to my bedroom door, her voice grows louder.

Wait? How did I get here? When I open my eyes, confusion takes hold. I was outside a second ago. Why is it dark?

"Nat? Sweetheart are you up for a call?" My mom is holding the phone to her shoulder to muffle the question giving me the chance to say no.

"Who is it?" my reply is scratchy with sleep.

"It's G.J.. She is really worried about you, as am I." Mom's silhouetted in the doorway.

"I'll call her back. Can I talk to you, Mom?" I ask, unsure of what I am going to say.

My mom tells G.J. I'll return her call in a bit and disconnects. She turns on my light and then comes to my bed. I blink against the brightness and focus on her as she sits. She rubs my hand that is outside my blankets.

"The neighbor saw you fall and came to get me. You are getting too big for me to carry. Your dad is flying home tonight, but I could have used him today." She smiles, explaining how I ended up here.

"Mom, I don't know what happened," I say, still confused.

"Can I just take peek?" my sweet, ethical mother is asking if she can read my thoughts.

"Mom, I am afraid for you too. I blacked out because of what these... people pushed into my head." I just can't bring myself to cop to the whole ghost thing yet.

"Who is pushing things into your head?" My mother's alarm is crackling in the room. "Nat, people should not be able to do that."

Sighing, I realize this is the moment of truth. "Well, they aren't exactly people. They were people."

My mom's face is now puzzled. "Were?'

"Mom, I have started seeing ghosts." There, I ripped off the Band-Aid.

"Oh Dear Lord." Mom stands up and backs away from me in obvious horror.

"Thanks, Mom, that's the love and support I was hoping for." My sarcasm is dripping, like a sieve full of syrup.

"Oh, Nat. Honey..." She is reluctant to come close to me, like I'm lying on a swarm of bed bugs. "Where is your father?" She looks to the door, as if hoping he will somehow appear and handle this.

"Okay, Mom, if you could stop freaking me out now that would be great." As if I wasn't already having trouble coping.

"Nat?" she asks in a whisper, "Are there any here now?" She looks around, reminding me of one of those classic Betty Boop clocks where Betty's eyes swing with the seconds.

"No, we are alone, for now," I whisper, mocking her ridiculous response.

"Sorry…" She rubs her hands down her pants.

I assume they are sweating from her fearful reaction. What a rock, my mom.

"Nat, I am sorry. I am sure you are more upset than I am, but, honey… you don't understand."

"Nope, I sure don't." I sit up higher, fluffing my pillow and resting back. "How about you clue me in?"

"I just never thought…" She starts and shakes her head. Taking a deep breath, she says, "You're my baby and we will sort this out together." I can actually see her straighten her spine, as if readying for battle. Awesome, my almost five foot tall mom, the warrior. Now I am brimming with confidence, not.

I take in a steadying breath, shaking my head. "Okay." I stretch out the word with all the air I need to expel.

"Nat. You know we are different," Mom starts awkwardly.

I nod. I'm certain if I speak now, her bravado will pop, like a balloon. Even though different around here is the new normal.

"Let me start again," she says, as if she has started at all. "We aren't human."

I close one eye and squint at her with the other in skeptical confusion.

"Humans can't read minds, Nat," she condescends, as if I should have already figured this out.

I sit quietly, waiting to hear the rest of this mind-blowing confession.

"We are the forgotten, some would say lost ones. Our kind left this world and we are who remain behind." My mom should really have her library card revoked. "Don't look at me like that. When I say that, I don't mean we are aliens. Aliens aren't real. We are what some call the wee folk. Others call us the Tribe of the Goddess Danu. Our world is not one of a different place but one of a different plane."

I rub my face with one hand massaging my temples with my fingers and my thumb. Am I still sleeping? As I slide my hand down, I look at my mother. She is still across the room and seems unwilling to get close to me. "Please get to the part that explains why you are acting like I am radioactive."

"Those of us who stayed in this world… We have no knowledge of how to exist in the other. That world is strange and unknown at this point. We stayed because we don't fit there. We fear returning there now. This world is where we belong." My mom's eyes implore me to understand this is vital.

"Okay, so what?" I ask, "You obviously know something that I need to know. Explain."

"Nat, the Shadow World is just that, another world. Another plane…" She looks at me, waiting for my brain to put it together.

"So I am seeing another plane?" I ask.

"You don't just see it, you can interact with it," Mom stresses again.

But I am simply unequipped to compute whatever equation she wants me to understand. I am so confused. "Interact?"

"Nat, if you can connect with one world, you can connect with all of them. It is just a matter of time. Among our kind, you are what we fear most. You are a bridge. You can create a space within yourself where the planes can cross. You could send us back. We cannot go back. Through you, beings from the other planes can come here. Nat, you can't let that happen. There are very good reasons the others left. They don't respect human life." My mother is still pinned to the far wall, as if by coming any closer I will fling her into another dimension.

"Who else is our kind? What do you mean they don't respect human life? Mom, I am still me. I won't hurt you. I don't even know if what you are saying is right. I mean other people see ghosts. Look at the TV. Half the shows have some guy with electronic equipment running around in the dark complaining about battery life. Are they all bridges too?" My nerves are completely frazzled.

"Nat, they are not our kind." She sighs. "The ones that left were driven out. Our kind, all of our kind, can live thousands of years. Human's lives are insignificant in comparison to some of the others. When they walked this world, they brought tremendous destruction. They held no concern for any repercussions, they found it entertaining to cause conflict. A small group of us cared for the humans. We saw value in their short lives and the creativity and passion held in them. There used to be many bridges and crossing back and forth was nothing. But when it became clear that this was not the way it should be, bridges were abolished. With the help of the last known bridge, we sent the others all back. It was extremely difficult, and we know the others will return to seek revenge if they can open a new pathway. You, Nat, apparently are a possible conduit for their return."

My mouth catches between spluttering my objection that I am this bridge and the gaping awkwardly in imitation of a fish.

"The Shadow World is the closest of the other realms, the shades can push through the fabric of this world far easier than the beings from the more-distant planes if there is an eager hand reaching for them. However, you said, without searching them out, these shadows found you and pushed into your mind. That is not the same thing at all. It has been a long time since there has been a bridge they too had this kind of connection forced on them."

Her face slackens.

"Our kind left this realm thousands of years ago. Should the worlds cross again, chaos will descend." Mom's voice grows hollow and distant, as if she is pulling words from somewhere within her DNA, not from her mind.

"Mom?" I'm not sure if she is here or in some kind of trance. "When you say abolished, do you mean murdered?"

She shakes herself and focuses back on me. "I need to speak to your father. Nat, you know I love you, honey, but I am not sure we can be close to you right now."

"Pardon?" I could not have heard her correctly.

"Let me talk to your dad." She scooted sideways, not turning her back on me, as she makes her way to the door.

"Mom?" hurt owns my voice as I ask, disbelieving, "Are you really afraid of me?"

Tears slide from her eyes, and she closes the door without answering.

Dear lord, my mom is scared of me. My heart skins at the concept of my *mom* being frightened of me. How can that be? She knows me. What does she think I am going to do? Somehow, whatever just happened broke our relationship. A vital piece of our mother daughter bond is missing and I instantly mourn the absence.

Chapter Five

I spend the rest of my night trying to think of anything but my conversation with my mother. It gets so bad I actually do all of my homework. What is the world coming to? I come back in my room, after I leave my evening bathroom ritual. Tossing my clothes in my hamper, I see Hugo sitting on my bed. At least he is alone this time. I quickly close my door, and in an angry whisper say, "Go away! If my mom knows you are here, she will need a horse sedative."

"*See,*" he pushes into my head.

"Cool it, Bucko! I appreciate the invite to the waking nightmare experience, but I'll pass." My voice never rises above a hushed tone. "Get off my bed."

Hugo looks around, like he doesn't realize where he is. "*You need to see.*" His gaze tries to connect with mine as he stands up and moves away from my bed.

"Look, Garet, please don't do this to me now." I am so tired and don't want to handle anything else.

"*You know me?*" Hugo's rich chocolate eyes widen. .

"Sure, you used to go to my school. Before…" I stop. I really don't want to upset him by discussing his untimely demise.

"*It never seemed like you knew I was there.*" Hugo's feelings in his mental connection are that of wonder.

I climbed into bed and pulled up the covers. "Hugo, I know people are afraid of me. I am not always the one to strike up a conversation. I tend to make people jumpy with the whole mind reading thing."

"*I never realized. I thought you didn't believe I existed.*" Hugo shakes his head.

"Irony is a comical bitch." I can't believe he only gets the nerve to talk when he shouldn't actually exist.

"*You have dangerous friends. You need to see.*" Hugo pushes his fear at me again.

I squeeze my eyes shut, but it doesn't stop the dread. Ripping and tearing. Teeth pulling flesh apart. The faces of so many as life leaves them. I fall into the blackness that consumes my consciousness like quicksand.

****

When I head for the bus, Mom and Dad aren't about. I know it is going to be a rough day since I can barely keep my eyes open. G.J. has saved me a seat, when I get to homeroom. "Nat, honey? Are you alright? You look like a possum that's had a scuttle with a Mack truck."

"What a nice thing to say," I return.

"I don't have to be nice, I'm your friend. Real friends get to be honest. If you're gonna drag your fanny in here looking like sundried-pond scum, I get to openly mock you. Call it a perk. Now spill, what on earth happened to you? The boys said you had to be carried home by your mama from the bus," she asked in her typical G.J. manner.

Unable to hold back the yawn, I say into the back of my hand, "I had a couple run-ins with my own personal Casper. And my mom is terrified of me. It's a really long story. I'll get into it at lunch. By the way, tell the boys, thanks for not helping scrape me off the sidewalk"

"I think your mama may have wondered about roofies if a couple birthday-suited teens dropped you home unconscious."

G.J. never likes to talk about the pack shifting and ending up nude. For a girl who is the Beta of said boys, I would think she would come to grips with their lack of clothing.

"Are you going to make it to lunch?" Her face loses her characteristic humor and brow creases in honest concern.

"I'm young. I'll make it," I say with false confidence.

I stumble through my day. By third period, I am closing one eye, then the other, resting half my brain at a time. By lunch, I collapse at the table and put my head in my pillowed up arms. Someone sits by me, and I know instantly it isn't G.J. "Go away. I'm too tired to deal with you."

"Are you all right? I can tell you are exhausted," Drake says in his cool calm demeanor I hate.

I pop up my head to give him the stink eye. "How nice of you to notice. Don't worry G.J. already covered the finer points of me looking like road kill today."

"You could never look like road kill. You are, however, lacking that certain Nat zest for life I am drawn to," Drake says, as if he... wait... what?

I shake my head. "I really can't fight with you today. I just don't have it in me." I put my head back down onto my arms.

"I wasn't intending on fighting with you." Drake's voice sounds a little offended. It changes to sneaky. "So you can't argue with me?"

I shake my head, still down on my arms.

"So, if I were to ask you to go to dinner this Friday?" The boy actually sounded hopeful.

I squeeze my eyes shut tighter. Where is the trick? I lift my head slightly so one eye can see him. I'll be damned, he actually looks hopeful. "You… want to take me… to dinner?"

He shifts his attention away for a second uncomfortable. Takes a quick breath… for courage maybe, and he says, "Yes."

"Why?" My face communicates the are-you-nuts expression it should; I can feel it.

"Because, I do," Drake explains without explaining anything.

"Okay." I put my head down onto my arms again.

"Okay what? Okay, we are going to dinner? Or okay, something else?" Drake asks, like the answer is super important.

I pop my head up. "Okay if I make it to Friday without dropping on my feet, I'll go to dinner with you." I put my head back down.

"Hey, Drake, you look happy," G.J. says, taking her seat.

"I'm pretty happy," Drake says almost gleeful.

"If you act chipper, I'm taking it back, no way I'm going to dinner with a chipper chap." I laugh goofily at the stupidity of my statement.

"Nat, honey, I think you are getting a little slap happy," G.J. says, "Wait dinner?"

"What's for dinner?" Hamilton asks, as he, too, finds his seat.

"Doesn't matter what is for dinner, G.J. can cook anything." Adam bookends G.J. with his friend.

"Shut up," Hamilton grumbles at him, sullen that Adam gets to spend time with her that he doesn't get.

"I'm not making dinner. Nat and Drake are going to dinner." There's an I-want-details note in her voice.

"You guys are dating?" Hamilton asks in surprise, and that sends up my hackles.

"No!" I say as my head shoots off my arms, bringing me to fully alert.

Drake looks at me with what appears to be caution in his eyes, as if I am some small woodland creature he doesn't want to scare off. "I asked Nat to dinner and she accepted. I consider it a date." He pauses for a minute before carefully saying, "We'll see how it goes from there."

He gives a perfectly respectable answer; my tired brain can figure no way to shoot that down. My unease grows. A date? Drake considers it a date? This would be my first date. And it is going to be with Drake of all people. I peer at him sideways, as G.J. turns into, of all things, a girl at that moment. "What are you going to wear?"

I shoot her a die now look. G.J. carefully folds her lips in, to seal her mouth shut, and focuses on her lunch. Drake watches me, so I put my tired head back down onto my arms with my face toward him and close my eyes.

Drake takes a deep breath and lets it out slowly.

From across the table Adam laughs. "Dude, you are done for."

"Hamilton, feel free to shut him up at any time," Drake says.

I open my eyes in time to see Hamilton reach around G.J., careful not to touch her, and smack Adam hard on the back of the head. Adam's eyes glow and he glares at Hamilton, letting him know that shot wasn't free. I remember what Hugo said about me having dangerous friends and sit up quickly, my exhaustion causing my focus to spin before settling on the three across the table. My brain is flashing through the images of ripping and tearing Hugo and friends had put in my head. These guys spent half their time in the form of a predator. Big predators. I have seen them like that in G.J.'s mind. They are not the size of a normal wolf. Dear God, is it the pack killing these people?

"Nat, darlin' you feeling all right?" G.J. asks in all innocence.

She would never hurt anyone. I know that, know her.

"Uhhh," is all my tired brain can muster.

"Nat?" Drake's warm hand touches my back, solicitous.

I eye him. He must see the fear in my eyes. His face changes, hardens. "What is it?"

I look back at the boys, having always considered friends. They, too, look alert, as if wary of danger. Alert for danger because I feel fear, because they consider me their friend, too.

"Nat?" G.J. starts to get up.

I shoot up backing away from the table. "I've gotta go." I bolt for the cafeteria doors.

G.J. is right on my heels. It isn't fair that her legs are three times the length of mine. She catches up with me and pulls me around the nearest corner. "Okay, lady, enough is enough, if you don't tell me what on Earth is the matter, this Amazon is going to get grumpy."

Tears fall from my eyes, as I explain, "I am apparently a portal for doom and destruction. My own mom won't come near me. That dead kid, Hugo, keeps overwhelming me with violent death scenes. And says my friends are to blame. And even though I am not conscious, I'm not resting. I am lying there terrorized for hours. I only have so much adrenaline."

G.J. wraps me in a big comforting hug. The one missing from when I talked to my mom. "Oh, poor kiddo." She rubs her hands up and down to sooth me. "Let's back up and tackle the first thing you said. Portal of doom?"

I whisper, so I think only she can hear, "My mom says we aren't human. I know, what a shocker in this town. We are the Tribe of the Goddess Danu?" I say in half-question. "And I am some kind of freak that can cross planes of existence."

"Whoa, you are Tuatha de Danann, I thought those were only myth," she says in wonder. "Well, so am I, so who am I to judge." She shrugs. "Continue.".

"What?" I have no idea what she just said.

"Too ahh thahh day Don ann." I pretty sure her southern twang isn't helping with the pronunciation of the strange words. "You are Fae. Like a Faery. No wonder you are small and gorgeous. That explains more than a few things. You can cross planes of existence? Wow. There are so many things we need to try." My genius best friend seems ready to play picklock with Pandora's Box.

"No, G.J., I am what will bring Chaos to this world. Or so went my mom's loving advice." I glare at G.J. in warning.

"Well that's no fun." She is only mildly disgruntled.

I shake her. "G.J., the dead kids are being ripped apart. Like by a wild animal..." I wait for her to pick up what I am saying, but she just stares blankly at me. "My friends are dangerous, is what Hugo said." I wait again.

Again, G.J.'s answer is silence.

"G.J., the pack is killing these people. You need to get away from them." My heart is brimming with fear.

"Nat, honey. I know you are upset, but my boys aren't killing anyone," G.J. says in blind faith.

"I can't believe it either, but it is the only thing that fits the vision and Hugo's warning."

G.J. pulls away from me. Her eyes full of disbelief shaking her head in small slow movements. "Nat, you are tired and wiped out. I am going to clear this up for you right quick. The pack has nothing to do with these murders."

I grab G.J.'s arm tight. "You don't know that. Look how violent they are. Look at Hamilton and Adam. You need to stay away from them."

A low growl sounds from behind us. We both turn quickly.

"You think we will harm her. You would tell her to leave us knowing how important she is." Hamilton's eyes are glowing the amber fire of his extremely livid wolf.

"Hamilton, I have this, back off," G.J. commands.

Adam holds Hamilton's shoulder, as if he can prevent him from lunging at me with such a small gesture.

G.J. turns on me. Fury in control of her beautiful features. "Listen here, I don't care who told you what. We are your friends. You know us. You have even invaded our minds and know us almost too well. Some dead guy tells you to fear those of us who care for you, and you turn on us like a light switch. My boys have done nothing wrong. Don't accuse them of such things. They are my family. Family is everything." G.J. has crowded my personal space and is yelling down at me in pure unadulterated contempt. "How dare you? Hugo is right, you do have dangerous friends. But my pack isn't half as scary as I will be if you ever come at my boys again with this nonsense."

Drake somehow squeezes his large form between us, which sets both Adam and Hamilton into attack mode. Drake has his back to me, pushing G.J. away.

In a low rumble, Adam warns him, "Get your hands off her."

Wow, I would have thought he was impersonating Hamilton.

Ignoring the two menacing boys, Drake addresses the still furious G.J., "Why don't we all settle down? Nat is really tired. She even agreed to go on a date with me so we know she isn't thinking clearly." His joke falls flat. "Just walk away." This he seems to direct at the two other boys.

"We aren't afraid of you, Aldrich," Hamilton says, and I believe him.

Drake repeats, "Just walk away. I will never allow you to harm her."

"Et tu, Drake." G.J. looks genuinely devastated. Ire deflated, she simply leaves, disgusted.

Hamilton, of course, won't leave it at that. "She is too treasured to spend any time with someone willing to hurt her. Stay the hell away from her, Nat. I mean it, Drake. If you want us to leave Nat alone, she has to stay away from G.J.. We won't lose her because some Tinkerbelle has nightmares."

Adam stood in silent agreement at Hamilton's shoulder. They turn as one unit and follow the wake of G.J..

I put my tired head to rest in the middle of Drake's warm back. His body tenses before he turns to embrace me. Wrapped up, I let go of the stress of the past few moments. He rubs his hand over my head and makes shushing noises.

His well-defined chest muffles the words I say, "Well, there are three less Christmas cards I'll have to write."

Drake's hands find my buried face and he uses his thumbs under my chin to gently tilt my face up to his. "They are just upset. You know how Hamilton and Adam feel about her."

His thumbs stroke my jaw. My stomach, which the bottom had fallen out of, lifts like I have sped over a small hill.

Looking at me intensely, he whispers, "I completely understand."

The bell rings sending kids bustling down the hall. I pull my face from Drake's hands. His hand runs down my arm, grabbing my hand as I try to move away. He squeezes it, saying, "It will be all right. If you need to talk, I am around."

****

It seems as if every minute is an hour. Finally, the day ends. I am so tired I can't keep my head up, and I fall asleep on the bus ride home. I stumble into bed and crash for a few much-needed hours.

The house is quiet, when I wake up. Hungry, I go to the kitchen to scrounge up something to eat, surprised Mom didn't wake me up for dinner. I snag the Special K with Red Berries, a bowl, and the milk. Setting them on the counter, I see an envelope with my name on it. As I open it, I am stuffing a handful of dry cereal in my mouth, but I can't swallow.

> *Nat,*
>
> *Your mother and I can't be around you with what you can possibly do. Here is some money and one of our credit cards to take care of your needs until other decisions are made. We will be in touch if we can figure out how without anyone getting hurt. We hope you are strong enough to handle what is to come. We love you very much. I simply can't put your mother in this position. We will set up a way for this all to work. Be safe.*
>
> *Love,*
>
> *Dad*

I can't breathe. Dry cereal begins to stick painfully to the roof of my mouth and cheeks. My parents ran away from home. How on Earth do I process this? I only just turned sixteen. I can't even drive. What do I do about groceries? My parents are gone. They are so afraid of me that they've abandoned me. When I finally work the prickling food down my throat, I call G.J.. Her phone goes straight to voicemail. I call over to the Wyfle's house.

"Hello," says a deep male voice.

"Hey... Umm... Mr. Wyfle. Is G.J. around? This is Nat," I ask hesitantly.

"Sure, Nat, give me a minute to get her." Mr. Wyfle says, and I hear him put the phone down and walk off calling for G.J. to come to the phone. Someone picks up the phone.

Adam says in a low growl, "G.J. isn't going to talk to you." The line goes dead.

Ugh! Really? Today is the day my parents pick to leave? When I am fighting with the only other person I can count on?

I fold down on myself and sit on the kitchen floor with my back to the cabinets. I take a few deep breaths. I call Gus. Sure, our last conversation didn't go well, but maybe he was just having a bad day. Everybody has a bad day now and again. Look at mine... today. Gus' phone goes straight to voicemail. "Hey Gus... I ...umm... Well, I could really use a friend right now, and G.J. won't talk to me because I told her some things she didn't want to hear. Could you give me a call when you get a chance? Please... Gus... just call me back when you get this."

I wander around the house, I guess checking to see if my parents are truly gone. Their closet is almost completely empty. Even their winter stuff has been taken. Photo albums are missing. Their computer is gone too. Dear Lord, I don't think they are coming back. I call my mom's cell; it goes straight to voicemail, as does my Dad's. What is the use of people having cell phones if nobody answers them?

Wow, I am totally alone.

In a desperate attempt to get my mind off my life, I do my massive amount of homework. If this keeps up, I might actually get decent grades without using my special skills to cheat on tests.

I never thought about being alone in my house before. It never bothered me. But laying here, trying to sleep, knowing I am alone is disconcerting. Every creak the house makes, every car door the neighbor slams, and the hum of every engine that goes by makes my mind race. Who is that? What is that? Where did that noise come from? Needless to say sleep is elusive until the early morning. When my alarm goes off, I feel as though I've blinked instead of slept. After I hit snooze twice, I realize I can't miss the bus. I have no other ride to school. I have no parents.

Chapter Six

When I stumble into homeroom, G.J. is talking with Ms. Stontz and another girl. I think my mom works with hers, but I have never actually met her. Before I get a chance to talk to her, Ms. Stontz writes a note and G.J. and the girl walk out of class without one word. I try to pick Ms. Stontz's mind for why G.J. left, but Ms. Stontz is a powerful Wiccan and blocks my mental perusal. She is one of G.J.'s coven, and she has always been cagey with her thoughts.

The highlight of my day is actually having my homework to turn in when requested. That feels pretty good. Who knew?

Lunch, however, proves to be less than awesome. Every member of the pack looks at me in utter contempt and surrounds G.J., like a rapper's entourage. I don't even try to get near her. I find a seat at the end of the table were the kids with hygiene issues sit and pretend that I am going to get any food down. The girl G.J. left class with is at my table. Her head is lowered and her fingers are stiff, but seem to be rotating from the knuckle joint in tiny circles each digit independent from another in that odd way someone on the Autism spectrum tends to do.

"May I?" Drake asks, and points to the seat opposite me.

"You don't want to sit with G.J. and friends?" I ask, smarting a little at my obvious shunning.

"I'll take any time I can with you," Drake says, folding himself into the seat across from me.

"Well that's novel." I can't believe Drake is the only person on the planet willing to say that to me. Who would have seen that coming?

"How are you holding up?"

Drake's seemingly genuine concern catches me off guard, and I have to take a deep breath in order to not let tears come. Rolling my eyes upward, I try to keep the overabundance of water from leaking out of them. "I can't say this is my favorite time of my life."

His hand grabs mine in silent support. I look at him.

"I'm here, Nat." He has a sweet smile on his handsome face.

Man, I hate that I can't read his thoughts. "Do you do that on purpose?" I ask.

"What?"

"Do you block me from reading your mind?" I have never asked him before.

He pulls his hand away. "No."

"Then why can't I read you?"

"Why does it matter?" Drake shrugs and starts to eat his lunch.

"Because it does," I respond, faking indifference, and picking at my own food.

"I really don't know exactly why. I can't change it, so now what?" he asks in a relaxed challenge.

"What do you mean 'now what?'"

"You can't read my mind. We have been over this before. I will tell you what I am thinking. Since you really want to know, I think you are incredible. I have for a while. I think about you all the time. I think I want to spend more time with you, and I know I like a very long list of things about you. If there is anything else you want to know, ask." Drake watches me carefully for my reaction.

I pick a piece of bread off my sandwich and roll it between my fingers, not quite courageous enough to meet his eyes. Holy moly, did he just say that? My cheeks are on fire. I thought G.J. handled complements badly, but I have no idea what to do with what he just said. "I don't know what to say to that. Were you just throwing down of a verbal gauntlet?" I do meet his gaze then.

Drake flinches a little, but he holds our connection. "You don't have to say anything. *That* was an exercise of my honesty. I said I would tell you what I think. I did." He shrugs and takes a bite of his sandwich.

"You don't expect me to tell you what I am thinking?"

"No." He pauses for almost a full minute. "I'm not sure if I want to know."

"You don't care what I think?" I accuse.

"No." he says, quick and sharp. He laughs a little. "I definitely care. I'm just worried ignorance may be bliss. And it's hard on a guy to spill his guts like that." He waits a beat. "I just don't want to get shot down in the same moment. I need a little time to rebuild my reserves." He flashes a shy half smile.

I take a bite and chew my untasted food. He, too, eats letting the silence stretch out. We watch each other. Drake is a handsome kid. His eyes are such an amazing green. What am I supposed to say? I really don't like not knowing what he is thinking. But I guess this is how everybody else goes through life. Wow, how do they stand it? I realize I can't hate the guy just because I can't read him. I can also use anyone in my corner right now, including him. "Okay."

Drake tilts his head still watching me. "Okay?"

"Yeah, okay. Let me know when your quote 'reserves' are back up, and I will tell you what I think." The corners of my mouth pull up in an unexpected smile.

"Keep looking at me like that and it won't take long," Drake responds, smiling back and shaking his head. "Man, Adam was right."

My smile falls at the mention of the wolfie connection.

"What's wrong?" Drake asks.

I shake my head and eat my lunch with my head down. Finishing up, I pack up my luncheon remains and stand up. "Still on for Friday then?"

Drake is halfway up; he lifts his head grinning. "Absolutely."

****

I hadn't realized our pantry was so well stocked. My parents have enough food in storage to possibly be considered an emergency shelter for the greater Spokane area. It looks like the chefs at Progresso will be providing my dining experience for the next few days. If G.J. was speaking to me, I could ask her what you do with canned artichoke or pickled herring.

Once again, I meander through the house revisiting the signs of my parent's exodus. Bored with the pity party, I knock out my homework again. If I don't watch it, this could become a habit. I get in my cozy clothes and go from door to door and window to window making sure everything is locked up. Maybe by practicing this ritual, I will feel more secure when it comes time to get some sleep. I try to reach my parents again, and again there is no answer. I don't bother to leave a message. What would I say?

It's funny how lonely it is when you live alone. We don't even have a pet. I am looking forward to school, just to have human contact. This is not something I would have ever thought my brain would generate in the course of its normal functioning. What is even odder is the fact that no one knows I'm without parental supervision. Nobody seems to need to contact my parents. Like their existence is superfluous. Maybe I am projecting that in order for me to feel better about their leaving.

****

Thursday G.J. isn't in homeroom again. I have no idea why and Ms. Stontz still remains un-tappable. Drake and I have lunch together again at the table of the exiled. He makes me laugh and flirts shamelessly. He does provide a nice counterpoint to the other unpleasantness in my life.

"So on Friday, do you want to meet me or can we pick you up?"

He catches me off guard by a question that may make me admit I am alone. "Uhhh… You're going to have to pick me up."

"Good. The restaurant is kind of nice, just so you know," Drake says, pulling at his collar as though it constricted from the start of his sentence nervously.

"Okay…" My cash resources are limited, and I'm not sure if I can get away with using the credit card. "How much money should I bring with me?"

"No, no, you don't have to bring any money. I'm paying. I just wanted you to know so you knew what to expect. You know, for how to dress and stuff."

"You're worried about what I am going to wear?" I ask stung and confused.

"I didn't say that. I am giving you information you can use at your discretion. I don't care if you wear anything." Drake stops, his face turns slightly red. "I mean…"

"You need help with an outfit?" comes the sweetest drawl I have ever heard from behind me.

Drake smiles relieved to be helped out of his verbal stumbling.

My heart actually squeezes in hope, as I face G.J., "I could use some friendly advice."

"I'm part of a special project so I won't be here tomorrow, and I have a ton of work to do tonight for it, but I will catch up with you at your house. Drake, honey, what time are you picking Nat up?" G.J. asks.

"6:30 alright with you, Nat?" Drake asks like an old-world gentleman.

"Ummm, sounds fine."

"Listen, don't mention it to the boys. They are still kind of prickly about what you said so I'm gonna have to sneak out. But I'll see you at your place around... let's say... five-ish?" G.J. asks with a big smile.

"That's great. Thanks, G.J." I think my voice actually cracks with emotion.

G.J. turns and says to the girl from homeroom, "Hey there, Megan. I found the missing equation. We can get together in math and I will run you through what I found."

Megan doesn't look up at G.J., keeping her gaze down, not really looking at her food but more like seeing through the table to some kind of white board in her mind's eye. G.J. elaborates; Megan starts rocking, her twirling fingers tapping her temple while she responds. G.J. sits across from her and the two go back and forth. After a while, Megan hesitantly makes eye contact with G.J. She only does it every so often and when she does, it's as if she's looking into G.J.'s head instead of her eyes. Her focus isn't on G.J. the person but the conversation itself. When they come to some point of consensus, Megan looks back down without saying a word.

"Okay well... bye then." G.J. left the conversation awkwardly and turned back to me. "I better get back before Tweedle Dee and Tweedle Dumber think it's time to put on the macho show. See you tomorrow." She waves as she moves back toward the sea of letter jackets.

"And all is right with the world," Drake says, grinning at me.

"Ha! Not even close but definitely better than it was."

"G.J. is pretty cool." Drake's smile is still big.

A flash of unexpected jealousy hits me out of nowhere. I beat it down internally with a vicious body slam. No way is a petty emotion like that going to screw up mending my fences with G.J., "Yeah she is."

But that little ember of green smolders down, deep where I can't extricate it.

Chapter Seven

Friday hits and I buzz around my house in the morning with a nervous anticipation. I am going on my first date of my life today. I call my mom's cell phone and leave her a message. I almost convince myself a voicemail box is just as good as a mother for a sounding board. Almost.

G.J. is not in school, as she had said she wouldn't be. I am still kind of hoping to talk to her, but it isn't to be.

Every time I see Drake, he gives me this humungous smile that just makes me blush and grin back at him. I have no idea how we are going to eat dinner if this keeps up. At lunch, he is his normal flirty self. But he doesn't stop looking at me. And at the end of meal, he confirms, "6:30 you'll be ready?"

"I'll be ready." I shake my head and move on to finish what has to be the longest day in history.

I get home and lay out a couple nice outfits. I'd borrow jewelry from my mom, but that went with her. This is a big day and I slam things around, angry with my parents for missing it. I call Mom's voicemail again and walk through my decision making process. Just to see if I can prompt a response, I tell her non-corporeal listening device I think we should address safe sex next time we talk. That has to get a reaction. What parent can let that one slide?

In an effort not to wring my hands and work myself up into a lather, I do a little homework and put away the dishes from the dishwasher. At five, I go to the front room to wait for G.J.. I sort the mail. I am not sure what to do with the bills that are coming in. Seeing the credit card bill, I open it quickly to see if I can figure out where my parents are. Sadly the billing cycle ended before they went M.I.A.. The electric bill is outrageous. Looks like I am going to be turning off the lights, no matter how soothing the extra wattage may seem when alone. Although, to be fair, this billing cycle was from when I had parents too.

In my futzing, a half an hour has past. Where is G.J.? I take out the trash and wipe down the kitchen counters. By six o'clock, I decide she must not have been able to get away from the pack. I try her cell, but it goes straight to voicemail. Should I call the house? If I do and she is on her way, I may bring the howling hooligans charging.

I get ready for my first date of my whole life by myself. I burn my ear on the curling iron. Man that is annoying. If G.J. were here, she would heal it right up for me. The more I do, the more peeved I get. Why tell me you are coming at all if you aren't? And would a phone call hurt? How can you not even make a phone call? She probably found some mathematical equation so important she had to talk it over with Megan and forgot all about me.

At 6:30 on the nose, the doorbell rings. I open the front door to find the already handsome Drake looking like the next James Bond. We both stand there for a second. I break the moment. "Hey, come on in. Let me just grab my purse."

"You look beautiful," Drake says in an awe-filled tone.

"Thanks, you too, pretty boy."

"Are your parents at home?" he asks, making me freeze to the spot.

"No, why?" My hyper cautious reaction startles Drake, making him pull his head back and peer around the room.

"I'd like to meet your parents. I am taking their daughter out. I'd think they would want to meet me. I want this to go well, so there's a chance we can do this again." He looks at me a little confused as to what the problem is.

"They aren't home." I whirl back and go to grab my purse.

"All set?" Drake asks, as I return.

"I'm ready if you are." I let out a nervous breath.

I lock up the house before I spin around to see a limo and driver waiting at the curb. I look at Drake. "Are you studying John Hughes films in order to pick up dating tips?"

He smiles as he ushers me to the car. "You have been hanging out with G.J. too long."

"She isn't the only one with an Amazon Prime account." I look up at the tree line behind my house. Gus stands in the shadows. I call out to him, "Gus?"

Drake turns around. Gus takes a step forward and the light hits him. He is a mess and his eyes… they are glowing like blue lasers. Drake pushes me farther into the car and stands between Gus and me. His voice is louder than I have ever heard him before, and it echoes off the surrounding houses, "Nat and I are leaving now, Sanzar. Whatever it is can wait."

"Drake."

He looks like he has been in a fight. I try to push past Drake, but when I look back, Gus is gone. "Gus?" I call out again. "Gus?" He just vanished. I give Drake an evil look.

"Gus is a big boy. He can handle himself," Drake says, trying to ease me back into the car.

"I know he can handle himself." I tap my head. "I know all kinds of things about people. That's why seeing him looking like he took a spin in the laundry machine with mud instead of detergent is a bit upsetting. I wonder if the wolves went after him too." That last part I really meant to keep to myself, but it slipped out my mouth.

"Nat." This time Drake actually gets me in the back of the car, and the driver shuts the door. Before Drake continues, he rolls up the privacy screen between the driver and us. Turning sideways to face at me, he says, "You know the guys in the pack. Why would they go after any of these people? I only know of one case where they killed a human and that was in defense of G.J., which was totally worth it in my humble opinion. Any other case where there has been an issue has been internal or when they have been threatened by something else. Not a human. There is nothing to suggest they're involved."

"Hugo." I wince a little admitting my phantom conversation to Drake. "Said I have dangerous friends. The pack is the most dangerous friends I have." I look out the window, when I confess, "Drake, the images and feelings of their deaths are so horrible. It is so violent." I shiver.

Drake slides closer to me and puts his arm around me. "Nat, I am so sorry you have to go through this. I wish I could stop it somehow." He rubs his hand up and down my arm, pulling me closer against his side.

"Thanks, Drake." I look up into his face. "I really wish you could too." I smile a little. His warm minty breath heats my cheeks. Both of us are startled, when the driver opens the door.

The restaurant is amazing and Drake has ordered up the royal treatment. As we wait to be seated, I surreptitiously turn my phone to vibrate. No way am I going to have a digital music embarrassment in this place. Dinner is astounding. After asking me a couple of preference questions, Drake asks if I mind if he orders for us both. We start with an heirloom beet salad. I am dubious of it, but one bite changes my mind. For the main course, Drake has the osso bucco pork shanks over grits and orders me the duck in a brown butter sauce with gnocchi. The server is so stiff I swear he starches and irons his shirt every time he goes in the back. I drink San Pellegrino, just to be able to use the pretty, stemmed glassware. I am certain I use the wrong utensil for most of our meal. But it's cool to have an experience like this under my belt.

Drake is funny, charming, and flirty. He disarms me way too often.

"So honesty time again. What are you thinking? You said I could ask, and I am a girl, so it is obligatory."

He resettles himself in his seat and wipes his mouth before meeting my eyes. Sighing, he starts slowly, "I think you are insanely beautiful, and I'm working really hard to remember what we're talking about instead of just sitting here staring at you. I think you are really funny, and I can't wait to hear what you have to say next. I think I'm the luckiest guy on the planet that you agreed to go out with me, and I am hoping like hell I don't screw this up somehow." He looks down at his plate. Bashfully, with his head down, he catches my eyes with his. "I'm also thinking I would really like to do his again. Often."

I let him hang there for a few seconds before I return, "Is that all?" My smile breaks hard to let him know I'm teasing.

He rolls his eyes heavenward. "I wish you could read my mind because these honesty moments are going to kill me." He smiles too.

Wow, I totally get what he means about just wanting to sit and stare except in reverse. "Is it really that hard?" I ask, unwittingly, setting myself up.

"Try it," he dares.

I open my mouth… it closes slowly. *He's right this is tough.* I try again. Shaking my head, I say, "You're a better man than I."

Drake shakes his head too. "Chicken."

His face lights up in a smile and I am now clear on what devastatingly handsome really means. We grin at each other for a beat too long, until the well-pressed waiter asks, "Will there be anything else this evening?"

Looking around, both Drake and I notice we are one of the last tables seated in the restaurant. "No, just the check will be fine."

After Drake takes care of the check, which I am dying to see but behave myself and don't peek, we head out to the waiting car and driver. I guess the waiter alerted the valet. It is amazing how little the wealthy have to take care of for themselves.

Drake helps me in the car and settles down next to me. "So." He slaps his hands on his knees. "Did you have a good time?"

"The food was great." I avoid answering.

"It was," Drake says, drawing out the last word, as if seeking more.

"The service was excellent," I add.

"That too." Drake watches me; only half-turned, his chin tilts in agreement.

I look out the window, but continue, "And… I enjoyed the company."

Drake's warm hand covers mine, sliding his fingers to entwine us together. With my head turned all the way away, I hide my smile.

"Me too," he leans over and says close to my ear. He settles himself back in his seat, and we ride along in silence for a little while. Drake rubs his thumb gently over the back of my hand. "So…" He waits until I face him. "If you had a good time and I had a good time, I think we should go out again."

I look back at him. He did not actually ask me a question so I let his statement lie.

"What do you think?" he asks.

"About what?"

"About going out again," stumbling over his words he adds, "with me?"

"When?" At this point, I am torturing him. I do have an evil streak.

"Is tomorrow too soon?" He gets this big devastating grin taking his handsome to a whole new level.

Before I have a chance to form a response, we stop in front of my house. I glance out the window, distracted by what I am going to say. My porch light outlines a large shadowed figure. I reach out with my mind to see who it is, and an image of G.J. with her throat torn out slams into me as the shadow races toward the car.

Chapter Eight

The door to the car rips open, pushing the limits of the hinge with a wrenching creak. A bare arm pulls Drake out, sends him flying from the car before returning and grabbing for me. Before it reaches me, I pin myself to the far door. The arm, too, is pulled from the car, and the door slams, not quite meeting its normal position. A bright flash heats up the whole car. The shadowed figure dives away from the light.

I go to open the door Drake had disappeared through, but the handle radiates heat making it too hot to touch. I am too afraid of seeing the image of G.J. to try to reach out to the attacker's mind again. I move back to the other door and slip out of the limo. The driver is outside and crouching behind the car. He motions for me to keep down.

A growling voice demands, "Nat comes with me now!" There is no humanity in it, but I recognize the voice. It's Hamilton.

"Not a chance." While Drake sounds calm, he isn't. Is he nuts to take on Hamilton, when he is spazzed out like this?

I pop up from behind the car. "What did you do to G.J.?" My best friend is torn apart; no way I am staying out of this, but at least I have a car between the wolf-boy and me.

Hamilton spins towards my voice. "Nothing! You are coming with me now." He leaps on top the car, his eyes glowing in rage. So much for the car.

Drake grabs one of his ankles, as he lunges for me, and pulls him off the far side of the car. "She's not going anywhere with you, Calhoun. Don't even think about it."

I scramble around the back of the car.

Hamilton is half-naked; sweat shorts slung low on his hips. His aggressive fury makes his chest heave in ragged breaths. "Nat, we need you to find out what happened to G.J.." While his features aren't changing, his eyes are radiating an intense gold. Every muscle he has appears taut, straining to remain in his human form.

"I saw her in your mind, Hamilton. I know what you did to G.J.. You ripped out her throat. What do you want from me?" I snap back at him, meeting his aggression with my own.

Drake glances my way before getting up in Hamilton's space. "What?"

Over Drake's shoulder, Hamilton's eyes widen in disbelief and horror. "Adam found her like that. We would never do that to G.J.. Are you serious right now?" He chuffs out a breath in utter disgust

"Explain," Drake commands.

Hamilton paces away in agitation. He clearly doesn't want to take any more time for this. He spins back. "I'll explain on the way. We have to know what happened. Please, Nat, she is unconscious and we don't know what happened."

Drake twists toward the car and winces. The door on this side appears as if it a meteor hit it. Turning, I gape at Drake, my eyes asking an unspoken question: "What did you do?"

Drake says, "Let's get in on the other side," ushering me around the car. As we come around the back, he sees the driver still cowering by the driver's door. "Ken, don't worry about the damage. I'll take care of it. If you could head towards the Wyfle's house." Drake looks to Hamilton, who nods his confirmation of Drake's guess as to where G.J. is lying damaged.

We all get in the car with Hamilton taking the rear-facing seat. The privacy screen is still up from before. Drake takes my hand again. Hamilton notices the gesture and glares out the window, pain moving across his face.

Drake prompts Hamilton to start talking. "Go on."

Hamilton takes in a deep breath and blows it out, clearing the frustration away so he can talk. "A little before five, Adam went looking for G.J. She wasn't hanging out with us in the living room. But she wasn't in her room, either. He followed her scent outside and to the woods. He tracked her down and found her with her throat…" Hamilton had to stop he couldn't bring himself to describe G.J. so mutilated. "Adam shifted and let out a howl. He wasn't sure if he should move her. When we got there…" Again this big brute couldn't continue. He closed his eyes, almost like the action would help him un-see the gruesome visage.

My eyes tear up; I can't believe I thought, for even one second, Hamilton could have done such a thing to G.J..

"God… Gosh… Hell." Again he stops. G.J. hates it when anyone curses, and Hamilton's internal struggle to do what she wants brings home how stupid my accusatory thoughts have been.

"G.J. is so strong. How does anyone get near her to hurt her?" Drake asks the logical question.

Hamilton grows angry again over his inability to do anything about what happened. "We don't know. That's why I came to Nat's. We need someone to get in her head so we know what happened. I would have taken any of your family, but since your parents seem to have moved out, we need you. I know you and G.J. are fighting right now—"

I cut him off, "How do you know my parents are gone?"

"I went in your house looking for someone to come help." Hamilton dismisses my concern.

"You broke into my house?" I ask, my hands balling in outrage.

Hamilton starts "G.J.—"

"Why do you say her parents moved out?" Drake looks from Hamilton to me.

"All their clothes are gone, there smell is old in the house, and there is that note from her dad," Hamilton says, as if it should be obvious to anyone.

"Hamilton! You have no right to break into my house and go through everything. There is such a thing as privacy."

"Ha! Seriously, Nat. *You* are going to talk about people's privacy." While he doesn't smile, his eyes crinkle at the corner finding the idea funny.

"Back off, Calhoun," Drake warns him.

"What? You don't find it hypocritical of a mind reader to have privacy concerns?" Hamilton asks.

"Stop now or she won't help you," Drake warns again.

"Screw that. G.J. is hurt. I'm going to help G.J. regardless of what this idiot says."

"I get so tired of you calling me an idiot all the time," Hamilton complains.

"I get so tired of you being an idiot all the time," I reply, my voice mimicking the notes he used.

"How bad is G.J.?" Drake asks.

"Adam stopped the bleeding as best he could, but she has lost so much blood." Again, Hamilton's eyes look out the window. "She just needs to wake up so she can fix it." His voice is resolute. "She's just gotta fix it…" His voice tapers off, like a whimpering puppy.

"She's alive, man," Drake tries to reassure us all.

We pull up to the Wyfle's enormous house. The place is swarming with men of all sizes. Our driver is stopped by a gargantuan dude who was standing by the gate.

Hamilton leans toward me, pushing the window button so he can stick his head out the back window. He commands the hulking man who stopped us, "Let us in,"

The guard gives the driver a nod and the car glides forward

We all exit the car through the non-damaged door. We don't even make it to the back of the vehicle before Jack Wyfle's colossal form fills the doorway. "What took so long?"

"They just got back." Hamilton, lowering his head and looking down and slightly away, takes a submissive stance in front of Jack.

"You can leave now, Mr. Aldrich," Jack dismisses Drake.

Drake puts his arm around my waist. "I know things are tense right now, but G.J. is a friend. I would like to help."

Silence falls as Jack and Drake have a silent communication. Jack nods, turning slightly to usher us in. The scene, as we enter G.J.'s room, is one from my worst nightmare. G.J. is lying on her bed, blood-soaked gauze clinging to her neck. Her Aunt Celia sits next to her, holding her hand, sobbing whimpering cries. Adam straightens from the wall where he has been slouched in despair, hope replacing his desperate features.

Celia's swollen gaze lands on me. She rushes over, pulling me against her pregnant body, her baby bump protruding. "Nat, thank God. Please help us."

"I'll do whatever I can," I promise her.

"We need to know what happened. Why was she in the woods alone? She knows better. Who attacked her? Why did she not defend herself? If you can get her to wake up so she can heal." Jack is listing off the reasons I am here.

Looking at the floor, I say, "She was in the woods because she was on her way to see me."

"What?" Jack asks, even though I know he heard me. Wolves have great hearing. "Why on Earth would she feel the need to sneak out to see you? She can see you any time she wants."

"She thought Adam and Hamilton wouldn't let her after…" I trail off, still looking down.

"Why?" Jack sounds incredulous.

"She tried to tell G.J. to stay away from us. She thinks we are the ones doing this to people," Hamilton defends himself, gesturing to G.J.'s neck with a fling of his arm.

"Look, I'm sorry. I know I was wrong. It's just Hugo warned me about my friends," I blurt out, tears filling my eyes.

Drake pulls me to his chest and holds me close, sheltering me from some of the hurt and anger filling the room.

"You two and I will talk later," Jack directs to Adam and Hamilton. "Nat, why would she need to sneak out? Couldn't you two have talked on the phone?" His voice is gentle, but he's still puzzling out the mystery.

"She was going to help me get ready for my date." Drake's chest muffles my words, and I hiccup a sob. Guilt truly overwhelms me. G.J. would have called. Why did I assume she wouldn't have called? Why didn't I know then something was wrong. I could have prevented this.

"What did she say?" Celia asks, unable to make out my garble.

"G.J. had promised to help Nat get ready for our date," Drake clarifies. "I didn't know she hadn't come. Nat looked so nice I thought…" He didn't finish and hugged me closer.

Jack takes a deep breath, trying to stay in control of his temper. "Nat, if you could try to see if you can get anything out of her. Please, there is much we need to do."

I nod and pull away from Drake, who squeezes me in reassurance before letting me go. Moving to the bed, I carefully grasp G.J.'s too cold hand. Steeling myself, I try to see what is going on in her head. At first, it is foggy. Nothing seems to be going on and I start to panic. G.J. always seems to have things happening in her head, and the stillness of her thoughts is more than upsetting. "Come on," I breathe out in encouragement, urging G.J. to think of anything.

After a few seconds, I sense her bewilderment. Her brain is trying to figure out where she is, what is happening. It starts slowly, her mind replays sneaking out into the woods. She is thinking about getting me gussied up.

I smile at what a great friend she is.

We hear the sound of someone or thing crunch foliage as they take cautious steps. Did one of the boys figure out we are gone already? But wait, no, the wolves are way more quiet when they stalk something. Why did we have to think about stalking? *Stop freaking out G.J..* The sun has passed the hillside. Feeling unsettled we speed up. We grow more and more concerned. We stumble, as we look over our shoulder more than where we are going. *You have grown up gallivanting around in the woods why today of all days do you suddenly become such an agoraphobic.* We hear a noise and she looks behind us. We, again, try to shake off our growing panic taking deep breaths and marching swiftly in false confidence.

About half way to my house, we know something is wrong. We spin one way and another, trying to see anything. We get out her phone wanting to call me, to just to have me on the phone while we walk. Before we can push call, vice-like arms grab us from behind. We fling our will at whoever or whatever it is. Nothing happens. We feel one hand slide up to the bottom of our jaw while the other arm holds us still against the immovable being behind us. A tongue licks the shell of our ear. We shiver completely disgusted.

"Now you will be mine." The breath from the whispered voice cools the saliva the tongue has left.

We fight as hard as we can. The hold on our jaw moves slightly and starts to squeeze our windpipe preventing us from screaming. Preventing us from even getting any air. As we fight, the pressure on our windpipe might make it break, and we struggle harder to simply take a breath. A horrible pain rips at the side of our throat.

We try again to make the person let go by using our will. Realizing it won't work, we grab a large log with our power and slam it into the all of us, throwing us all to the ground. Her effort rips her throat even more, as the teeth, maybe, that held us are pulled from our neck without releasing the jaw. Our fear rises, as we lay there, unable to move anything but our eyes.

Someone is moving around. Laughter. We see Gus.

Gus?

He screams, "No!"

He is gone and we don't hear anything else. For some reason an image of Mrs. Ackers flashes through our head but it, too, is gone.

G.J. is in so much pain. She is terrified. She tries to heal herself, but it isn't working.

We are both sobbing. I've deeply connected myself to G.J.'s thoughts and pass out when she does.

Chapter Nine

Coming around, I am in a room I have never been in before. I push up a bit to see where I am exactly. Mr. Calhoun, Hamilton's father, who is also a pack member, is by the door. Drake is in a chair by the bed. As I prop up on my elbows, he comes to me.

"Hey, easy. How are you? Can you sit up by yourself?" Drake smoothes my hair away from my face.

I nod my response. My throat feels like I decided to take the metal shavings from around a key making machine and swallow a hand full without a chaser.

"I'll go let Jack know she's awake." Mr. Calhoun heads out into the hallway.

"You scared the hell out of me," Drake says, pinning me in place with his gaze. But he pulls me to him and hugs me, as if it is his instinct to do so and not a choice.

Braving using my voice, I croak, "Gus…" Talking hurts as bad as I thought it would. I try to swallow and start again, but there is nothing but dry goo in my mouth to swallow. "Gus was there, Drake."

"What?" he asks in disbelief.

"Gus was there. I saw him in G.J.'s memory. She doesn't believe or doesn't want to believe he did this to her. But he was there. If I tell the pack, they will kill him. No explanations." I pull back and look at Drake.

His eyes are distant.

Mr. Calhoun comes back in. "Are you well enough to go to them. Celia won't leave G.J. and Jack won't leave Celia."

I nod again. Drake helps me off the large bed, keeping his arm around me. I can't tell if he is trying to keep me from falling or just keeping me close, as some form of protection.

We walk down the hall two doors and enter G.J.'s room. Celia's red-rimmed gaze falls on me again. "What did you see?" she begs me to answer.

I clear my raw throat.

"Let me get you some water." Drake shifts me closer to G.J.'s form.

My friend is laying there so still.

"Nat?" Celia pleads again, her voice cracking as she melts into tears.

Drake hands me a cup, and I take a sip; the water washes the sludge down. I make one of those awful hacking noises that get things to dislodge from your vocal chords.

"What happened?" Jack asked.

"She was attacked by someone in the woods," I begin.

Hamilton throws his arms up. "Well there's a news flash."

"Hamilton let her finish," Jack quiets his outburst. "Go on Nat." He turns and prompts me to continue.

"She was walking to my house like we thought. She felt followed and was weirded out. When the attacker hit, they came from behind so she couldn't see who it was." I stop and shake off the memory of her pain and fear.

"Why didn't she pull them off with her power?" Celia asks, as if she can change what happened with the suggestion.

"She tried, it wouldn't work. The person grabbed her, and she tried to use her will, but it wouldn't work. Then they…" I take a deep breath to control the shaking of my voice.

"What? They what, Nat?" Hamilton half-screams at me.

Jack makes a low growling noise, and Drake eases closer to me, nudging me right next to G.J..

"Whoever it was licked her ear, and said, 'Now you will be mine.'" I close my eyes unwilling to see the reaction of the men in the room.

All of the wolves are growling. When I open my eyes, not one pair of theirs are without the telltale glow promising someone's death.

Jack says in a low menacing voice, "Continue."

"Then—" I take another fortifying breath. "—then, whoever it was bit G.J.'s neck. She realized she couldn't use her will on them so she slammed them both with a piece of wood she saw on the ground. That caused the teeth to rip out of her neck and for the person to lose their hold on her. They had been squeezing her windpipe pretty hard."

"Luke. Call the pack. NOW!" Jack holds his teeth together, as if he can prevent his canines from descending with the effort. After nodding one quick bob of his head, Mr. Calhoun leaves the room.

From behind me on the bed, someone grabs my hand. I turn and look down into G.J.'s worried eyes. I drop to the bedside squeezing her hand. "She's awake."

Everyone rushes toward us.

"G.J., honey, thank God." Celia takes G.J.'s hand from mine.

"She can't speak," I inform the room.

G.J. prompts me expectantly with the expression on her face.

"Okay, but go easy on me, last time I was in there, I passed out."

Drake puts his arm around me for moral support. I pop in G.J.'s brain again. This time the normal G.J. things are happening.

"Don't tell them about Gus. I don't think it was him. You know how they are. These boys will string him behind two cars and play tug of war if they think he did this. Nat, I'm scared. I can't fix this. I am so weak and I can't heal myself like normal. All I'm able to do is try to keep the blood from getting to that part of my neck. The area itself won't heal. Tell them."

"She says she can't heal the wound. She is trying to keep the blood from the area, but the tissue won't actually heal."

"Why the hell not?" Hamilton directs his anger at me and not G.J..

"What an idiot. If I knew why not, I would have told you, all I can think of is my powers don't work on Gus. So maybe if he did this, I wouldn't be able to heal it? But, Nat..." G.J. pushes the image of Gus' face, when he saw her on the ground. *"He was far away from me, devastated and shocked, I really don't believe he did or would do this to me."*

Or he couldn't believe what he had just done. Gus is zippy quick. G.J. must have read the skepticism on my face because she catches my eye so she can continue.

"Nat, don't tell them about Gus. Please."

I nod my agreement.

"What? What is she saying?" Hamilton doesn't like our nonverbal communication.

"She is saying she will be okay. She is just tired." I lie.

"Of course she is. Good lord look what she has been through," Celia says. "We will get to the bottom of this. You rest right now." Celia pats G.J.'s hand.

"Nat, call Gus and see what is going on."

I nod at G.J. again.

Hamilton narrows his eyes at the two of us. He sits in the chair by G.J.'s bed making his huge body comfortable.

G.J. slants her eyes at him and then rolls them heavenward. Adam makes himself at home next to her on her queen-sized bed. Hamilton lets out a low growl.

"Boys, the two of you will not fight around her when she is injured like that," Celia lays down her dictate.

"Fight? We are just relishing the possibility of silence when G.J. is in the room," Adam quips.

G.J. smacks him with the back of her hand, which he catches and keeps, holding it to his chest.

Hamilton leaves the chair and sits on the bed, but on G.J.'s opposite side from Adam. G.J. fixes her gaze on the ceiling and gives a minute shake of her head.

"I'm serious, you two." Celia's tone grows sterner.

"Ceily, this is a pack thing. They have to be close to her. I'm fighting the urge to crawl up there and hold her to keep her from any more harm. The boys won't possibly do anything to hurt her, and it puts me at ease knowing they are there. Please let them stay. There are things I have to do, and I will be able to keep a clearer head if I know she is safe." Jack puts an arm around his pregnant wife's waist and leads her out of the room. "I also need you to rest. I am worried about you."

At the door, he stops and walks back over to G.J.; leaning down, he kisses her head before putting his nose right on top of her bleeding gauze bandage and sniffing long and hard.

G.J. scowls at him, and I don't have to even read her thoughts to know she is thinking: *seriously?*

Chapter Ten

B ack in the car, I ask Drake, "You ready for more honesty?"

Drake glances at me and gestures with his hand for me to ask away.

"Can I trust you not to say anything to the pack?" I look directly into his eyes, hoping that somehow I will see in his face what I can't read in his mind.

He sighs deeply. "About Gus?"

"Yeah, G.J. is adamant, and he and I have been close for a really long time." My focus still intent on Drake's face.

"How close?" Drake asks in a tone less calm than his normal suave.

I squint. "Extremely."

Drake crosses his arms and looks out the window at the passing houses, his jaw flexing and relaxing in his profile.

"Can I trust you?" I ask again.

"You said Gus was there." Drake turns back to me.

"G.J. saw him," I confirm.

"I'll make you a deal. I won't tell Jack, if you don't see Gus," Drake bargains.

"What?"

"I don't know what G.J. saw, but you know and I know what Gus is capable of. Or at least you said you knew." Drake's full mouth purses in worry.

It's my turn to look away.

Drake gently grabs my chin and turns me back to face him. "Nat, if you know so much about Gus, then you know a neck bite is completely something he can and would do."

I avoid meeting his eyes. I know what Gus is, and that is why I am not as confident as G.J. that Gus wouldn't have done it. But I don't want Drake to read something in my expression that would convict my old friend in his eyes.

"Please, Nat. If it is even possible that Gus is involved, I really need you to promise you won't be alone with him." Drake strokes my jaw with his thumb. "We saw Gus before we left for the restaurant. He looked like he had been in a fight, and he was coming from the woods, which is where Adam found G.J. It doesn't look good."

I sharply jerk my gaze to Drake's. "You think he did it?"

He lets go of my face and sits back, eyeing me as if trying to find the best approach.

"Stop that. You promised honesty. So be honest. You think he did this?" My question is direct and aggressive.

Drake's jaw muscles flex in a clench and he squints a little in a show of temper. "You want honest, here it goes. I'm worried he did do it. Gus' been my friend for a while too. But I know what he is capable of. And although he handles it pretty well, it is his nature to go after what he desires. He wants G.J.. I thought he was willing to wait until she was older, but something might have changed. Maybe he can't take her getting so cozy with the wolves. Maybe she said or did something that changed his thoughts on the matter. Or maybe he just couldn't take not being with her any longer. I can actually relate to that. But Gus bites necks and Gus drinks blood and that is what happened to G.J.. You said whoever it was said, 'She was now theirs.' Gus is the logical answer as to what happened. For the sake of our friendship, I am willing to hear the guy out, but what I won't do is risk *you* being hurt. So stay. Away. From Gus."

"So *you* are going to confront Gus? Gus who is capable of God knows what. But I'm not supposed to do the same? Who are you Fred Flintstone? What kind of cave do you live in? Gus is my friend, and I need to know what he knows. I am going to talk to him. You don't control me." I poke Drake in the chest, but only notice when he glances at my finger.

The car stops, and I open the door before the driver gets out. Drake is right behind me. "Nat, wait."

"For what? More directives from Mr. Big shot." I storm toward my door.

"No, just stop for a second." Drake reaches for my arm as I reach my front porch.

"Damn it, Hamilton! What kind of moron leaves a house wide open? If you are going to break in, at least have the courtesy to close up after," I vent at the boy not present.

Drake firms his hold and stops my progress. "Nat, stop."

"One date, Drake. One date." I turn on him. "You don't get to control me ever but definitely have no say in what I do when we have only been on one date." I project my fury through my eyes.

"You," Drake starts, just as angry but stops to take a deep breath. In a calmer manner, he says, "You are right, Nat, what I want from you has nothing to do with control. I care about you. I think I've made that fairly clear. I'm concerned, can't you understand that?" He examines my face. "Nat, I don't want anything to happen to you." He cups my cheek, his fingers sliding into the hair near my ear.

I pull away and into my open doorway. "Don't worry about me, Drake, I'm not your responsibility." I fling the door shut with a loud whack in his face.

A soft thump sounds from the other side of the door. I stand there for a moment gathering my strength. Sighing, I turn toward my dark, silent house. The events of the last week stun me. I was a happy person, then whammo. I stare blankly around my empty living room. Only… it isn't.

Gus peels away from the shadows, and I let out a small shriek.

His face isn't normal. The blue of his eyes is electric. The neon-like glow the only thing I can make out on his obscured face. "Did you have a nice date with Aldrich?" Gus sounds like there is something in his mouth making several of his words seem to have S's and his voice almost guttural. "It sounded like there is trouble in paradise already. How sad."

"What are you doing here, Gus?" I ask what I consider a perfectly legitimate question.

"You left me a message. I'm here to find out what it was you told G.J.," Gus replies, moving closer to me.

"What?" I forgot about the message.

"Your message said you told G.J. something she didn't want to hear. What was it?" Gus is persistent.

"Gus, why don't you tell me what the hell happened in the woods today," I demand.

Gus looks away. "I couldn't stop—"

A knocking at the front door interrupts Gus. "Nat," Drake calls.

"Make him go away." Gus is on me, holding me from behind. His actions remind me of how G.J. felt in the woods.

"Gus what are you doing?" I yell.

"Nat…" Gus whispers my name angrily right in my ear, just as the front door explodes. Splinters, debris, and smoke assault the room, and Gus quickly turns away, shielding me from harm.

Gus squeezes me tighter to him. "That wasn't polite, Aldrich," Gus taunts Drake, turning us back, as the debris settles to the ground.

Adrenaline courses through my body. Drake looks scarier than the wolves do when their eyes are glowing. I swear he has fire in his eyes. Oranges and reds push out the normal green of his iris. Terrifyingly beautiful.

"Gus, I will fry you if you don't let her go," Drake says, as he tosses my purse on the table next to him.

I must have forgotten it in the limo.

"I'm afraid you will fry me if I do release her." Gus acts bored, but the tension in his muscles presses against me.

Smoke rises from Drake's mouth and nose as he exhales slowly. "You get that you are holding Nat hostage? What about this scenario works out well for you in your mind? You do anything to her and you are gone. You leave here with her, and I go to the pack and tell them it was you who attacked G.J.. I won't even have to lift a finger."

Gus relaxes his hold a little. "If I let her go, will you hear me out?"

"We start with you letting her go before anything is on the table." Drake pulls his phone from his back pocket. "Funny thing happens when you spend a good part of your evening at Jack's house watching your girlfriend be comatose because she was trying to help him talk to his injured ward. He insists that you put him on speed dial." Drake's thumb scrolls on his phone and shows Gus, Jack's name and number listing on the screen.

"G.J.?" Gus seems shocked. "Is G.J. alive?"

"Barely," I answer. I collapse a little, as Gus releases me, but before I can blink, he disappears.

Drake scoops me up into his arms and just holds me to his chest. I hold him right back. After a minute, he says, "Nat, I have to tell Jack what just happened. G.J. is in danger."

I replay the moment in quick mental flashes and nod. "Call him."

Drake moves me to the sofa, and we sit as he hits call on his phone's screen. I am close enough to hear the tone of Jack's low voice when he picks up.

"Hey, Jack, this is Drake Aldrich. I'm at Nat's house and Gus just left. Jack, we think Gus may be involved with what happened to G.J.."

Jack rumbles his reply.

"Gus is acting really strange, and he just took Nat kind of hostage. He was also surprised G.J. is alive."

The low buzz of Jack saying something else is the only sound in my empty house.

"After Nat told him she was, Gus took off."

Jack must be saying something important because Drake is listening intently. He looks at me.

"Let me talk to her. We will see you in a little while." Drake ends the call and pulls me closer to his side.

I slide my arms around his waist, still unsettled by everything going on.

"Nat? Are your parents really gone?" Drake asks, softly, his lips on the top of my head.

Chapter Eleven

Realizing I am alone in the house with Drake and he knows my parents are gone, I stiffen. He rubs my back and pulls back, and he angles his head down at me.

"Why?" I ask with my eyes narrowed.

"Are you kidding?" Drake's eyes widen at me, like I've lost my mind.

"Drake, we don't need parental supervision." *What does this boy think is going to happen?*

Drake laughs a little. "While I like where you are going there, and don't get me wrong, being alone with you when that should be a concern is definitely on my top ten most wanted moments list. Right now, I don't think is the best time to take advantage."

"Wait... What? I wasn't saying..."

Drake takes my hand and kisses my palm. "We'll get there. If there is a God, we will get there." He puts my hand between both of his, as he gets serious. "With everything going on, it might be best if you stayed at Jack's house."

"You are telling me to stay with the pack?" While I now know it was misdirected, my mind can't quite make the one-eighty from me thinking the wolves have been responsible for all of the attacks.

"Heaven forbid I tell you to do anything. I'm a quick study. I have no control issues. Jack would appreciate it if you were on hand so they can communicate with G.J. while she can't talk. You would be safer with people around, and while the idea of you sleeping under the same roof as Adam the Flirting Machine makes me a little jumpy, I'm willing to deal if it means you aren't alone. Unless, of course, you want to invite me to stay with you, then I can work with that, too," he says the last part hopefully.

I think about it for all of three second. "Okay."

Drake eyes me like I am wearing a suit made of money. "Okay what? Okay you are staying at the Wyfle's, or okay you and I are now roommates?"

"Okay." I lean a little closer to Drake's face and glance at his mouth. I whisper, "I'll go get packed," and push up from the sofa.

Drake collapses back. "You are an evil woman, Natalia," he calls after me, as I head down the hall to my room.

Giggling to myself, I lay several clothing items on my bed for me to take. I grab my laptop and book bag, I shove my cell phone charger and as much bathroom stuff in that will fit since my school stuff is still in it. I try to find a suitcase and realize I don't have one. I don't have one because my parents took all of them in order to escape the terror that is me. I slump on the bed, my nose tingles and I fail miserably at holding back tears.

"Hey, what's up?" Drake asks from my doorway.

Hiding my face, I wipe the unwanted liquid on the back of my hands. It doesn't work so I stay facing away from Drake. But it doesn't faze him either. He waltzes in my room, like he has been there a million times before, and sits next to me. Drake pulls me to his warm body again. We sit there awhile, with him holding me, while I try to get it together.

I make an awful snot sucking sound trying to get my nose not to dribble without a tissue. This makes it even harder to face Drake. Let's just add embarrassment to my emotional Molotov cocktail. *Sexiest woman alive right here ladies and gentlemen.* I say weakly, "I don't have any way of carrying my stuff. My parents took all the luggage." I sniff again.

"You want to talk about where they are yet?" Drake asks.

I shake my head: no.

He rubs my arm and leans over to kiss my head. "Honesty time?" he asks.

I shrug. I'm not sure if I want him to be honest right now.

"I think you are exhausted. I think we both have been through enough today. I know I want you to tell me what is going on with your family, but I want you to do it on your own terms. So I'm not pushing you about it. But I do want to understand at some point. So get up."

I look at him, teary eyes and all.

"Man, you are killing me," Drake says, as he takes his hand and wipes the tracks from my tears off my cheeks. He puts his forehead to mine for a long moment. The heat from his long exhale warms my face. Pulling back, "Up!" he commands, as he lets me go.

I stand up. "What?" I search around.

"Is this everything?" Drake indicates toward the stuff on my bed.

I nod. "I think so." I take one more glance around my room to be sure.

"Okay." Drake takes the ends of my comforter on my bed and makes a giant hobo sack. He picks it up, like Santa headed for a chimney, and heads out the door. "Come on, it's almost 3:00 AM, let's get you to Jack's."

I laugh at this boy as he leads me from my home.

This time, when the battered limo pulls up, three *Weres* are standing at the gate. There didn't used to be a gate, but when Celia and Jack got married, and he discovered he was going to be a daddy again, security measures went up like a flag on a pole. To say Jack is protective is an understatement. The men search the car and open my blanket full of stuff on the driveway. I'm not overly pleased to have my belongings riffled through, but I figure I can suffer this indignity quietly if it means my head finds a pillow soon.

Sentries are scattered across the lawn. Nothing will catch Jack off guard. I'm not sure a gnat could get past these guys unnoticed.

Jack meets us at the door, still dressed and with a grim face, looking as though he is planning a war. "Drake, Nat." He motions to someone on the lawn, who comes, takes my things from the driver, and brings them into the house. "Nat, you'll be down the hall from G.J.."

This apparently gives my burly bellhop directions, and he passes Jack with a nod.

"Celia will be glad you are here. Tomorrow we are going to discuss why it is Drake and Hamilton believe your parents are unavailable. But we are all tired now so come inside and get settled." He turns slightly to allow me entrance and it is clear he is indicating Drake should go.

"Jack, can I just have a second?" Drake asks, grabbing my arm to halt my progress.

Jack crosses his massive arms but shows no indication he intends to give us privacy.

Drake faces me darting his gaze nervously from Jack to me. "As crazy as it was, I still would like to go out with you again, Nat."

I tilt my face up to his. His eyes are so earnest I feel like I have to throw him a bone. "You made today bearable."

My face breaks into a smile letting him know I am teasing. "I'd like that."

Drake shoots one more worried look at Jack, whose features are set in a stone mask back at him in warning. With his head slightly turned, focused on Jack, I lift up my toes and press my lips to Drake's. It takes him all of a second to realize what is happening and forget Jack is there. He slides his arms around me and starts to get more involved in the lip lock. Too soon Drake's arms are being pulled apart and I am dragged away.

With me in tow, Jack calls over his shoulder, "Drake, you asked to put her under my protection, which means she is mine to watch out for. Hope you enjoyed it because that's the last time you're going to get one of those from her for a long time." With that, Jack slams the door closed.

Jack squints down at my beet red face and shakes his head. "Get to bed."

I put my head down and move toward the stairs.

"Nat," Jack calls.

I glance back at him from the bottom step.

"We're glad you are here." Jack smiles.

"Thanks, Jack. Me too." I really like Jack.

My room is the one I had been in earlier. It is huge and beautiful. I have my own bath, which makes me do a little happy dance. My sack-o-stuff is off in one corner. I untie the big knot and sort through the items, finding my bedclothes and finding my bathroom items. I put my cell on the nightstand before taking care of my nightly bathroom ritual. Once in my jammies and fully ready for bed, I dig out my cell phone charger and find a plug near the bed. As I go to plug it in for the night, I see I have a text message.

"Good night, Nat," from Drake.

I reply, "G'nite Drake."

Even with the insanity that is my life, I go to bed holding my fingers to my lips, remembering the feel of Drake's. I fall asleep with a little grin.

Chapter Twelve

In the morning, I take time to put away some things and organize. Still in my jammies, I decide I will sneak down to check on G.J.. Sadly, there is no sneaking happening in this house right now. Mr. Calhoun is standing right outside my bedroom door. Several men are also standing at different posts up and down the hall.

I smile a greeting and point toward G.J.'s door in a silent request to pass. The big man nods and lets me by.

If I think the hallway is full of the brawny sort, it doesn't compare to G.J.'s bedroom. G.J. is asleep under the covers, curled onto her side with her head on Adam's chest. Hamilton spoons around the back of her. Both boys are on top of the covers, still in their clothes. While that's in the "I never thought I'd see that in this lifetime" category, what really shocks me is the number of boys strewn about the room.

The huge bulk of Stanzi, a kid who graduated last year, takes up the bedside chair, his feet propped on the mattress. Mikey and another smaller boy lay at the foot of the bed. Several other boys are on the floor, one on the desk, another on an ottoman, and as I stand there, a boy wanders out of the bathroom. All of their eyes have opened, with the exception of G.J.'s, staring at me.

Adam grins and whispers, "Who knew, after all these years, my house would be where the hot chicks flock?"

"Shut up, Adam," Hamilton says, quietly trying not to wake G.J.. In his mind, he realizes he is wrapped around her, unable to decide if he is happy where he is or should remove himself before she wakes up and catches him. He chooses to incur her wrath because he snuggles closer and closes his eyes again.

"What's up, short stuff?" Adam asks quietly. "You need something?"

I stand there not quite sure what to make of the scene. I peer around at all the eyes that come with ears that are on me. A private conversation looks to be out of the picture. "Umm. I need a little Best Bud time, but since she is asleep, I can come back after I get dressed."

"Ha!" Adam lets out a laugh, making his whole chest move and stirring G.J.. "Nat, you're covered from neck to foot in flannel p.j.'s, decorated in rainbows and clouds. Trust me, you are dressed. You'd need to wear things like G.J. does to bed to be worried."

G.J. smacks Adam on the chest in sleepy protest as she, too, now opens her eyes. Hamilton, realizing he is about to get busted, hops off the bed and heads for the bathroom. In doing so, he knocks Stanzi's feet to the floor. G.J. looks down, to where his arm had been, and narrows her eyes toward the now closed door.

I smile; some things never change. I tap in to G.J..

"That boy better not be spraying down the toilet like a fire hose on the loose cause I'm next. And if he leaves the seat up, I'm slamming his hand in it next time like a gator bite."

I laugh. "The bathroom might not be his fault, I'd wager all of these guys have tried their hand at hit the Cheerio throughout the night."

As she sits up to look around, G.J. winces in pain. She grins a little at this new family, who came to be near her.

"And heaven closes its doors." Adam sighs. "Next time let's have the slumber party with Nat and skip Hamilton." He half-begs G.J..

G.J.'s gaze slides toward his; her lips curve up again as shakes her head. As soon as she starts the action, by the look on her face, she regrets her mistake. Her hand goes to her neck.

Adam puts his arm around her in an effort to ease the pain, but there is no way he can. "Sweet, you can't say no to me. Marry me, G.J.?"

G.J. gives him the evil eye.

"Oh, I guess you still can," Adam shrugs, "It was worth a shot."

Hamilton comes out of the bathroom, and G.J. makes her way to the side of the bed. As she stands, I see what Adam meant. G.J. wears a tank top cami and sleep shorts. *Is she nuts?* I look around the room. I could have stolen the crown jewels out from under this pack of boys. Not one soul would have seen a thing until G.J. shut the bathroom door, and they took a minute to shake off the image. Thank heavens I've learned by now, when I see things like that, I have absolutely no desire to know how boys are seeing it.

Before G.J. can reappear, Hamilton snarls, "Get out!" at the boys lying about the room. He stares them all down, which is impressive with Stanzi, who has him by thirty pounds and two or three inches.

They all file past, sniffing me and murmuring hellos and good mornings. Hamilton settles himself on the chair Stanzi vacated and tries to look bored while watching the door G.J. will open at any second.

Adam being Adam takes a pillow and puts it behind his back, getting comfortable and waiting for G.J. to come back to bed. I stand near the door still. Adam pats the bed next to him, "Come on, Nat, make my dreams come true. Come over here and we will wait for G.J.."

"I would but I have enough nightmares," I shoot back.

"You wound me." He grabs his heart. "That's all right, I wouldn't want to be in the hot seat with Aldrich." Adam makes kissy faces and slurping noises.

G.J. opens the door at this point. Her eyes grow round, she points at me before the bed, insisting with only her hand gestures that I sit and tell her all. I don't budge. Giving my bestie a pointed look I glance from Hamilton to Adam, I shake my head. No way am I spilling my guts with those two around.

G.J. makes shooing motions with her hands at first Hamilton, then Adam.

Hamilton takes on his bored, no-way-I'm-going-any-where face and settles himself farther back into the chair.

Adam claps his hands perkily and says, "I love girl talk."

G.J. now takes her finger and points first at Adam, then at Hamilton, and then swirls it around her head before pointing to the door. The boys remain where they are. Frustrated, G.J. stalks from the bathroom door over to me. Adam and Hamilton watch every motion the back of her makes. Their eyes work slowly up from her bare feet and linger around her rump. Man, these guys are so blatant I'm embarrassed for G.J. without sneaking a mental peek. I am buying her a big, fluffy robe for Columbus Day. That's the next holiday, right?

Oblivious, G.J. grabs my hand and pulls me into the room. Her arm once again directs the two unmovable boys to vacate the premises. Again, they lounge. She stomps her foot and points to the door once more. No response.

"In case you missed it, I think she would like you to leave," I put forth dryly.

"Well, we aren't, so she should stop jiggling and give up already," Hamilton, in his absurd way, says to our collective stone faces.

"Ham, I love you, brother, but some of the things you say are truly stupid," says Adam.

G.J. recovers from the jiggle comment and scowls at the interlopers. Then, and I saw this coming even if the boys didn't, the two almost-men start floating up and out of the room.

"G.J., stop," Hamilton yells.

"Come on, G.J.," Adam objects.

At the door, Adam misses the frame, but Hamilton snags it with his fingers. Using her will, G.J. slowly lifts each finger. All the blood has left Hamilton's now white fingertips. With triumph in her eyes, his last finger gives and she slams the door closed in Hamilton's angry face.

It takes only a bare moment for the pounding on the door to start, and the perturbed duo to voice their annoyance, muffled by wood.

"Do you think the door will hold?" I ask.

G.J. gives me a one-shouldered shrug, heads back to her bed, and climbs in.

"Be glad the boys weren't here to watch you do that. They might never get their tongues back in their mouth." After watching my best friend unknowingly crawl around on a mattress, like she is starring in a Katy Perry video, I shake my head. "By the way, we need to have a serious chat about respectable sleepwear."

G.J. looks at my ensemble and lets me know with a look that there is no way she is donning my attire.

"I grew up in the south. It is hot. This is what is comfortable to me. I would feel smothered like a gravy covered biscuit in your getup."

"There has to be a compromise," I say. "The torture you are inflicting on these boys will employ therapists for decades."

G.J. rolls her eyes and gives her head a small dismissive shake. Sitting tailor-fashion on her bed, she plops a pillow on her lap, half-hugging it, makes a talking sign by mimicking a bird with one hand, and aims her finger at me. When I don't respond, she puckers up her lips miming smooching.

"Oh, yeah, I kissed Drake." It is my turn to do a one-shoulder shrug and look out the window.

Her pillow smacks me in the head. When I glance back at her, her eyes narrow at me and she taps her temple.

"From the beginning. Start with when he picked you up and end with is he a good kisser? Skip nothing."

I laugh. "Man, you are nosey. He was on time. We had a nice dinner, Hamilton came to kidnap me. A meteor hit the car. My best friend was attacked. I passed out reading her mind. I went home. I was taken hostage by an old friend. And I packed all my belongings and moved in with your family." I stop counting on my ninth finger for a second; this makes G.J. take her foot and push my leg in prompting. "Oh yeah and I wouldn't mind kissing him again." My cheeks heat up with my confession.

G.J. makes a continuous circle in the air. The banging and yelling continue from the hall.

"Really, out of that whole list, you think the kiss is the most important thing to re-hash?"

G.J. nods gently, eager but trying not to cause herself pain.

"Go kiss one of your own boys," I sling, "I'm not spilling."

G.J. puts up her hands, as if to say what boys.

"You want me to go open the door?" My expression's clear; I'm not buying it.

She taps her temple again. *"One of them is my brother and the other just compared me to a Jell-O product. No thanks."*

"I'm fairly sure Adam, in no way, considers you a sister and Hamilton..." I sigh.

"Hamilton loves to find new exciting ways to abuse me with the English language. Besides he and Sara have something going on." She gives a little shiver. *"I don't have time for all that. I need to live vicariously through you. Details."*

I shake my head. "Nope, sorry, not going to happen."

The banging turns to a loud pounding knock.

"Uh-Oh." G.J. opens the door with her will. A very sleepy and angry Jack is standing there with his hands on his hips.

"Good morning, ladies," Jack says in a way that lets us know he sees nothing good about it.

G.J. waves, and I return a mumbled, "Morning, Jack."

"Would either of the two young women, who were attacked last night, like to explain to me why they have removed the guards I posted?" Jack's nonchalance is a little disturbing.

I point at G.J.. "She did it."

Again, her foot finds my leg this time almost unseating me.

Jack moves his massive form into the room. "G.J., we have talked about this. You can't go around tossing the boys here and there. For one thing, I want to know you are protected. For another, they don't handle it well. Finally, I have a pregnant wife who needs her sleep and can't get it if those two are banging on your door." He reaches G.J. and towers over her with his massive arms crossed, stretching the limits of his T-shirt sleeves. "You and I have a deal."

G.J. tilts her face down in that same submissive way Hamilton had last night.

Jack carefully takes her chin in one of his huge hands bringing her attention to him. "Not again."

G.J. looks at him and begrudgingly acquiesces with a slide of her eyes.

"How is your neck today?" Jack asks.

G.J. swallows and in a painfully hoarse whisper-croak manages, "Hurts but better."

Jack tilts her head and examines the bandage. "The bleeding looks to be slowing down. Is that you or is that happening on its own?"

G.J. pointed her thumb back at her body.

"What happens if you stop holding it back?" Jack asks.

While it doesn't look like she does anything, the bandage at her neck starts to turn red quickly.

"Enough!" Jack commands. Hamilton and Adam are right behind him. "Go get cleaned up. I'll talk to both you girls after breakfast. Are you up for coming downstairs or do you want me to have yours sent up?"

G.J. points out the door toward the stairs.

"All right, stay with at least one of the pack," he warns her again, and walks out of the room rubbing his eyes.

"I call shower detail!" Adam says.

"Adam!" Jack leans back in the door, glaring at his son.

Chapter Thirteen

After readying for the day, I go back to G.J.'s room. She wears a new tank top and a pair of jeans. Her hair is wet. It has grown out since last year, when she lost it due to a head injury, and now makes a slicked back bob. Adam's normally jovial face is stern as he gingerly tries to put a clean bandage over her wound. When G.J. flinches, so does he and his face becomes even grimmer.

"You got it, or do you want me to give it a shot?" I offer my assistance.

"I got it," he says, "I get lots of practice playing nurse maid to this klutz." Adam gestures at G.J. with a nod.

G.J. sends him a sarcastic ha-ha-very-funny face.

"Whatever it takes to get you on the mend," he says, leaning over her. "I'm up for the job. Besides, who can resist spending time alone with G.J.?"

G.J. puckers up and smooches the air up toward Adam's face in a pretend kiss. Adam becomes immobile, fixated on her mouth it seems, as if he is about to dive for it.

"Easy boy," I coach. "She truly has no clue."

Adam shakes his head and peers at me in longing dismay. As G.J., the girl with the genius I.Q., peers at me in innocent question, I'm not sure if I do or don't want to be here when she figures it out. Adam puts on the last piece of tape and uses his fingers to smooth it in place.

G.J. smiles and stands, forcing Adam to back up a step. She grabs a zip up hoodie on the bed next to her and mouths, "Thank you," to Adam.

"Anytime." He means the word more than she realizes. "Umm you might need to re-tape that in a little while. Your skin—" He swallows before he continues "—is still damp from your shower." Poor Adam, he may put up a brave front, but she has his insides so tied up it's a wonder he can breathe.

G.J. touches the tape and tests how secure it is. She slides on her sweatshirt. As she does, Adam is mourning the view of each inch of skin as she covers it.

I shake my head. "You ready?"

In response, she heads in my direction. I'm glad she is with me. I would have felt awkward making my way to the kitchen by myself. Even though I'm a guest, I still have the feeling I don't belong.

The house smells of all the beautiful things breakfast should smell like: bacon, sausage, cooking dough, melted butter with a hint of citrus. Dinner last night was great, but I am so looking forward to this breakfast.

Celia is sitting on a stool at the counter with her head over a cup, inhaling deeply. Jack is facing her, spatula in hand in full on lecture mode. "Ceily, you told me not to let you have any coffee."

"I'm just smelling it," Celia protests. "Our lives need to be a bit less exhausting if I'm going to live by that rule."

Jack comes around the island and steals a kiss along with his coffee cup. "What is little stuff up for this morning?" he asks the woman he so clearly loves.

"Right now, I think maybe an egg?" She puts her hand

on her stomach thinking about the food, then changes her mind. "We'll start with toast."

"Toast it is." Jack moves to make it happen.

Celia realizes we are there. "Hey, you're up." She starts to rise in order to go to G.J..

G.J. motions her back and comes to her instead.

"Good Morning, Nat. Welcome. Did you sleep well?" Celia asks.

"Yeah, thanks for having me," meaning the often spoken return.

"G.J., up for giving me a hand?" Jack asks. "I have to feed all the men I've called over."

G.J. starts pulling out pans and heads to the fridge to see what else is available. I sit next to Celia on a stool and settle in to watch.

Adam, who followed us down, says, "Dad, I'm gonna go grab a shower if you got this?"

Jack nods his permission for G.J.'s assigned protector to take his leave. Adam jogs out, hurrying in order to return quickly.

Celia shakes her head, as if she still can't believe the world she married into. She turns to me. "Okay, Nat, let's hear what happened to you last night."

I'm a little unsure of where she wants me to start. "Uhhh,"

"How about we start with where are your parents?" Jack says, his back to us, sliding the toast in the toaster.

G.J. looks at me with a question on her face as she tries not to drop all of the refrigerated items she has bundled to her chest.

"I don't know where they are," I answer honestly if not helpfully.

"What? What does that mean?" Celia has turned her fully concerned parental figure aim on me.

"They left. I woke up from a nap after school a few days ago, and I realized they were gone. They might have left the night before, or they could have left while I was a school. I really don't know." I shrug desperately uncomfortable.

"They hadn't planned a trip or anything?" Celia asks.

I shake my head, waiting for the unwanted, obvious next question.

"Why?" Celia is utterly baffled.

"Oh, G.J., didn't mention it. I'm a bridge to other dimensions that could mean the end of humanity. Thanks for having me over." I try to act like this means nothing, but the twisted remnants of a napkin I found on the counter give away my fear.

Jack glares at me. "Come again?" He seems to be judging the distance between his wife and me, holding his spatula, like he might use it to fling me away from her if it becomes necessary.

If my parents really felt it was necessary to leave; I should tell these people I care about I might be a danger to them. I blow out a breath and start my confession. "So apparently the whole mind reading thing is because I'm a Faery."

Celia throws her hands up in the air, as if she has officially given up on the world she used to believe was her reality. Jack, however, just nods.

I tilt my head and look at him. "You knew?"

"You smell different. I didn't know what you were until the boys told me, but I know you and your parents aren't human." The man really doesn't seem to be phased by my Faery-ness.

My features pinch in hesitation as I avoid meeting anyone's gaze directly. I continue, uncertain to their reaction, "So I have been seeing ghosts for a while."

Celia barks out a little laugh of incredulity.

I go on, "They have been sort of invading my head. When I told my mom, she freaked out. She said I am a bridge to other planes of existence and all the other bridges have been killed to prevent the other, I guess, Faeries, from coming back. My parents think I can send them there if I touch them."

Again, Jack mentally measures the distance between Celia and me.

"Look, I didn't even know I wasn't human 'til Tuesday, so I have no clue if this is true or not. But because of this, my parents went walkabout."

Celia puts her hand on my arm, which makes Jack tense up. "You have been alone since Tuesday?" Her care is so genuine; I envy G.J. more than a little.

I nod.

"Nat, I'm so sorry," Celia says in a soft voice. "They left you with people going missing left and right?"

"Uhhh yeah," If I'm confessing I'm going all out, "So about that." I shoot a look at G.J., who knows where this is going and is waiting to see what I do. "I know the guys said I thought it was the pack that was mauling these people. I only thought it because my new dead pals said I have dangerous friends. At the time, your gang was the most dangerous I could think of."

"We still are," Jack states, not boasting just informing.

I don't disagree. "So, I'm sorry. I know none of you would do anything like that to G.J.."

Jack turns his back to me and works on getting his wife some toast.

"Nat, this has to be so terrifying for you," Celia says.

"Tell me about it. The ghosts like to let me feel what it was like the moment they died." I shake off the memory. "It is truly awful."

Jack puts a plate in front of Celia. "Do they all die the same way?"

"Jack. Please. I am working on the concept of keeping the toast down. Can we not go there right now?" Celia asks.

Jack nods and shoots me a direct gaze saying we will be going over this later. I nod back acknowledging I know.

"I'll have to say I was more than a little jumpy thinking that way and having Hamilton show up all ticked off. That is why he and Drake got into it," I explain.

Jack raises his eyebrow at me.

"Oh that's right. You two were on a date last night. I'm putting in a post-it there, and we will come back to that later," Celia says, her face in the same expression as her niece's when wanting details.

I blush a little. "Anyway, Hamilton said he had broken into the house and so when we got back from here, I thought he was the one who had left my door open."

Celia gives Jack a "You are going to speak to him about that or I will" scowl. Jack's reply is a bland face.

"But it was Gus. He was waiting in my house, and when Drake came back to the door, because I had forgotten my purse in the car, Gus grabbed me from behind and kind of held me hostage 'til Drake told him G.J. was alive."

G.J. drops the pan she is working with and looks at me in horror. Jack slides over to turn off the burner and hustles her over to a chair.

"Then he disappeared," I finish.

G.J. taps her temple. "*I told you not to say anything about Gus.*"

"You told me not to say anything about him with you. I only told what happened to me," I say, and we both realize I am speaking out loud when three growls erupt in the room. Hamilton and Adam have returned.

Celia brings the moment of tension to a head. "Girls, this is not a time to keep secrets. I won't have it, G.J.. Nat, if you know something, I insist that you tell us."

I turn to G.J. who makes her go on motion with her hand dejectedly.

In trying to mitigate the damage, I start with G.J.'s disclaimer. "G.J. doesn't think Gus did anything. She thinks he was just there." All eyes are on me, and I am feeling shorter by the second.

Jack's puts his hands on the counter, glowering and giving a clear indication to get on with it.

I run back through what happened in G.J.'s mind. She holds her neck as she remembers. Celia's fingers are on her mouth to hold in the one bite of toast she has gotten in it; Hamilton and Adam pace.

When I finish, Jack asks, "Is that everything?"

"Yes. I think so," I answer trying to run over the details again in my mind.

"He's a dead man." Hamilton growls.

"Settle," Jack commands.

"Dad, we can take him." Adam's eyes are the color of the sun through honey.

"I said settle," Jack snaps at the two younger men.

They immediately expose their necks in submission.

"Sanzor didn't attack G.J. I have no idea about the rest of the missing, but his smell is nowhere on her or her wound," Jack informs everyone.

G.J. huffs out a relieved breath.

Hamilton stalks over to her and grabs both shoulders, pulling her to him so he can smell her neck. G.J. stands there, startled by his sudden action. He releases her quickly and turns on Adam. "You!" and he charges for the other boy.

Adam braces for impact, but before he can take his second step, Jack has Hamilton on the ground by his throat. Jack's eyes are molten amber. "You dare to attack anyone in front of my wife who is carrying my child." The words are so low the rumble makes the glassware around the room tinkle as it shivers in vibration.

Hamilton goes limp in submission.

Jack picks up the boy a little and slams him back on the ground. "You... will... never... put... my wife... in harm's way." He isn't worried about Adam, who had been Hamilton's target.

Everyone in the room can tell, without being a mind reader, that Jack needs a minute if he is going to stop himself from doing some real damage to Hamilton. We all sit very still in the tension soup the air has become. I take the opportunity to do a spot check on what in is running through everyone's head.

Jack is thinking exactly what I guessed. Don't kill this impudent pup and Hamilton is going to be put through some "manners" classes until something gives. He may be a leader someday, but he has gone far too long without a humility check.

Adam is stunned that his best friend could think he would harm G.J.. He isn't worried about fighting Hamilton, though, and, at the moment, eagerly anticipates the opportunity. Adam hopes G.J., nor anyone else, will believe he would do such a thing. He is worried about Celia and me. Adam really is a sweet pea. But he starts flashing though what he intends to do to Hamilton when he gets a shot at him. That sort of kills my aww moment. I leave him to work that out and move on to Celia.

Celia is taking full but shallow breaths, trying not to vomit, the stress of the moment not helping her morning sickness. She is worried about Hamilton and wants Jack to let him go. She wants to comfort her husband, who she can tell is strung tight right now, but feels hesitant to step on some unknown pack law. But Celia is a sharp cookie and takes mental notes to address later.

G.J. is ticked. She is not happy Hamilton grabbed her. Not at all pleased he was about to start a brawl in her kitchen and thinks he is way too violent. She, too, has plans to teach him a lesson if she gets him alone. I kind of feel for Hamilton, his little outburst has three people wanting to catch him in a dark alley so to speak. G.J. is also annoyed he stopped Jack from explaining about Gus. She is glad she trusted her instincts about him. Gus didn't do it and she is now determined to talk to him. This makes me nervous because I am not as positive as she and Jack, not after my run in with him last night. But G.J.'s mind moves back to the food that was being prepared and, bustling, she makes sure it all remains edible.

Hamilton is actively trying to think of ways to get to Adam, even if it is through Jack. His brain placed Adam's scent signature on G.J.'s neck. He doesn't understand why Jack is protecting Adam, other than favoritism. Hamilton doesn't care if he has to take on Jack himself, he will destroy Adam for marking G.J. He is distraught; G.J. has a wound that will mark her. He is helpless and that only adds to his frustrated anger. He wants to lock G.J. away. My face screws up in a you're-bonkers-if-you-think-that-is-going-to-work way.

To ease the tension, I figure it's time to share. "Hamilton, Adam changed G.J.'s bandage today. I am pretty sure that is why you smell him on her. Jack, while I am not defending his actions, because I think Hamilton needs to take it down a few notches, he thought Adam did that to G.J. to mark her as his. While he should have, he didn't register anyone else was in the room."

Jack looks down at Hamilton warning clear in his eyes and his voice. "Never again." Regaining full control of himself, he lets go of Hamilton's throat.

Hamilton stands up tentatively, not meeting anyone's eyes. No one seems sure how to get from what just happened to the next moment. Of course, G.J. is never truly speechless. She walks over and slaps the counter in front of me to get my attention. She points to her temple and then back at me. This seems to be her new way of turning on my translator mode. "Here we go," I murmur.

"You tell that obtuse testosterone junkie if he grabs me like that again, I'm going to pin him to the wall like an entomology exhibit. He needs to use his words, if he can figure out how to string them together. I will not be his personal scratch and sniff. And if he thinks he would have made it to Adam, he is delusional. If Jack hadn't have gotten to him, I would have set him up the nearest tree."

"Whoa, settle down, you might be able to memorize the Gettysburg Address after one recitation, but you are going to have to spoon feed me what you want me to tell them." I stop her mid rant. "Hamilton, you're a moron." I look back at G.J. very proud of my edited version of what she wants to say. She seems annoyed that I somehow missed the highlights.

Throwing her hands up, G.J. turns back to getting the breakfast stuff to some semblance of order.

Adam's normally quick-with-a-smile features turn on Hamilton, as if they had never been friends. Adam's breathing is slow and even, yet it seems it takes him a great deal of effort to accomplish. Hamilton faces Adam in the same impassive masque; each of them silently determined there would be a reckoning in the future. Jack watches the two younger men before letting out an enormous tired sigh. He looks over at G.J. who has her back to him at the moment, then at Celia.

Celia rubs her forehead. "If you thought this was going to be easy, you aren't as smart as I thought."

"I never expected easy but this is…" Jack shakes his head. "Let's all have something to eat."

G.J., in silent agreement, starts placing some of the food out on the table and the rest goes into buffet trays she has pulled from the large pantry. Celia takes her now cold toast and sets it at her place before grabbing place settings for everyone. The rest of us lend a hand and soon sit at the large kitchen table.

"Are you sure you don't want to try that egg?" Jack solicits Celia.

"I'm good." She tries to avoid looking at all of the rest of the food on the table.

Jack takes a helping and slides things onto G.J.'s plate he knows she likes until her hand goes up to stop him. From there the food is passed around. Hamilton getting the plates last. Once Jack starts eating, we all dig in except Hamilton. After a few minutes, Jack inclines his head to him, which is the indicator he, too, can eat. There is an awkward bite to the air and no one is particularly talkative.

G.J. taps my arm. I should have guessed she would be the one to break the reigning silence by making me do it.

"Ask Hamilton how he could blame any wolf for what happened."

"Really? Now? Can't we wait until the sharp objects are out of reach?" I ask, hoping to put this off 'til maybe sometime in the next decade.

"What is it?" Jack directs his inquiry to me.

"Sometimes being the mind reader is really a pain in the butt," I grumble. Taking in a resigned breath, I relay, "She wants Hamilton to explain how he could think any wolf could do this?"

Hamilton brings his gaze up to meet G.J.'s. He opens his mouth to respond, but before any words make it out, Jack says, "What makes you think it wasn't a wolf?"

All eyes fall on the head of the pack.

Adam in incredulity verbalizes the stunned question on all of our lips. "Dad, you think a wolf did this to G.J.?"

Instead of being vindicated, Hamilton is just as stunned as the rest of us.

Jack puts down his fork and steeples his hands over his plate, his elbows on the table. "I don't know that it was a wolf. But it easily could have been. I have nothing to prove it wasn't. And you aren't the only ones who see G.J.'s potential. I've—" Jack pauses, "—dissuaded a few suitors since she joined the pack. I worry one of them might have decided marking her was worth the risk. But to be fair, the scent is not one I know."

Everyone sits, blinking, in the face of this news. Both Hamilton and Adam's hands ball into fists as they do what they can to hold on to their civility. They are resigned that one of them will be with G.J., in the end, but woe to any other male who makes an attempt.

She taps my arm asking me to translate again. G.J. puts her hand to her neck and she falls back into the memory of the attack.

"Okay, just don't relive that moment again, or your voice box will pass out. I admit I'm a wimp."

G.J. carefully bobs her head. "*Tell everyone to hear me out before they jump to conclusions.*" She waits as I do. "*It wasn't a wolf.*"

"She says it wasn't a wolf."

"What makes you say so?" Jack asks her.

"*My will wouldn't work on my attacker. I can use it on wolves.*" Her eyes encourage me to share.

"G.J.'s power didn't work on her attacker. Remember, she had to hit them with that wood."

"Has that ever happened before?" Jack asked.

G.J.'s face pinches in worry, showing discomfort in what she is going to say next. "*It didn't work on Gus. But Jack already said it wasn't him.*"

I look at her, not sure to be as secure in her faith of my old friend. "It doesn't work on Gus."

Chapter Fourteen

Jack pins G.J. with a long stare. You can see him re-evaluating his previous determination. "You could have mentioned this before."

"*Remind him, he doesn't think it is Gus,*" G.J. prompts me.

"She says—"

Jack puts up a hand. "I know what I said, I also know I wasn't given all the information." Again, he scowls back at G.J., perturbed by her omission.

"Gus has been after her since she got here," Hamilton the Helpful chimes in.

G.J. rolls her eyes. Jack seems to be going over some memory and nods.

"Why wouldn't your powers work on him?" Celia asks.

G.J. shrugs in utter bewilderment.

"Gus isn't human, either," Jack informs her.

"Werewolves, Witches, Faeries, Ghosts…" Celia counts off on her fingers. "Who are we missing… oh yes, vampires." She thought she was joking around until Jack reluctantly nods. Celia closes her eyes for a silent moment before opening them in horror, and snaps to G.J., "A vampire bit G.J? Oh my god, what does that mean? What will it do to her?"

G.J.'s hand is on her neck as her scared brain runs through her own millions of questions.

"I don't know." Jack tries to sound reassuring, even presenting his lack of knowledge. "Why is it you don't think it was Gus?" Jack faces G.J..

G.J. tilts her head down examining her plate. She peeks up at me for help.

I sigh. "I am not sure you can trust him, G.J.."

She shoots me a betrayed glare and taps her temple. *"Look at his face."* She again shows me her memory of laying on the ground and Gus. *"He thought I had been killed. Whoever did this to me knew I was alive. They did something that paralyzed me, but they knew I was alive."*

While I still am unsure, I try to explain as best I can, "Gus was there when she was attacked." G.J. corrects me with a nudge. "I guess he was there just after. And he looked horrified by what happened to her. He also thought she was dead. He did seem surprised when Drake and I told him she is still kicking."

"G.J., do you think you can't heal your wound because of who it was that inflicted it?" Hamilton asks. It always surprises me when he proves not to be so stupid.

G.J. gives a thoughtful half-shrug, indicating it is a possibility.

Jack communicates to Celia with one of those spouse gestures that presents themselves as a facial tick to those not in the relationship.

Celia says, "I need to go lie down."

"G.J., will you take Celia upstairs?' Jack requests.

G.J. quickly moves to help her Aunt upstairs.

When they have gone, Jack turns back to the rest of us. "I want a meeting with Gus. Which one of you can make that happen?"

"You think he did it?" Adam asks.

"I don't care if he did or didn't, he left her for dead," Hamilton says, focusing on a point that makes him crazy.

Adam nods at his old friend in silent deadly accord.

Jack's hand slams on the tabletop making us all jump. "Nobody in this pack makes that kind of decision other than me." His warning skewers the two boys. "Gus will not be harmed. For God's sake, think, you two. G.J. can't heal herself. And we don't know how to. She can't keep blood from flowing to that area forever. Infection will set in soon. Gus is our best chance of figuring out how to fix her neck. We need him on our side, or she *could* end up dead. We will not risk it. Are we clear?"

Hamilton nods, lost in worried thoughts.

Adam looks down, then up at his father. "When this is over. Either way it ends up. I make no promises, I'll leave it at that with Gus. Hamilton is right. If I hadn't had been right behind her, she could already be gone, and Gus did nothing to help. I can't, Dad. If it were Celia, you wouldn't, either."

"Celia wouldn't feel the need to hide from me. The two of you need to understand anyone you are trying to protect has to know you will care about that, above any opinions you might have about their lives. If the ones you are protecting try to hide things from you, that is when it gets exponentially more dangerous. They should never see you as a jailor. This happened because you both seem to want to control G.J.. You never will. She is not submissive, and if that is what you want, you need to look elsewhere. Celia is a strong, smart, incredible woman. She knows she is my partner. Celia understands I need to keep her safe and accepts it as just who I am. My caring for her doesn't mean I think she is helpless. She gets that it means I think she is precious. She also knows I would never allow her to be hurt like that." Jack's eyes blaze with his wolf, and the younger men absorb their lesson.

"Gus wants to talk to me. I can see if I can make it happen," I jump in.

"Soon, Nat. I am worried about this." Jack puts the weight of G.J.'s life on my shoulders.

I give Jack an "I understand" glance.

"Adam, go let the others know it's time to eat. Hamilton put on some sweats, I'll meet you in the gym. I hear you went a round with Aldrich. It's time you and I worked on a few things." Jack let Hamilton know this was not going to be fun for anyone, except maybe him.

I find it strange they think Drake is such a threat. It makes me wonder why.

****

I run into G.J. coming down the stairs as I am heading up. She turns and we walk back to my room. Stanzi meets us at the top of the steps. G.J. makes an eating motion and points down toward the kitchen.

"I'm not hungry." He falls in behind us.

G.J.'s face shows utter disbelief with her jaw wide open, and she steps awkwardly backward to show him her shocked face. She apparently knows his appetite.

Stanzi just grins and continues to shadow us.

At my door, Mr. Calhoun steps forward from the vicinity of G.J.'s room "I have the girls, you go grab some food." He smiles at Stanzi putting him at ease.

G.J. and I continue into my room. She puts up her hands, like a game show prize model, and silently asks what I think of my new digs.

"Pretty cool, I can definitely get into having my own bath."

She sits on the bed and pats the mattress. When I join her, she prompts me to talk. Before I begin, my cell shimmies as it buzzes with vibration. She leans back and grabs it, handing it over to me.

I can't keep the huge grin from my face.

"Good Morning." Drake greets.

"Good Morning." Apparently, my voice has an auto set to flirty. Who knew?

G.J. makes a kissy face and gets off my bed to give me some space. I roll my eyes at her, but my grin doesn't waiver.

"I was out for a drive and thought you might be up for breakfast," he asks hopefully.

"I have already checked that off my 'to do' list."

"Coffee then?" he presses.

"Ummm," I know I need to get a hold of Gus and don't want G.J. to get twitchy. "That could work."

"Don't sound so excited."

"Sorry, it sounds great. I have to run it past the powers that be," I remind him of having to report to parental types.

"Good, I'm already on my way. I should be there in a few."

"That confident, huh?"

"Optimistic," he corrects.

My smile gets even bigger. "It might take me a minute."

"I'm actually pulling onto your street now, but I can wait."

"Okay, pushy. See you soon." I am about to hit end, when I hear a loud thumping smash against the far wall. "Oh my God," I scream.

Mr. Calhoun has G.J. by her damaged throat pinned against the wall. "Submit!" he growls at her. Blood is seeping through his tight fingers.

The pain is wrenching to even watch G.J. experience it.

Distantly I hear a tinny voice. "Nat?"

I fly at the attacker's back, "Let go of her." He flings me off with one arm, but with his wolfie strength, I slam against the desk knocking everything on it to the floor as I slide and fall off the opposite side. I groan.

G.J.'s agony-filled eyes search out what happened to me with worry. She can't breathe.

Mr. Calhoun leans close to her ear. "You are making this harder than it has to be. Submit quickly and things will go back to the way they were. You aren't meant to be beta. You aren't even a wolf. Submit and it is all over." He seems to think he is having a rational discussion while squeezing the life out of my friend.

G.J. picks him up so his feet are floating outward, but she can't quite seem to break the hold on her neck.

"You're killing her!" I scream at him.

"Shut up or I will end you, Nat," he snarls over his shoulder.

G.J. struggles with renewed vigor. She pries at his hand and manages to tear away from the one on her throat, losing her bloody bandage in the process. Sadly, he has a hold of her arm with the other. G.J.'s blood pulses wildly out of her wound with every rapid heartbeat.

In a move of sheer intimidation, he licks his fingers cleaning off her blood. "Mmmmm." He growls low enjoying the flavor.

Ugh.

"That's a taste I could get used to. I might have to mark you myself."

G.J. twists her arm while forcing Mr. Calhoun farther away. He manages to keep hold of her sleeve. He grins down at her, proud of himself for stopping her attempt to dislodge him.

"What in the world?" Celia says from the doorway.

"Sorry, Celia," And he seems genuinely sad this is happening. "G.J., just needs to submit and we will be all done here. This is a challenge fight. No one can get involved."

G.J.'s face turns wrathful. She slams him with objects from around the room. "*You never claimed challenge! You snuck up on me!*"

Mr. Calhoun manages to pull himself toward her and backhands her across the face. "Not so easy this time," he taunts, floating in midair.

"Jack!" Celia cries.

I tap his mind: *"This girl is no beta. No wound makes a beta weak. She is nothing but a breeder. She isn't even aware when an attack is coming. Weak."*

I love G.J.'s brain. Because even standing there, fighting for her life, bleeding to death, it comes up with her next move. She unzips her hoodie and flings it and Mr. Calhoun out the window.

Celia and I race to G.J., who doubles over, sucking in air and regaining her composure. Adam is in the doorway, trying to make sense of the insane scene he's ran in on. Before he can react to anything, there is an explosion from the yard. And then another.

Jack is yelling for Celia from down the hall.

"Dad," Adam yells to direct his father. Again, an explosion wobbles my room.

Jack is in the room and has Celia wrapped up in his arms. With his neck, he motions Adam to look out the window. Hamilton has now made it to my room. He, too, can't figure out what is happening. His gaze falls on G.J., her bare neck wound covered in blood, and his large frame tumbles toward her.

By just saying his name, Jack commands his son to give him information, "Adam."

"It's Aldrich." His eyes drop to Hamilton. "It looks like he fried Luke."

Chapter Fifteen

J ack examines Celia, who wholly focuses on G.J.. The big
man lets out a roar-like noise. "I don't care what that kid
is, he is over." Jack starts to stand.

Celia comes back to herself. "What? Jack, no!" She holds
tight to Jack, pulling his attention from his rage.

"Celia, I have to go deal with this." He gently tries to
extricate himself from his wife.

"Jack." She grabs a stronger hold and makes him pay
attention to her. "Luke attacked G.J," Celia spits out before
her husband can break free.

"What?" Jack asks, as if she has started to speak a different language.

Hamilton, too, gapes at Celia, unwilling to believe
her words.

"Dad, Drake is submitting to the guys on the lawn. He
isn't doing anything and they aren't using kid gloves," Adam
informs his father.

I defend my best friend, "Jack, Mr. Calhoun attacked
G.J. with no warning, and then after the fact claimed it was
a challenge fight. He had G.J. by the throat before she knew
what was happening. He wants to be beta again and doesn't
think G.J. has the right."

Hamilton turns his face toward G.J., who centers her mind on trying to heal in his arms. G.J.'s neck is still bleeding badly and her body is shivering.

Jack says in a wounded voice, "He was to protect you. He swore to protect you." He gingerly strokes Celia's head and his equally wounded gaze lands on G.J., like he can feel her pain.

"He was so mad about not being beta," Hamilton says, "I knew how mad he was, but I never thought he would hurt her, Jack. He knows what she means to—"

I cut him off. "After he squeezed her already shredded neck, and tore off her bandage, he licked her blood and said he should mark her. This is who he is, Jack. This was what he did and what he thought. Don't delude yourself. Look at what he tried to do because he thought he could take G.J. while she is injured." I stare down the massive form of Jack Wyfle and point at G.J.'s ravaged neck and face that is swelling from the blow. Werewolves can really pack a punch.

G.J. shivers and goes limp. Hamilton pulls her over his lap and cradles her to him. He puts his head down, whispering something I can't hear, but it sounds repetitive. More men begin to crowd the room.

Jack pulls Celia's face to his and kisses her. "I will take care of this. Please go with Stanzi." He helps his wife up and hands her off to the big young man. "Hamilton, take G.J. with Celia. Go to the safe room until I can sort this out. Nat, please…" Jack's orders fall short on me.

"I'm going with you," I insist.

"Not now, Nat," Jack rumbles, distracted.

"If Drake is attacking you, I can find out why faster than you can," I argue.

"Nat, I know your gift doesn't work on Drake. You have made it clear several times." Jack is unmoved by my argument.

"Drake has promised me honesty, Jack." My direct stare conveys my belief this will work. "He will tell me why he did whatever Adam thinks he did."

Jack studies me for a moment. "Adam, stay with Nat. The first sign of trouble and you get her out of there."

We all follow his instructions.

Outside, the air smells a bit like struck matches and overcooked meat. Scorches mark the lawn. Drake is face down in the grass with two men sitting on his back.

When we are about twenty feet away, Jack calls out, "Let him up."

Drake's scans me head to toe as soon as he finds me before to focusing on Jack. "Where is G.J.?"

"You don't get to ask questions. Why are you here?" Jack returns.

"I came to see Nat. I was going to take her to coffee," Drake answers.

"And you just happened to blow up my lawn and attack a leader in my pack?"

"He's still alive. You can do what you want with him." Drake's face is impassive.

Jack's head motion moves all of our attention, magnetizing to the form of the badly burned man motionless on the ground. "You left him alive?"

"It was hard, but yes," Drake admits.

"Why?" Jack asks, genuinely curious.

"I was on the phone with Nat when I heard something happening. She was trying to stop someone fighting. I stayed on the phone so I could hear the fight, but I couldn't do anything about it. I heard Mr. Calhoun threaten Nat and attack G.J.. I then saw him—" Drake gestures with his head "—come flying out the window. I can't let what he did ride. He started to run from the house, and I took care of it. I left him for you. I didn't cross the line."

"It is not your place to get involved in our business." Jack levels Drake with a stare.

"I left him alive." Drake is nonchalant.

Jack asks the men around Drake, "Is that what you saw?"

A chorus of "Yeah's" come from the more verbal of the men, the other less loquacious only nod.

"You should have let him run." Jack shakes his head and rubs his hair. "What a mess."

"He threatened Nat. I left her in your care, Jack. I only hurt the one who threatened her." Drake looks at me. I really do hate that I can't tell what he's thinking.

Jack nods. "I failed you and Nat. Christ, I failed G.J. and Celia." His disappointed gaze moves to the former beta of his pack. "Take him to the cage, when he heals, I will call a pack meeting."

"Nat, are you okay?" Drake asks.

"I'm doing better than that guy. Do you carry a bazooka or flame thrower or something?"

Jack laughs at Drake saying. "Good luck! Why don't you come in for coffee? I need to get back and check on the girls."

Agreeing, Drake walks over to me.

Jack stands close to us with his arms crossed. Drake gently takes my face and turns it toward the light. "Is this your only injury?"

Jack looks at my throbbing cheek and swears.

"My hip caught the desk when I went over it, but I'm fine. G.J. though…" I shake my head and my eyes well with tears.

We all move toward the house at a swift pace and we head inside.

Jack clears the house of all but a certain few wolves. Only when everyone else leaves does he open the safe room. Celia holds a bandage to G.J.'s neck, and Hamilton still holds G.J. in his lap. All three are sitting on a sofa. Stanzi sits in a substantial office chair over by a bank of monitors keeping an eye on what looks like the entire Wyfle compound.

"How is she?" Jack asks, as he moves to his wife's side.

"There are new scratches," Celia says. "When she woke up a minute ago, I told her that. Then the blood started flowing really badly. The new scratches started to heal, and then G.J. passed out. Jack, she is losing so much blood." As she takes air in for strength, Celia's breath shudders.

Jack gently turns G.J.'s head and removes the cloth too see the wound. Again, he swears and covers it back up.

Hamilton faces Jack with hopeless eyes. "Dad went right for the injury. No mercy. He would have killed her to be beta again. There is no making this right." Hamilton looks down at G.J. and puts his forehead to hers. He softly voices, "I am so sorry. God, I am so sorry."

G.J.'s hand slaps Hamilton's arm that weakly encircles her, in an almost soundless whisper, she manages, "Don't swear."

Hamilton holds her even tighter. "Stay with me and I promise I won't. Stay awake, you have to stop the bleeding." His hand brushes the side of her face, trying to keep her attention.

G.J. looks at everyone watching her and finds me. "*Tell everyone I just need a minute and I'll be dandy. I need to be able to close this thing up, Nat. Can you find Gus and see if he knows how?*"

"She is putting up a brave front and wants me to lie to everyone," I say.

"*You should never seek employment as a translator for the United Nations.*" G.J. is doing the best glare she can in her debilitated state.

"G.J., are you sure Gus didn't do this?" Jack asks.

With barely a motion to move her head, her gaze gives him her answer.

"So to me, this means either she is wrong, or we have another vampire in town. One who isn't up on all the local rules or doesn't care." Jack's gaze moves to each of the other men in the room.

Drake nods slowly. "That would explain a few things. Nat, can you talk to Hugo and see if that is what is going on?"

Jack directs his attention to me, "Who is this Hugo?"

"This dead guy I have been chatting with on occasion." I waive my hand dismissively. "Every time I talk to him, he overwhelms me. I can try, but I am not sure how long I will be out for."

Drake shakes his head. "I don't like it."

"Is there anything you can do?" Jack asks Drake.

Drake glances at G.J. in concern and then at me. I really am beyond frustrated I can't tap his mind.

"That should only happen as a last resort. There are ramifications to me being involved that I'm not sure many of us could live with." Drake tries to communicate with Jack some unspoken consequence.

"Are you saying you can help her, but you won't?" I challenge.

"It's more complex than that, Nat," Drake says.

"But you think you can help her?" Celia asks.

"Whatever I do will hurt like hell and may not have the outcome desired. If there are other options, I won't do anything until we have exhausted them." Drake sighs. "Hugo it is."

"Adam, Hamilton, see if you and Drake can work on that other thing," Jack directs.

"Umm, not until I'm there, Gus I can read," I chime in. Jack nods his assent.

Chapter Sixteen

Hugo doesn't want to come out and play, so the boys and I head out to find Gus. Mrs. Ackers responded but says she doesn't know what happened to G.J.. That woman gives me the creeps and always seems like she is lying. I would have hopped into her mind, but after my run in with Hugo's, I won't buy that ticket to horror town.

I call Gus' cell a few times with no luck. After a few minutes, Hamilton, still bloody from holding G.J., pulls her cell from his pocket. "Try this." He hands it to me.

"I don't even want to be in a ten mile radius when she finds out you have this." I look at the phone, like he is trying to hand me a used tissue.

"She can't talk right now. She doesn't need it," Hamilton defends his thievery.

"She can text. She can use the internet. She can take selfies and Snap Chat. She *can* kill you when she finds out." I say, but he shrugs.

"She needs to rest," is all he says.

"I'm sure she'll get all kinds of rest when she is worn out after tearing her room apart looking for her lost phone." I shake my head in a nonverbal Hamilton-you-are-an-idiot way. I try Gus from her cell.

"G.J.? I am so glad you are all right. Where are you?" Gus panics into the phone.

"Outside Drake's limo. The better question is, where you are?" I ask.

"Where is G.J.?" Gus demands.

"She can't talk, she is busy bleeding, which is why I ask again, where are you?"

"Bleeding? Why is she still bleeding?" Gus asks.

"Other than another unfortunate attack on her life, she hasn't been able to heal the bite from yesterday," I say. "Now, we need to talk, Gus. Where are you?"

"Again?" Gus says, but this awful creaking and crunching noise fills the speaker, and the line goes dead.

"What in the world?" I ask.

"He crushed the phone," Adam informs us.

"How do you know?" I ask.

"Because I'm friends with Hamilton and the son of Jack Wyfle. It happens—" Adam's unapologetic smirk says it all "—those things are too delicate."

"Great *now* how are we going to find him?" I ask the group.

Adam and Hamilton remove their clothes, shirts first. Sweet sexuality tsunami, now I get why G.J. is uncomfortable with their nudity. When they go for the buttons on their jeans, I fidget and make my eyes find some other place to gawk, but my female responses won't seem to let me. Finally, when they slide their thumbs to the side of their waistbands, I spin to avert my gaze. Sadly, the next thing my eyes land on is Drake's face.

Less than pleased, he asks, "Enjoying the show?" His tone is dry and he keeps his cool-green glare on me.

"They're not normal," I equivocate, as heat fills the apples of my cheeks.

Drake lets out an annoyed breath.

"Drake, you can't really blame the girl. I'm a fine spe-ci-mine." Adam changes the last word so it rhymes.

Drake's gaze flicks over my shoulder to where Adam must be standing. I glance down, not even wanting to catch a glimpse of them in the reflection of Drake's eyes.

"Shut up and shift, G.J. needs us to find Gus. Man, can't you do anything without joking around. Be serious!" Hamilton grumps at Adam.

"Dude, I am just as freaked out as you about G.J., if not more. This is how I deal with it. Get over yourself," Adam says before a weird popping and grinding noise happens.

When I turn back, two ginormous wolves stand side-by-side. "God, they're big."

One of the wolves chuffs, and the other turns his muzzle away in bored contempt.

"You have done enough for their egos for today," Drake says, as he gathers up their clothes. "Get in the limo."

"Are you kidding? Are we all getting in the car? What about your driver?" I ask in quick succession.

"We will ride around 'til they catch his scent and then they will follow it, and we will follow them," Drake says, "Don't worry about Ken. He understands the local scene."

"Is this a normally scheduled activity for you three? How does everyone know the plan but me?" I ask, as I scoot in the car.

"It makes sense." Drake climbs in next to me, deposits the clothes on other bench seat, and closes the door.

"Hey, I thought they were coming with us," I object, as one of the wolves barks.

"They are but this day isn't going as I had planned, and I need to get a hold of it again," Drake says.

"Wha—" is as far as I get before he pulls me to him and kisses me. He is gentle and sweet, and, although I am surprised, I am not unpleasantly so and apply a little pressure of my own.

He pulls back, his eyes twinkling. "Now, we can get on with today's drama. I just wanted to do that real fast." He leans away and opens the car door, letting the wolves in.

We arrange seating so Drake and I are on the rear-facing seat and the wolves get the windows. I grin, like an idiot, but both animals have their heads out the windows, so they don't notice.

Starting at school, we drive for hours. No luck anywhere, not even the coffee shop where Gus tends to hangout. The second time we pass the strip mall, the wolves' whine wanting out. Drake tells Ken, the driver, to pull behind the string of buildings. I tap into the wolf that proves to be Hamilton's mind and translate what he is thinking to Drake, before we open.

"He smells blood," I explain.

Adam hangs back with us, but Hamilton stalks forward through the open door, cautiously.

Softly, I pull on Drake's arm so he will lean down to me. In a hushed voice, I tell him, "He now smells blood and Gus."

Drake nods and ushers Adam to catch up with Hamilton. Adam scrutinizes Drake for a long moment, then complies.

In an alcove behind a dumpster, one of my oldest friends is feeding on a kitchen worker from one of the restaurants. The young man is glassy eyed, oblivious Gus' mouth on his neck, and Gus is making the most disgusting slurping noises.

Adam has gone to the right and Hamilton to the left, flanking Gus. Pulling his head up, Gus levels distain upon them, in turn. His mouth is red and his eyes burn in blue brilliance. Gus half-growls and half-shouts in frustration. He leans down to the kitchen guy and goes back to his neck, only for a second, and nudges the guy back toward a door.

The worker walks away in a stunned trance.

"So you found me. Now what is your plan?" Gus asks.

Screw coy, I hop into his head. "He is planning to attack Hamilton first. Then use his body to toss into Adam. He hopes that will block Drake," I rattle off as fast as I can.

"Natalia! Stay out of my head," Gus yells.

"Gus, why are you so hungry?" My stomach rumbles in response to his need. "You haven't been feeding. That kid was your first meal in weeks?"

Gus' head drops. "Nat, if you get involved in this, you will die."

Heat flashes so hot next to me I reflexively close my eyes and twist away from it. When the air cools again, I turn. The wolf form of Adam is on top of Drake. Wolfie Hamilton is pinning Gus to the corner where the wall meets the street. Above Hamilton and Gus is a scorch mark on the wall. "What in the hell just happened?" I ask the group.

"Drake! I am not threatening Nat, I am warning her," Gus shouts.

"Let me up, Adam," Drake says quietly, but it is a scary serenity.

Adam looks at Hamilton, and slowly backs off Drake. I smell burned hair. Adam has a burn on his shoulder. I ask, "Are you ok?"

"I'll be all right. Your boy has a hot temper." Adam is as good-natured as always, even if I feel his pain.

"Drake? You did this to Adam?" I am dumbfounded.

"I'll talk to you about it later." Directing his attention to Gus, Drake continues, "We believe G.J. was wounded by you or someone like you. She is unable to heal the bite. How can we fix it? The longer it is like this, the worse this will get."

Gus puts his head back, resting on the filthy ground. He is unwilling or unable to answer. Hamilton growls in his face.

As I jump back in his thoughts, images of G.J. and an overwhelming desire to be with and have her crashes over me from Gus. I knew he liked her, but this feeling is intense, bordering on unstable.

Obsessed much?

He flashes to an image; G.J. far away in the woods and someone attached to her neck. Now the jealousy is crippling. *MINE!* Hunger again swamps my senses. *Her blood is mine and only mine!* His need for her blood blends with an incredibly strong lust. He remembers the smell of her flowing blood, and it excites him to the point of frenzy.

Yikes. That is not the kind of thing you want to know about your friends.

"How… do… we… help… G.J.?" Drake asks slowly.

Now the image in Gus' head is of him feeding on G.J.. He is lost in a drunken power twining, twisting longing, sex, and bliss. It slithers through his veins, warming him and making his flesh tingle. *Not yet. Too young. She is too young.*

"She won't get older if we don't do something," I shout at Gus.

His gaze flicks to mine. *Will not lose her!* In his head, he licks her wound and it closes. But he can't stop himself. He has to drink. He has no control. He wants what he sees as his. Some old, distant piece of Gus does not want to claim her without consent. It is not strong enough to govern the craving in him for G.J.'s blood.

"He can lick the wound to close it, like with other feedings. But he is afraid he won't be able to stop from feeding on her," I explain his mind.

"Is there any other way?" Drake asks.

A quick flash of a wolf licking her wound flashes but goes. "*NO!*" shrieks from Gus' mind.

"Licking the wound and it helps somehow," I say, trying to comprehend what I saw in Gus' mind, but I am only half-thinking out loud.

"NO!" now escapes Gus. His eyes are full of fear. He fidgets showing both anger and anxiety.

Hamilton and Adam watches me confused and then at Gus.

"She will not be yours!" Gus' chest is heaving in contained rage.

Hamilton shifts right before our eyes. That must be painful as bone and tissue move to make his human form again. It seems to take less time than when I listened to it earlier. Other than a more-pronounced grimace, Hamilton pays no attention to what his body has just done and keeps his livid glare on Gus. I stay focused on Gus, too, to give Hamilton the privacy he apparently doesn't care about.

Hamilton grabs Gus and pins him to the brick wall behind him. "You will tell us what you know. G.J. has a gaping wound on her throat and unless you want one to match, you will explain... now."

"I will not just give her away like that." Gus pushes through his clenched teeth.

I find it interesting his mouth can accommodate his fangs.

Hamilton pulls Gus away from the wall and slams him back, hard. Adam, still in wolf form, growls to add pressure on Gus to talk.

"How can we help her?" Menace drips from Hamilton's words.

Gus stares him right in the eye before looking away. I am trying hard to sort through his thoughts, but the idea of losing G.J. is sending them swirling like a cyclone.

"He is a dangerous friend to have."

"Crap. Now? Really?" I say to my unwanted friend Hugo.

"Nat?" Drake asks.

"You guys have to handle Gus. Hugo just showed and I don't really have a choice but to talk to him."

"You have many dangerous friends," Hugo adds in that special way of his.

"Yeah, I know. What I don't know is who did this to you? My best friend was attacked and my guess it is the same creepoid who had you for a snack. So, do you know who it was?"

Hugo pushes the images of his death through my head.

"Ahhhgh! Will you cut it out! I am going to pass out if you do that." I put my hands on my head in a vain attempt to make them stop.

"Nat!" Drake yells right next to me.

Thanks. The extra volume is super helpful when my brain is exploring the chaos theory.

"*You need to see,*" Hugo says again, but stops pushing images into my mind.

"What? What do you want me to see?" I ask him, still shaken by the previous mind blitz.

Hugo holds out his hand and I grab it.

Chapter Seventeen

Despite a dense fog, I can see far in the distance. Shadowed forms move, some slowly and others darting. The slower ones are less present. The faster ones are more vibrant. These forms are spirits. Hugo is still holding my hand. Horrified, I gape at him. I am no longer in the alley. While I have never been here before, this must be the world of the dead.

"Did you just kill me?" My mouth forms the words, but the sound is distorted and distant.

"*I brought you to see,*" Hugo says.

"WHAT! That there are such things as ghosts? I know! I have been playing peek-a-boo with them for months now. Why did you bring me here?"

"*Your friends are more dangerous than you know.*" Hugo spins the same line, like the hook of a really annoying pop song.

"I think we have covered that. Why did you bring me here? Explain." My words dance back to me, as though the wind has the sound in an eddy.

"*This is the Shadow World,*" Hugo says.

All I can think is, "Duh."

"*The beings that remain here are the troubled. The energy they held when they left the last world has to be tremendous.*

These souls died violently or with an unresolved concern that continues to feed their entity holding them together. Do you see the mist?"

"The fog? Yeah."

"That is a being finally finding peace. The energy that once held it together has dissipated enough, it can no longer hold the shade form."

As I breathe in, I feel as though the air is viscous, full of the shades dissipating forms. The idea makes my stomach roll in disgust.

"This world has a natural cycle, a way to wind down the life still in these beings, so they can be one in the next world. Not all death comes here. Those who die at peace never see the Shadow World. Only the ones who cannot rest come here."

"Okay, so why do I need to see this?"

"This world can hold only so many. Always a great number die with unsettled energies. War, hate, murder, disease all leave energy behind. Starvation, those at peace, and old age usually bypass this world. Each way someone leaves their last world has a different energy."

"Okay, so what?"

"Your friend's kind needs to stop sending too many souls with too much vitality and newfound curiosity of what might exist. The boundaries of the Shadow World were never meant to contain, or imprison. It is here to allow a soul to find peace.

"The shades will start crossing into the other realms. Human energy is unique and others hunger for it. They are prized in other worlds. Especially ones with so much energy."

"What do you think I can do?"

"This is the world closest to the human world. It acts a buffer. Should enough human shadows cross other boundaries, they will lead other beings here and then lead them back to your world. The kind that brings violent end is becoming greedy. She told

me, you must come here to see so you can stop them."

I blink at him. What on Earth—or wherever we are—do I say to that?

Hugo pulls on my arm and we glide at a bewildering speed. When we stop, it takes a moment to orient what I am seeing. Light and dark meet, kind of like dusk. The fog is thin here and drift by in slow wisps. We are standing in the dark. In the light, colors are unlike any I have ever seen. The brilliance is mesmerizing and jewel-like.

A shadow reaches into the light. Stretching for what looks as if it could be a tree if a tree has clean sharp lines and a fuchsia top similar to liquid glass in place of leaves.

"That is a human shade. It is curious. Instead of going back to the human world to address any issues or waiting here to dissipate, it wants to see what other worlds are like. This happens more frequently with the shadows, introduced to death by what they believed to be fictional creatures until the attack kills them. They have enough power to leave the Shadow World, and they know now there are other things out there. What they don't understand is there are worse things than death."

A lithe form steps from the woods. I have never seen such a beautiful being. It is lean and graceful; its movements are hypnotic. When it reaches the shadow, its eyes grow wide and lustful. The being smiles but it is not joy. Something much darker. It touches the shadow and a vicious struggle begins. Pulled toward the beautiful beast, the shadow shrinks and screeches in agony. It is horrible and tears well in my eyes. The shadow is being decimated. When its life force is all but gone, it starts to break into the particles forming the mist. The lovely creature holds out its arms and waves the fog toward itself, inhaling, devouring every last remnant of the former shade.

"Hugo, what does that mean?" I ask in grief, knowing I just watched the final end of a soul.

"*Don't Speak!*" Hugo shouts in my mind.

The creature in the light turns and looks right at me. My heart seizes. It seems to recognize me.

It connects with my mind. "*Lost one? Your kind was said to be no more. Come to us and we will show you what you could be.*"

Images of life with no time, total dominance, and control over other races floods my head with the corrosiveness of an oil spill. The burden of them weigh down my own memories and thoughts.

My mind feels as though it is being ripped apart like Velcro.

"Nat!" Drake shouts. He slaps my face lightly.

"If you are into hitting girls, I am going to rethink this whole dating thing," I mumble, as I bring my thoughts back to this world.

Drake's strong arms fold me to his chest, and I had been lying on the ground. The rusty dumpster is oozing something, and I am pretty sure my shirt is not sticking to me due to sweat. Ew —I wonder how hot Jack's water heater gets and if he has antibacterial soap.

"Hey what happened?" Drake kisses the top of my head and runs his hand down the back of it.

"I went on a little tour of the Shadow World. That was fun." I wonder if I can get a Master's in sarcasm. I do have a talent for it.

Drake leans away slightly to look at my face. "The Shadow World? You didn't die. You just passed out."

"Nope." I wriggle free of him and stand. Drake is trying to be helpful but really just getting in my way. "Hugo wanted to play tour guide so off we went."

"You have been to the Shadow World?" Gus asks, still pinned to the wall by the completely nude Hamilton.

Okay brain, what am I supposed to do with that image? That kind of eye candy can give you mental diabetes.

"Yeah, I wouldn't rate it above two stars. Drab scenery and the service is awful," I try joking to shake off my unease. It doesn't work.

Drake presses me to him again. I think, somehow, he gets that, *Holy crap I was just in the world of the dead.* I take a second to absorb the comfort Drake gives. His warmth slows down my racing heart easing my freak out. Steeling myself, I turn on Gus, who Hamilton is still trying to muscle a response out of. "Hey, we need an answer about G.J. and then, you and I need to have an important pow-wow about another issue. So let's skip this whole boring 'I'll never tell' moment."

"We…" Gus stops. "There are more of us than there ever have been. I try to stay away from others like me. Each of us tends to be … domineering. Living as long as we do has an adverse effect on our humanity. Several battle it out for money and power and those who live in communities are sadistic to put it in the most generous way possible. They love controlling politicians and dabble in world domination. I have plenty of money and have no need to rule. So I stay among younger humans. I was turned at an early age so it works for me."

"G.J.," Hamilton growls his prompt.

"Ahh…" Gus sighs. "She is something special."

To that comment, Hamilton slams Gus against the wall. Gus stares at Hamilton with bored distain as if he were a mere annoyance.

"She is rare. Rare things are coveted. Like our Natalia here." As flattering as that sounds, I am totally good if Gus keeps that obsession needle pointed at G.J.. "Others of my kind discovered her existence. They were invited to our area to take care of a problem for another. I thought she was safe with the wolves." Gus scowls at Hamilton, like he was as worthless as an old chicken bone. "I had been tracking the other one who had been feeding so greedily in my territory while they, apparently, waited for their opportunity to strike." Gus stops and closes his eyes. A tremor vibrates his body. After a moment, he continues, "I was not in time. Why was G.J. alone? You did not care for her."

"You left her for dead." Hamilton sends his anger into Gus, shaking him.

Adam growls low.

"What would you have had me do? I had not fed in order to heighten my tracking skills to find the other. She is," Gus pauses, "what I desire most."

Again, Hamilton starts his rumbling growl and shakes things around us. The chains on the dumpsters rattle. Adam is adding his own menacing vibration.

"Guys, let him finish," Drake intercedes.

Gus and Hamilton have a staring contest. "Go… on," Hamilton bites out.

"Had I gotten anywhere close to her, I would have turned her," Gus says.

"So you left her to die?" I ask.

Gus' blue gaze finds me. "That is forever. She is too young to live forever without it being her choice," he says the words, as if he is trying to convince himself.

"You won't live forever, needle teeth," Hamilton says as a promise.

"If the options are death or forever, which one do you think G.J. would have chosen," I shoot back.

"Some things are worse than death."

Gus' words throw me back to the image of the beautiful thing that devoured a soul. I think about my brilliant, curious friend and what she would do if put in the Shadow

World. She would never stay there. G.J. would go to every realm she could find. My voice is pensive. "That there are."

Drake looks at me with worry.

"How can we fix G.J.'s neck?" Hamilton stays on the only topic he cares about.

"I am trying to feed enough that I can be near her. I am almost there," Gus says.

But I know that is not the truth. I felt his hunger.

"Gus, G.J. has lost a lot of blood. We can't just wait for you to go to the buffet. You are nowhere close to not being hungry. If there is another way, you have to tell us." I jump in his head.

"*The wolves' saliva will combat the vampire. If they do it, she will be marked. I will never have her,*" Gus thinks.

"Crap." I know I'm eloquent. "I need to talk to Jack. Now."

"NATALIA!" Gus roars.

Drake and I turn toward the car.

"Do whatever it is you have to do. G.J. cannot stay like this. But if you turn her, I will end you," Hamilton says behind us.

Chapter Eighteen

Both Adam and Hamilton are their less furry-selves and thankfully have donned their clothes for the ride back to Jack's. "What is it you saw?" Hamilton asks.

"I need to talk to Jack." I frown toward the window.

"Nat! Just freaking tell us. You are making us crazy," Adam insists in an un-Adam-like tone.

Drake examines me. He is curious, too, but he backs me up. "Settle down. If Nat thinks something needs to be run past Jack first, I trust her judgment. So should you." While the other boys aren't happy, Drake holds some kind of authority and they sit back and grumble.

I am starting to like having Drake in my corner.

****

Celia is sitting on the corner of Jack's desk, and Jack is in his chair when we enter his study, which had been G.J.'s room briefly when she first moved in. Drake and I stand near the plush visitors' chairs that sit in front of his desk.

Jack asks, "Did you find him?"

"Uhh yeah." I look at Adam and Hamilton. "I need to talk to you alone about that."

"If it has to do with G.J., I am staying," Celia says, propping her crossed arms over her small baby belly.

"Really what I mean is Adam and Hamilton can't hear this." I rip off the adhesive.

Hamilton does that thing where he crosses his arms in the I'm-not-going-anywhere pose he loves.

"Out!" Jack uses a booming voice that makes the room seem like an echo chamber.

Celia puts her hand on her belly. Adam and Hamilton glare at me, but they do as Jack commanded.

"Warn me next time, will you?" Celia says, after the boys close the door behind them. "This little tyke might start following orders sooner than we would expect."

"Are you alright?" Jack asks with a sincerity that makes me feel he has forgotten Drake and I are here.

Celia waves her hand dismissing his overabundance of concern. "I'm fine. Nat, what is it you wanted to talk to Jack about."

"The wolves saliva can heal G.J.." I say.

Jack puts his face in his hands, and Drake blows out a deep breath.

"Well that's great news isn't it?" Celia picks up that the men are not so thrilled to hear this news.

"Actually it is ... well... kinda awkward news," I explain.

"Jack?" Celia asks.

"Ceily, if one of us fixes it where she is injured, we mark her as our mate." Jack's unshaven face is haggard.

Celia's hand goes to where her neck meets her shoulder, and her eyes grow distant in thought. That's a little TMI about their physical relationship.

"I presume this is the same issue you were talking about if you were to fix it." Jack flicks his gaze at Drake.

Drake nods once. "As far as long term consequences go, yeah."

I turn and gape at him. "What?"

"We'll talk later," he assures me.

My eyes assure him he better bet on it.

"No." Celia shakes her head and repeats the word a few more times. "She is sixteen. Jack, she can't mate anybody. There has to be another way."

"Gus is too hungry," I say. "He will turn her if he gets near her right now, and I don't know how much longer she's got. He is… obsessed with her, add that he starved himself to find this other vampire, and G.J. could be on a permanent liquid diet. I fear even if he isn't so hungry, he will turn her."

Jack nods. A loud knock sounds on the door. Jack barks, "Come."

"Sir, Adam and Hamilton are in with G.J.. They ran upstairs and relieved me. But then they closed the door locked it, and I think I heard them shift."

"Oh my God!" Celia wobbles her pregnant body off the desk and runs for the door.

Jack grabs her arm. "Stay with Stanzi."

"I am—" she starts, but Jack cuts her off.

"I need you safe!" Jack leaves the room expecting Celia to stay put. Silly man.

Drake and I are right behind Jack as he takes the stairs three at a time. With no preamble, he crashes into G.J.'s door. I get there just in time. Adam and Hamilton, in wolf form, skitter back from G.J.'s bed.

A pulse of fury so enormous terror shoots through me leaves Jack. With no thought for his clothes the big man shifts leaving the tatters clinging to him and strewn on the floor. He lunges for the other two. You might think two against one is an unfair fight but Adam is just taking the beating and not fighting back while Hamilton only plays defense.

"Dear God, Jack, don't kill them," Celia begs from beside me. She had finally gotten to the room, with Stanzi doing his best to stay between her and the fight.

All of the sudden all three wolves are floating in the air. G.J. sits up. "Ya'll need to quit." Her southern voice sounds scratchy with sleep but her throat mended.

Jack shifts back to human, which makes G.J. throw the covers over her head.

"Put me down," he commands her.

"Promise not to hurt my... the other wolves," she calls from her hiding place.

"Put me down," Jack repeats.

"Promise?"

"Stanzi, please go get the boys and Jack some clothes," Celia says calmly, if not slightly embarrassed for her husband's nudity.

"Young Lady, you do *not* float me in the air. We have discussed this."

"Yeah, we sure did, but I was not aware at the time you would be mauling my... uh any wolves in my bedroom. I think we need to revisit that topic," comes her muffled argument.

Stanzi returns bringing three pairs of workout shorts, handing one up to Jack and putting the other two on the floor beneath the two other wolves. Jack slides his on trying to stay vertical. "Shift," Jack commands of the other two.

I turn away to avoid getting hit with their nakedness. At least Jack had his back to me but... I would have had an all access pass to the other two.

"You can put us all down now. I need to reach my pants," Adam instructs G.J..

They all float down. Before Adam and Hamilton can pull up their shorts, Jack goes to the bed and rips off G.J.'s covers. She squeals in protest. He leans down and smells her neck as she cringes back into the sheets on the mattress.

Hamilton and Adam both advance toward Jack, who turns to face the two boys and asks disconsolately, "What did you do?"

Chapter Nineteen

"Dad, we helped her. We heard what Nat said through the door. And we fixed G.J.," Adam says softly, yet proud of himself.

"Oh Lordy, I knew it." G.J. slams her hands over her face. "Why did it have to be you?" She peers through her fingers at Hamilton in annoyed despair.

Hamilton appears, for once in his life, a little sheepish.

"You can't do this." Jack sounds hopeless.

"What? We wanted to help. She can't stay like that." Adam tries again to explain.

I jump in Jack's head. "*They both licked the same wound at the same time. That is how you turn a wolf.*"

"Holy crap!" I blurt.

Jack turns to me lost.

"What?" G.J. asks, feeling her neck and sitting up. "Hey, how about that my neck is all patched up. Good job fellas!" She's cheerful and unwitting. "What's all the fuss about?'

"G., they licked the same wound at the same time. That's not a good thing," I hint.

"We did it that way so neither of us could lay rightful claim. We will sort it out between the two of us when the time comes," Adam says, trying to convince his father all would be well.

"Adam! Your love life is the least of our concerns right now!" Jack bellows at his son.

"What do you mean?" Hamilton asks cautiously.

"Oh dear heavens! Am I gonna get all furry now?" G.J. asks Jack.

"What? Why would you get furry?" Drake asks.

"'Cause what they just did is how you turn a person into a werewolf. Becoming a wolf is a pack decision. It takes at least two wolves agreeing to change a human into a wolf. That is done by licking the same wound at the same time. I didn't even think about that. Saints help me." G.J. puts her face back in her hands. "What kind of grooming maintenance is that gonna take? Hurry everybody go buy stock in Gillette, I will be blowin' through razors like Sweeney Todd."

"G.J., this isn't funny. I told you in your lessons we don't change anyone, especially our mates, because shifting is hard. Few survive." Jack's forehead is wrinkled in worry..

"Oh God. Dad, we," Adam started.

"We were only trying to heal her. We talked about the mate thing and decided we could work it out," Hamilton said. "We didn't mean to turn her."

"No one has been turned in so long… We didn't think abo—" Whatever excuse Adam is about to give, Jack shoots down.

"No! You didn't think about anything beyond one moment. You are right, Adam. No one has been turned in a long time. Because they don't survive the shift. Not because we haven't tried." Jack loses his volume control.

"So… can't I just not shift?" G.J. asks hopefully.

Jack lets out a long breath shaking his head.

"Wait? What?" Celia's brain catches up with the conversation. "G.J. is now a werewolf Witch?"

Adam and Hamilton take a step back, as if they can distance themselves from what they've done.

"Man, you two are idiots," I chime in.

"We were trying to help," Adam says.

"By dual mating her?" I ask, stupefied.

"Pardon?" G.J. turns her attention fully on the two younger wolves.

"You couldn't heal, so we did what we had to," Hamilton says defiantly.

"Dual what?" she asks, like she needs clarification, but we all know she understood.

"You were injured," Hamilton says. Adam at least has regained enough sense to keep quiet.

G.J. faces Jack. "I thought I couldn't be mated without consent."

"Consent is giving your neck in submission," Jack explains in defeat.

G.J. gapes at the two boys, who have their gazes fixed on the ground, and then back at Jack, whose concerned gaze is on her face. She puts her hand up to try to gain control. "Hold up a sec. Are you telling me after having been mauled by a strange vampire, on the neck because that's their M.O., I am now mated to not one but two werewolves, all without the benefit of a pretty dress or at the very least a trip to Vegas. *And* I could potentially die on the next full moon from growing unwanted body hair and trying to contort like a balloon animal?"

Jack too averts his gaze from G.J.'s.

"I need to sit down." Celia says, and Stanzi ushers her to a chair.

"Where is my phone?" G.J. demands.

I pull it from my pocket and walk it over to her.

"Why do you have my phone?" G.J. asks with suspicion.

I would NARC on Hamilton, but I have a feeling he is in enough trouble. So, I just shrug.

"Who are you calling?" Jack asks.

"Ms. Stontz, she might be able to help." She's focusing on her phone scrolling for the number.

"G.J.? Have you told her about us?" Jack asks horrified.

"Oh... Shoot, no." G.J.'s hand holding the phone collapses to her lap her gaze falling in defeat.

Jack focuses on her.

"No. I really haven't. I promise. I just... I need to stop this. I feel out of control." Tears well in her eyes. "I usually can figure out what to do.... I don't know what to do." Her voice is pitiful.

Adam and Hamilton both move toward her, but Jack's fury holds them back from comforting her. I sit on her other side from Jack and hold her hand.

"Let me email Pa..." Celia starts.

I jump in Celia's head to catch "*trick.*" Lemons, popsicles, and then, "*Get out of my head, NAT!*"

I look at her.

"Keep that to yourself young lady if you caught anything," Celia cautions.

"Celia?" Jack asks in warning.

She gets up to leave the room. "Jack, I can't tell you. We have been over this. Let me see what I can do."

"Celia, have you told this guy about us?" Jack asks.

"He already knows," Celia says, and exits the room, Jack right behind her.

"G.J.," Adam says, his posture still submissive. "We were trying to help."

"Thank you, Adam, I do know that. I do truly. Just... you didn't, honey. You made things worse."

"Your neck is better. How is that worse?" Hamilton challenges her.

"Did you miss the part where I could *die?*"

"Well, you aren't going to die today." Hamilton throws his hands up, angry she isn't more grateful.

"I'm not sure what's worse, being mated to that idiot or knowing he is my wolf I have spilled my guts to." She looks to me for help, but I have none.

"So I *am* your wolf?" Hamilton has a stupid grin on his face.

"How do you know who is who?" Adam asks. "You were under the blankets when we shifted."

"Because you and I were together when that moron tried to come through the window that time." She sighs dismally. "I guess I knew it all along, I just really wanted to be wrong. I built a luxury residence in denial."

"Is it really so bad?" Hamilton asks, hurt evident in his scraping whispered tone.

"Man, I'd hold off on that question until she has had some time to process. I am pretty sure you don't want that answer right now," Drake schools the larger boy.

"You know what? I am being awfully selfish right now. You all are the ones who should be upset. Doesn't this mean you're stuck with me? That's a lot to give up just to try to help me out. I mean unless the whole shifting thing kills me," G.J. asks, still totally oblivious what she does to these two.

"G.? Really? You are mated against your will to two guys, and you are worried these boneheads can't date?" Her heart is too big for her own good.

Both Adam and Hamilton are using their eyes to plead with her to get how they feel.

"They're fine. You only have to worry about them killing each other. Focus on you," I direct her.

"You best not." G.J. pins them with her gaze. "I'm serious. I won't speak to you for the rest of your lives if you get in a tussle over me." G.J. is so serious. "What a mess. How can you be mated to two people at once? I mean how's that work?" Realizing what she just implied, she turns beat red. "I don't... umm... Ew." She stops herself.

"We will *have* to 'tussle'... at some point. But it will be a no kill match. The loser will just live like a bachelor," Hamilton says, finally uttering something that actually puts G.J. at ease. But this is Hamilton, so he follows up with, "Until we do, we'll need to get a bigger bed in here because we will all have to sleep together. We can't sleep without our mate. And last night was a tight squeeze."

G.J. isn't the only one who can't speak. All of us just stare at him.

Adam breaks the silence. "He's right."

G.J. moves her saucer-like gawk to find Adam still speechless. Drake bursts out laughing. I, too, start to giggle. I know she is my friend, but the look on her face is priceless.

"This isn't funny, Nat. I am not ready to have bed buddies. Last night was one thing, I was hurt and needed a snuggle but every night! Until whenever? And how does losing a fight make it so they don't need to sleep here 'cause I'll whip both your behinds right quick if that solves the issue."

"The bachelor will still have to live with us," Hamilton says, as if he has already won and everyone knows the loser will be Adam.

"Yeah, you will have to get the room next door," Adam taunts, "Hope we don't get too–"

"ADAM!" G.J. puts an end to that fast. "I won't have this. This I will fix." She is panicky. "I will find a way and make this right. Until then, neither of you will imply anything about bedroom activities. Good Night! I have spent my whole life living like I was raised. You know I don't like when anyone acts like I have no control over my libido. We may not have to worry about any of that because I might not make it through the next full moon. Until then, if that sleeping thing is true," her finger shoots out in warning, "And I am checking with Jack on that. You two are sleeping in wolf form!"

The two boys grumble.

"And what happens if I fall in love with someone else on this planet? Then what?"

The two boys growl.

Chapter Twenty

G.J. and I wanted time to clean up so, after I grab a much-needed shower, Drake and I head downstairs to grab something to eat. On the steps, Drake starts laughing.

"Okay what is so funny?" I ask.

"Are you kidding? G.J. is probably on the short list for the most virtuous teens, and she now will be sleeping with two guys every night. I don't know who I feel sorrier for. G.J. and her panic-based denial of her own sexuality, or Adam and Hamilton who will be in bed with the girl of their dreams... every night... and can't touch her. Because if she doesn't stop them, which I would lay money down she can and will, and if they don't stop each other in an errant attempt in the night, Jack will destroy them. They really didn't think that one through at all." Drake smirks and shakes his head.

"Nope. I've said it before and sadly I know I will be saying again... often... idiots." I agree smiling and shaking my own head. "So... you mark people too?"

"You do like the jugular, Natalia." Drake finds the chandelier with his gaze and takes a deep breath, then jerks his head to pop his neck.

"You said we would cover this later. It's later."

"I ... need this conversation to be much later."

"Why? You said you would be honest with me and tell me anything I wanted to know."

Drake's smile turns into a frown. "It isn't exactly the same. It is similar though. *I* want to tell you about it. *I* am sure. I have been for a while. But I think *you* aren't ready."

"What is that supposed to mean?" I really hate not being able to just pilfer the info I want out of his skull.

"It means, when we talk about it, it will be because I am about to do it."

"Do what? How is it the same kind of thing like the wolves do? Wait. You think I am going to mate you?"

Drake sighs. "Nat, I am positive this is not something we can address right now. I promise I will talk to you about it at some point. But I … can't right now. It has taken me years just to get you out on one date. Don't make me rush you. You deserve time. I really want to give you time."

I give him my unhappy face.

"How about your excursion to the Shadow World?" Drake tries to change topics.

My mind wanders back to the terrifying, beautiful being. I must give something away because Drake stops our progress at the kitchen door.

"Hey, what's wrong?"

I shiver to expel the mental chill the images give me. "I think my parents might have had a reason to fear me." I bend my head, gazing at the ground, and the hurt, anger and fear I've tried to push away since my parents left overwhelms me. I am not a weepy chick, but all those emotions well the water in my eyes.

Drake pulls me into his arms and simply holds me. He doesn't say anything, and I draw comfort from him for an unknown while.

"Everything okay here?" Jack's deep voice rumbles, as he heads toward us from the stairs.

We separate but Drake keeps his hand on my lower back and rubs in a comforting way. "Nat's had a rough day."

"Seems to be going around, I need to get something to eat. Are you two hungry?" Jack passes us and leads us into the kitchen.

"Yeah," Drake admits.

"Let me find the leftovers from the gumbo G.J. made the other day. That's if the boys left any." Jack heads to the double sized fridge, as Drake and I sit at the bar.

As he digs around, I hear the triumph in his voice, when he finds what he is looking for.

"It's hard to hide good food from the super sense of smell we have. But since G.J. has moved in, I have started finding ways to block them from finding the things I want. I keep our coffee beans in the fridge now." Jack smiles as he places a large container on the counter and unwraps it.

"G.J. cooks?" Drake asks, surprised.

"Man, can she cook. I'm mainly a meat guy, but she makes eating like an adventure." Jack heats up the gumbo in a pot.

"She is a girl of many talents," Drake says appreciatively, which puts me in a bit of a sour mood. "Do you cook?"

That makes me glare at him though my slitted eyes. "No, do you cook?"

Jack barks out a quick laugh and says, "You could say that." He has a huge knowing grin, so I pop in his head. *"Fire breed."*

"What is a fire breed?" I examine Drake's face for any clues.

Drake glares at Jack, who puts up his hands.

"I can't prevent Nat from mind reading. If I could, I would have a long time ago."

"I can control fire," Drake says, but somehow I don't feel like he is telling me everything.

"How and why can you control fire?" I ask.

The flame under the pot Jack heats leaps to Drake. He holds his hand up, and with small gestures and movements, he makes the flame hypnotically dance and wave. He makes the fire bigger and spells out my name. As I sit in stunned wonder at the pyrotechnic display, Drake keeps his gaze on me. My focus shifts to his eyes. Warmth of the flames heats my skin but I don't care. All I can do is stay connected to his intense watchful gaze.

Jack's clapping breaks the moment. "Okay, sparky, put the fire back so I can get this food heated up. I'm starving."

Drake grumbles under his breath, "Sparky," as the flames find their way back to the stove or disburse.

"Well, that's a cool trick. Now how about the why part of my question?" I have to admit I sound much calmer than I feel.

Drake shrugs, but, when G.J., Adam, and Hamilton all come in, the subject changes.

"Hey, Jack, you are about to lose a kid if these two don't back off. I am fairly sure being a mate doesn't mean I can't go two steps without having them follow me. And we need to talk about this whole sleep thing."

Jack glowers at Hamilton and Adam. "You two knuckle heads better go get changed. You have a few fights to get through. You know taking a mate puts you in adult Gamma. Until that gets sorted out, you don't get to sleep or eat."

"Well, there that solves a minor issue. Thanks, Jack," G.J. says with triumph gleaming in her eyes, as she gloats over the two boys, but shakes her shoulders, like she's trying to dispel something.

"Don't get too excited. If they aren't there, you won't sleep either," Jack explains.

"What? How is that?" G.J. asks.

Jack sighs and confirms her fears. "You won't be able to relax unless they are with you. It is part of the bond."

"Can we head to the store then and get a couple dog beds?" G.J. is hopeful.

Jack laughs. "Absolutely."

Adam and Hamilton look far less pleased with the subject.

"All right, now on to other topics." G.J. shifts her gaze to me. "Did you catch up with Gus? What did he say? Is he all right?"

Hamilton crowds G.J.. "Forget about him."

The doorbell rings; Jack answers it.

"Yep, this is the kind of *awesome* I expected." G.J.'s tone is flat. "Listen here, Mate-y, I might be stuck with you for the moment, but there are gonna be some ground rules you need to get. One." G.J. advances, wielding her finger like a fencing foil and jabbing at him to emphasize her points. "You are not the boss of me. I'm not only your Beta and can kick your fanny, if need be, but I am also *not* in any way subservient to you. Your thick skull better get a hold of that right quick. Two, I did not volunteer for this job. Therefore I am in this situation under duress. So before you get your big bully mojo rolling, you better remember that I am starting from a ticked off position, and I won't take kindly to any of that guff. And three, I have friends and activities that I will continue to keep up with, and you don't have any say. So back off!"

Hamilton backs up against the counter, and G.J. is right in his space. If I didn't witness it, I would not have believed the idiot takes that moment to kiss her square on the mouth. G.J. squeaks in surprise, and Adam jerks her out of Hamilton's lip lock. The two large boys get in a shoving match.

"Do that again, Hamilton, and you are a dead man," Adam growls out, as if he is holding on to his human form by sheer will.

Hamilton's aggressive eyes glow signaling his anger. "She is my mate. She was close. I took the opportunity she handed me."

"She is my mate!" Adam decks Hamilton, and they both tumble to the floor fighting.

"Adam! Hamilton! Enough!" Jack shouts, and he and three other large men rush in the room.

The two boys float apart at that moment. "Okay, that's it! I've had it. I told you I wouldn't have this. Hamilton, you need to catch up on what is appropriate in this day and age. You don't get to smooch a person based on proximity. Adam, I appreciate your assistance, but I would prefer you don't scuffle over me." G.J. turns to the men who have just come in. "Hey there, fellas. Good to see you again."

The men say in low, deferent tones, "Beta."

"You can use the sparring ring in the basement," Jack says, finishing a conversation we had not been privy to. "Looks like the boys are eager to start."

The two floating fools try that weird aggressive posturing thing men can do, but it comes across as ridiculous with them hanging out in midair.

"Head down, the others will be here soon so we can get this rolling," Jack instructs them. "G.J., let the boys down so they can get ready for their challenge fights."

I have seen some scary things in my life. Trust me. But, to date, the scariest thing I have ever seen is my best friend's menacing face as she turns on the men with Jack.

Chapter Twenty-One

G.J.'s eyes, which are normally a grey-blue, have turned an eerie color, like the sun trying to get past a storm cloud. "You challenge my mates?" her voice growls. And she moves Hamilton and Adam behind her and sets them down.

"G.J.." Jack uses the kind of voice you use when trying to quiet a raving lunatic. "The boys have to challenge into adulthood. You have studied our history, you know this is how it works."

G.J.'s gaze never leaves the three men. Her head tilts in a predatory manner. The wind in the room picks up and the feeling of static electricity has every hair on my arms and neck come to full attention. The power G.J. draws is massive. If she lets that go, there might not be a Wyfle house any more. Drake moves me behind him, but I peek around his arm.

She repeats her question, "You challenge my mates?"

"We have to do this, it is our rite of passage," Adam reasons with her.

"G.J., settle down," Jack tries again.

"They have to earn their place in adulthood. We won't bow down to any young pups if they don't earn it," one of the three men says.

While I don't actually read his thoughts, I am sure his next thought is, "*Whoops!*"

G.J.'s fingers flick, and, with the force of an unseen explosion, the three men fly backward and she now pins them to the wall. "Submit!" she demands.

The three werewolves growl back.

"SUBMIT!" she stresses again.

"G.J., the boys have to do this." Jack tries once more.

"Aunt Celia did not fight. My mates will not fight." G.J. is something primal, but she still has a bit of her brain.

Adam and Hamilton glance at each other. "G.J., we want to do this. The challenge fight is what gives us our place in the pack," Hamilton explains, using a gentle tone he doesn't usually display.

"You are my mates. That is your place in the pack." G.J. still holds the men to the wall glowering at them.

Jack judges the situation before him. "*There has never been a female beta. She is right. Celia didn't fight in. No mates in recent history have fought in. But none of them have been unranked wolves. If the boys don't fight in, what will they ever be?*" Out loud he uses his controlling voice. "Release them!"

G.J. visibly winces. As if she will challenge him, she scrutinizes Jack for a moment. Adam comes to her and pulls her into his arms, rubbing her back and settling her down. Hamilton sandwiches her between them, and they nuzzle her neck, which surprisingly she allows.

Jack turns to his men. "Go. We will have to handle this before we begin."

The men watch the three for a minute. One asks, "Jack, is she mated to both of them?"

Jack blows out a breath and nods once, curtly.

"Why would they do that? What does that even mean?" All of the men are incredulous.

"We have a good deal to sort out," Jack answers solemnly. The men file out of the kitchen, and he walks them toward the door.

"Uhh, G., you all right over there?" I ask, cowering a little behind Drake.

As she extricates herself from them with a rather startled look on her face, Hamilton and Adam growl a little.

"What in the name of all that is good on this green earth did I just do?"

"I'm not sure, but I think you may have just wolfed out a little," I suggest.

G.J.'s mouth opens and closes in an attempt to say anything, but she is stunned speechless.

Adam comforts her again, "It's fine. That is a perfectly natural reaction. You want to protect your mate. It will be okay." He rubs her arms gently.

Hamilton turns her to look at him. I guess he can't stand Adam that close. So he chooses to be helpful. "It is what wolves do." Have I mentioned Hamilton is abysmal at helpful?

G.J. is thunderstruck but finally finds her voice. "Wolves? I thought I wouldn't change until the full moon? Why did that just happen? I thought I had time." Her eyes are wide and unfocused, terrorized.

Jack returns and says, "You won't transform until then, but it doesn't take long to begin to feel different. Or so the few that have attempted this have told me. You are in a unique position. Our histories don't cover this kind of a thing. No one, that I know of, has been mated by two people. No wolf can stomach their mate with someone else so it has never been tried. To make matters worse, you hasn't yet made the change. We haven't had a female wolf beta. So there's a problem there as well. And then we've never, that I am aware of, had a Witch werewolf. So we are *really* on uncharted ground."

"Why is the female beta a problem?" G.J. asks.

"Well..." Jack's shoulders hunch as he winces trying to

tackle a sticky subject. "Wolves fight for a position in the hierarchy. That is who we are and what we do. You're right, Celia didn't have to battle to become my mate. But she isn't a wolf. When we had female wolves, they fought into our social order before mating. So they knew who would suit by their own level of Gamma.

"Because of size, males always take the top two spots of Alpha and Beta, although there've been great warrior females who were high-ranking Gammas. When you have a fifty to eighty pound weight advantage, odds are on your side, no matter how skilled a fighter you're up against.

"We want mates who will challenge us and stand by our side. All mates would be given deference as a wolf's equal, usually within a level or two. Females mated to Betas or Alphas aren't women to mess with. That whole romance novel crap about Alphas and Omegas is hilarious. No truly strong man wants a woman who skitters away from us.

"As we began to take human mates that sentiment has carried forward. We have never had a situation where the female was the Beta first. Even though you are pack, I thought whoever your mate would end up being, they would have a rank already. Adam and Hamilton are genetically born werewolves. They need to challenge fight. It is part of them. It is part of the pack's DNA to only respect them if they fight for their rights."

A small growl escapes G.J. and she puts her hand over her mouth, as if a burp surprised her.

"But now," Jack continues before G.J. can say anything, "you are hopefully going to survive the change and be a female Beta werewolf. There's a bond between wolf mates. You won't tolerate an attack on your mate. Or mates rather. Other wolves won't feel confident you aren't going to take offense. And your abilities are a real threat to them. The boys should've had their challenge fights before they claimed a mate. So we have a problem. Actually, we have two problems."

"I'm fighting," Hamilton insists.

"No!" G.J. growls.

"We need to do this," Adam calmly explains. "You have to trust that we can handle ourselves."

G.J.'s eyes get a strange glow. "No one hurts you."

"Nah, we'll be fine. If we have to live by your rules, you gotta live by ours." Adam has a way to smooth ruffled feathers with his easy demeanor.

G.J. closes her eyes and takes a deep breath. When she opens them, she is back to regular G.J.. "My mind gets what y'all are saying. But there is this weird part, I don't understand, that is having a real hard time letting my head be in control."

"That's the wolf-mate instinct. It is an extremely strong bond. You'll become more accustomed to it over time. You're going through a lot right now, you are adjusting to your wolf nature growing inside you, and you have a new mate bond. Both of those things are going to be tough to handle, particularly at the same time." Jack directs his next statement to Adam and Hamilton, "You two need to measure what your mate needs from you. There are strong emotions and urges that are a part of this bond. Things the newly turned wolf in her will make worse, and G.J. may not be in control. To take advantage of those situations will hurt her. Your first concern should always be her welfare. Remember that."

"I got it, Dad. We would never hurt G.J.," Adam replies.

"Adam, by doing this, you've already hurt her. She can't take you challenging other wolves. If your plan to challenge each other pans out, how do you think she is going to deal with that? Unfortunately, she is bound to you both." Jack points out something none of us had considered.

"Why can't vampires bite someone on their big toe? If

that was where I had been bitten I would only have to worry about shifting not mating times two." G.J. grumbles rubbing her temples. "I can't think on this anymore. I need to go for a walk or something."

Jack fixes his food he has been working on. "You go nowhere by yourself right now. We just got you back up and running."

G.J. is fidgety. She rubs her arms and peeks at Hamilton and Adam. She spins away quickly.

"Well this is awkward." Drake says.

"Adam, Hamilton, head down stairs," Jack instructs them, after he had eaten one bowl full of his gumbo.

G.J. takes two steps to follow, but stops herself. "I'm not gonna make it. It feels like a train rumbling toward me. Inside I feel the building rattle foretelling something is coming that I can't stop. It is making me all kinds of jumpy."

"Speaking of something coming, I had an interesting encounter in the Shadow World I think you guys should know about." I fill them in on what Hugo had shared with me.

"How do the other beings cross through the Shadow World? And why have they not tried before?" Jack asks.

"I don't know," I offer.

"Well, now, wait a minute. I think getting in wouldn't be a problem. You said it wasn't to contain so I'd bet you can get in there if you are shown the way. If these escapee souls are showing them how to get in, then I can see how they would be able to get there."

"But it is really foggy in there. I don't think I would've found my way around if Hugo hadn't played tour guide."

"What is the fog made of?" G.J. asks.

I swallow a little in disgust over breathing it in there. "Souls."

"Well, that's just about the worst answer," G.J. says with her mind thinking ten steps ahead face.

"Why is that?" Jack asks.

"'Cause if those other beings, Nat talked about, eat souls, or whatever, all they have to do is roll into the Shadow World. Eat like they are at a Chinese buffet and then they will be able to see how to get past the boundaries of our world or any other."

"People die all the time. Why is this different? How many of these people are the Vampires killing? It can't be more than a war zone or a natural disaster," Drake says.

"Hugo said something about if the shades are killed by a creature they had thought mythical making them try to explore instead of seeking resolution back in our world."

"That falls in line with our history," Jack says, and takes a drink.

"How?" G.J. asks.

Jack's massive chest expands in a deep breath, as if this is going to be another long story. "I can only speak for pack law. But we are forbidden to expose ourselves to humans. Not because of what folklore says. We don't fear humans taking us hostage and doing experiments." Jack laughs. "Our history bans it from a time long ago. It speaks of other beings sent away, and their only way back would be if the Shadow World is compromised. It's said that if humans believe us to be real, it can unlock the way for the others to return."

"We have a similar story in our traditions. I can ask my father to explain why they feel that is what will happen," Drake says.

Jack nods his approval.

"I kinda remember a part of an old book of the Wiccans that says something about a seer who talked about the time of the return. Maybe this is what they meant. I can go research it," G.J. adds.

Celia comes in the kitchen and goes over to Jack, who is now standing at the counter trying to eat his second bowl of gumbo. "We have a problem."

"We have the whole kit and caboodle of problems," G.J.

says in a way that seems to say "now what?"

"What is it?" Jack asks, as he wraps Celia into his arms.

Celia leans back and to peer up at Jack's eyes. "Is there a way to un-mate that you know of?"

"No. Once it happens, we are bound. You know that," Jack says, as if he explained this to her before.

I, for one, am glad they had already chatted about the subject, which would have been weird if they hadn't.

Celia sighs deeply. "I don't know how to say this, but G.J. can't be mated to the boys. She is already promised to someone else." Celia's shoulders are up around her ears, as she waits for the reaction from the rest of us.

G.J. is blank faced.

"Promised to whom?" Drake is the only one of us whose brain can get past the comment.

"It doesn't matter. She is already mated. Whatever the promise, it has to be broken," Jack lays down the law.

Celia examines G.J., worried. She knows, and I know, silence is just a build up to a heavily worded rant. I pop in Celia's noggin to find out who my BFF is betrothed to. Wouldn't you? "... *breeding witches so they can repopulate.*"

I bark out a laugh. "G., you are gonna love this one."

"Not helping, Nat." Celia shoots me an exasperated and rather annoyed expression.

I shrug. "Sorry, but if I know G.J., that is more of a jagged pill than anything Alanis Morissette dreamed up."

Drake leans down and asks, "What?" right in my ear. His warm breath across my neck gives me the tingles.

"How in the world do I go from having never, in my whole life, been on a date to having not one, not two, but three permanent life partners?"

"Four, if you count Gus." I do like to be helpful.

"I don't," she says, taking a breath to finish her rant.

"He does." My face holds that I-hate-to-tell-you-expression only a close friend can give.

G.J. puffs out a little of that big breath. She sucks it back into her lungs and sets her jaw a little. "Well, too bad, I have enough trouble from the dogged dastardly duo. I have no need to add to this list at the moment."

"Or ever." Jack crosses his arms in his super dad pose.

"Why am I suddenly the hottest ticket in town?" Her head moves, asking each of us with her eyes for an actual answer.

Drake asks, "You want the long or the short list."

I feel the muscles between my shoulder blades tense. My little jealous ember just had a flare up. Try having a friend like G.J. and see if you feel secure. I don't look at Drake. I don't have it in me to watch him joining G.J.'s ever-growing dance card.

"Short," she demands.

"You're gorgeous. Guys respond to it," Drake replies.

I glare at him. So, Drake finds G.J. gorgeous? Is the line too long for her and that is why settled to date me? I hate being jealous of my best friend. Bwahh. I do not have time for these kinds of insecurities. I have enough going on. But I can feel my annoyance pour out of my pinched face.

"Other guys. Not me. I mean, I do but…" Drake shifts his gaze from one of us to the other.

"Wow… you did that to yourself," Jack says to Drake, and laughs at him.

G.J. waves her hand at the comment and dispels it, like she does all compliments. "I don't think that has anything to do with it. I have a mirror, so I don't subscribe to that hooey. Do I even know the latest suitor? No. So there is no suiting happening here. Mark that one off the list. Aunt Celia, you tell this P person, G.J. don't play that."

"G.J., it isn't that simple. This was something your parents agreed to a long time ago," Celia starts, but solemnly finishes by dropping the bomb of, "You are needed to breed the next generation of Witches."

Five… four… three… two… "Excuse me? You are saying I am the means to an end, the end being repopulation. I'm to give up any chance at my own happiness or life so I can end up the Witchy version of '19 Kids and Counting'? And hold up, you said parents. Plural. Meaning more than one. I only had one parent, I have ever been introduced to, and she never said a word about my need to help out the census numbers for Witches. So, whoever else you think has a vote doesn't. The only one who has ever come close to being my daddy is Jack." G.J. turns her attention to him. "Jack, do you want me to be in the knocked-up-a-thon prescribed in repopulation attempts."

"Absolutely, not." Jack puts some growl in his voice for emphasis.

"Done and done. Aunt Celia you can just go on back to P and tell him, that there is a no go." G.J. crosses her arms, as if to end the discussion.

"It is more complicated than that," Celia says, as I check behind the scenes in her head for more info. *"There is no breaking the promise to the Old King."*

"Who is the 'Old King?'" I ask aloud.

The reaction that gets is shock, but Celia isn't who is the most upset. Drake gawks at me in horror. Jack and he exchange a stare. His handsome face becomes pallid and Drake stumbles back, shaking his head. When he reaches the doorway, he says nervously, "I have to go," and he rushes toward the entry door.

I glance at the group bewildered before racing to catch up with Drake before he can make it outside. "Hey," I call, but Drake keeps going. "Stop!" I command.

Drake stops with his hand on the door but doesn't turn around. "Nat, I can't do this right now."

"Do what? Talk to me? Tell me where you are going? Explain why you turned whiter than the Stay Puff Marshmallow Man? Say good-bye?" I am a little disgusted with how pitiful I sound. *One date Nat. This guy owes you nothing.*

Drake's shoulders lift in a heavy sigh. "I have to go deal with a few things. I can't stay here right now."

"Who is the Old King?"

"Nat… please don't." Drake still has not faced me.

I walk up and pull his arm so he turns. His forehead is wrinkled and his eyes are so full of torment it is heartbreaking. I just want to make it better, whatever "it" is. "Drake? You promised honesty."

He leans forward and kisses my forehead so gently, with such sorrow, I can't breathe. "I lied. Good-bye, Nat."

I stand there shocked. As Drake opens the door, five men come in. I don't move, as he makes his way out.

Chapter Twenty-Two

G.J. greets the men who have just entered the house, as she walks up beside me, but I can't see her. My stupid eyes are full of water and everything is blurry.

"Hey, why did Drake rush out like that?"

I face her, G.J.'s form distorts by my welling tears. My lungs expand, but pain shoots through my chest, as if someone is pushing on my sternum. From head to toe, my body stills, freezes; it wants to remain motionless, as if the act would lessen the devastating impact of Drake's last words, his actions.

"Nat? What happened?" G.J. asks gently.

My throat seizes, and it's impossible for me to speak. I give the slightest shake of my head and close my eyes; it is the only way to find control. I close in on myself. *One date, two kisses.* A month ago, I hated the guy. *Why does this hurt so badly?* One more person walking away from me; one more person I counted on leaving. He had no right to make me like him if this is what was going to happen. Why did he leave?

G.J. pulls me to her, hugging me close. She doesn't say a word, just holds me. Which makes me know she must care because G.J. always talks.

"He left, said he lied to me. Why would he have done that?" I leave "to me" unsaid.

"Honey, something that happened back there scared the bejeepers outta that boy. He'll be back." G.J. rubs my back to soothe me.

"How do you know?" I say, after I hiccup a little sob. I have all manner of facial drippings soaking G.J.'s shirtfront. That's what friends are for, I guess, and I make the worst sounding snot-sucking noise with my runny nose.

"Oh, sweetie, you can just tell."

"What? Now you are the mind reader?" I pull back and set my dismal gaze on her.

"Shoot no. I'm a people reader. That boy turned white as a sheet and bolted like a cat when a pack of pit bulls is set loose hungry." She pushes me an arm's length away to give me a once over. "Come on! We need to hold up in a dark room with snacks and streaming videos until you feel better."

I follow her only because I don't have the will to break her grip as she pulls me along. My head is racing with a million questions, but they all come back to why? What happened that made him leave like that and why would he lie to me? What had he lied about? Everything? Was this all some sort of stupid joke to him? Did he set me up? Was this all just a way to get close to G.J.?

****

Knock, knock, knock. A light tap interrupts our viewing of the most recent BBC production of "Persuasion." I, for one, am relieved; G.J. might love her regency romances, but I'm more in the mood for a horror film. Not that I had been paying any attention to the flat screen. When she was asking what we should watch, I hadn't said anything, and it became her choice by default. She had pulled her curtains causing the room to dim, but not darken, and cut the glare on the T.V.

Pausing the movie, G.J. calls, "Come on in."

Celia peeks around the door. "Hey, is there room up there for an old, pregnant lady?" She motions toward the bed with a small jut of her chin.

"If you are here in support of Nat, permission to board granted. If you are going to try to talk me into bachelor number three, you need to keep sailing sister," G.J. says, making it clear what topics she's approved for entry.

Holding her hands up in mock surrender, Celia makes her way over and scoots onto the bed, less awkwardly than I would have thought the baby bump would have allowed. She says, "So anyone want to clue me in on the need for the girl time happening here?"

G.J. studies me waiting for my lead.

I sigh deeply. "Not particularly but I will. You know I have never been able to read Drake. It has made me dislike him for a very long time. He said he liked me. He said he would always tell me the truth. He said a lot of really nice things. Things that made me like him back. Then, up comes this Old King guy and Drake bolts. I remind him he promised to tell me the truth and he said he lied." I focus on my hands that I am twisting in my lap. "Then, he said good-bye. The way he said that sounded like the big good-bye... Boys suck."

"Hear, hear!" G.J. says in solidarity.

"Mmmm." Celia murmurs ambiguously.

"Don't mmmm Nat. Just because you have your dream guy doesn't mean the rest of us no longer have woes to deal with. Get with the 'boys are no good rotten scoundrels' or hit the highway," G.J. admonishes her aunt.

"You can't judge the entire male populous because of one or two," Celia says.

"Or three," I chime in.

"Or four," G.J. adds. "Really, if we start adding them up we might be here a while."

Celia huffs out in exasperation, "Whatever. There are good men and bad men. But bottom line is they are all people. They have thoughts and feelings behind why they make their choices. I'm sure Drake has a very good reason for why he acted the way he did. We will have to see what it is. In the meantime, we have other things that need to be addressed and moping around over what could very well be a non-issue seems like a gigantic waste of time." Celia flicks a stern gaze at each of us in turn.

G.J. and I glance at each other. I don't particularly feel my woes are unworthy but there are bigger fish to fry, so, in silent agreement we attentively focus on Celia, to lead us to whatever she wants to address. So many things have happened I really have no idea what topics will make her top ten list.

"Nat, tell me what is happening. I have tried to reach your mom and I've had no luck. Jack wants your dad's cell number. Your mother's phone seems to be turned off, we can't track it."

"I told you I give them the heebee geebees so they took off. I'm a bridge to other planes of existence. And I have now proved it by taking a little jaunt into the Shadow World. What else do you want to know?"

"Well," Celia starts, "Can you control your visits to the … Shadow World … or can anyone… um … any ghost or spirit just pull you there?"

I blink at her. "I have no idea."

G.J. peruses me speculatively, which makes me uneasy. "Can you try it?"

"Try what?" I know what they want; I just can't acknowledge it to myself.

"Can you try to go there?" G.J. says it slowly, playing along with my ignorant act.

"Why would I?" I ask, honestly perplexed and just sure they have both lost their marbles. "End of the world as we know it stuff, remember?"

"If you can figure out how to control it, then you would have the power over the situation. Some wacko spirit would not have the ability to come grab you and pull you out of this world without your okay," G.J. explains.

"That and you would be able to check if the boundaries are stable," Celia adds.

G.J. and I both whip our gazes toward Celia.

She shrugs her shoulders up. "You said your ghost friend said there's a possibility of that happening. We need to know if it does. The world will change in very scary and unknown ways if things that don't belong here come over. When I mentioned this to … my contact … they were very concerned. Someone has to make sure that doesn't happen. And if the strange killings that've been happening might cause this to occur, we could all be in very serious trouble."

"You want me to cross over?" I shake my head as my stomach flips in objection.

"Of course, I don't want you to, but you have the ability to do this, and no one else seems to. You can be our warning system," Celia says.

"I'm not as concerned about the warning system as I am you with you being able to control this ability. You said Sara's mama has come to chat with you. She is just the kind of crazy to pull you over and then what happens if you can't hop on back as you please. I prefer you here not there on a permanent basis," G.J. says, rubbing my arm.

I like her argument a whole lot better than Celia's. At sixteen, I have no interest in playing inter-dimensional spy, but I definitely see trying to avoid being stuck in the Shadow World as pro.

"Leslie has visited you?" Celia eyebrows jump half way to her hairline.

"Yep. She wants me to be a conduit for her to talk to Sara. I've told her no of course."

"What does she want you to tell Sara?" Now one of Celia's brows lower, leaving the other one arched.

"I don't know, it's all nonsense. 'The time is coming. Stay focused on your skills. Only ones with true power will survive. Practice spells of possession.' Yada yada…" I say quoting Mrs. Ackers in my best ghoul-y voice.

"You never told me what she said." It's G.J.'s turn for her eyebrows to wing up. She pulls her whole torso away in surprise.

"She's nuts. Death hasn't changed that," I reply.

"No," G.J. says, "I'm sure the grim reaper's sickle can't knock the crazy out of her, but, Nat, that sounds like an omen of what we're chatting about. And possession? Can you imagine if that chick gets back? Who does she want to possess?" Her pretty features screw up in a that-might-just-be-the-worst-news-ever face.

"How do you propose I find out how to go to the other world?" I ask, resigned to trying to figure this out. "If I am the only bridge around, I doubt there is an online course I can take on the subject."

"Do you think Hugo could help you?" G.J. taps her finger on her chin contemplating more than what she verbalized.

"I'm not sure. He kind of just dumped me back here after I drew the attention of that … whatever that thing was." This is the first thought I've had about Hugo since then and guilt crept over me. I should've been concerned for him. What if that thing had gotten to him? I shudder.

"Can you call him?" Celia wonders.

"I don't think he has a cell," I say dryly, remembering the worthless yelling for Hugo I had done, when I was out with the boys. The image of Drake flashes through my mind, and I focus at my hands again.

G.J. gets up and paces around her room.

"I will give it a shot... again." I'm completely convinced this is just going to be an embarrassing waste of time. "Huuuugoooo... Oh Huuugoooo..."

I repeat the call several times, as G.J. appears more and more agitated. About five minutes of this passes to no avail, when G.J. bolts out of the room.

I squint at Celia and I'm positive her what-just-happened expression mirrors my own.

Chapter Twenty-Three

Strong wind rushes through the house making the blowing curtains reach for us, as we pass them. The odd thing is that the windows are closed. Celia hurries past me and calls out for G.J..

Somewhere, at that same moment, I hear the distant bellow of Jack's command, "Settle!" The ground shakes with the intensity of the control he uses.

Several whimpers echo up from the basement stairwell Celia has led me to. When we make it to the bottom of that set of steps, we follow a large hallway to a huge room on the right. In the room, there is a mat and a Gold's Gym worth of exercise equipment.

In the crowd gathered in the room, I follow the beeline Celia is making with my gaze and find Jack. Jack is holding G.J., who has eyes that are emanating their own light source. Several of the men are backed up against the wall, a few of them a bruised and bloody. Wind is ruffling hair and sending towels rolling and curling across the floor. Adam and Hamilton are covered in blood. *Oh boy.*

"You need to leave this," Jack says low, still using his controlling rumble.

"Not my mates." G.J. is back to cave-chick speak.

"I need you to go back upstairs," Jack is commanding, leaving no room for arguments.

"Not my mates." G.J.'s voice growls in an imitation of the control Jack uses over the pack.

If the look on Jack's face is any indication, he thinks it is a pretty good one too. G.J. is agitated and pulls toward Adam and Hamilton. The two stay where they are with their heads lowered in a submissive gesture.

"Jack?" Celia says in a way that sounds like she just asked a whole line of questions about what on earth is going on.

"No Magic." The force of Jack's command is as strong as anything I have ever felt.

G.J. lets out a small whimper, which makes Adam and Hamilton twitch. Her eyes also seem dimmer, but they are still a long way from normal.

Jack's gaze finds Celia and once again gives some non-verbal spouse cue.

"We were upstairs and then a few minutes ago G.J. started getting jumpy. All of the sudden she bolted for the door," Celia tells Jack, who seems to be trying to gage if his command will hold G.J..

At her words, Jack moves his attention back to furious girl in his arms. "Only a few minutes ago?"

"Yeah, she was fine and then all of the sudden she freaked," I add.

Jack looks to me. Deciding, he says, "Draw!"

G.J. slumps a little and Jack holds her up. Every other person in the room gapes at Jack, like he has lost his mind.

"*You called for me?*"

"Now? You show up now?" I ask Hugo the Invisible to everyone but me.

"*Did you want me?*" Hugo seems a little annoyed at his reception.

I sigh. "Yep. I need you to take me back to the Shadow World."

As Hugo reaches for my hand, G.J. yells, "Wait. Nat..." she is gone and the mist of souls surrounds me again.

"Give a girl a little warning, will ya?" I grouse, as I shake myself to get used to the new surroundings.

"*I did as you asked.*" He sounds defensive.

"I know, but the world jumping thing isn't exactly playing hopscotch."

"*What was it you wanted?*"

"I am hoping you can show me how to go back and forth."

Hugo looks at me for a long moment, but shakes his head. "No? Why no?"

"*I'm not sure how I do it will work for you. I don't have a body any longer. That is how I make the transition. You have well—*" Hugo stops himself.

You can take the soul out of the teenaged hormonal boy, but you can't take the... you get the drift.

"I need to be able to control when and how I move between worlds. How do you bring me here?"

"*When I touch you, I pull your soul.*"

"Explain."

Hugo's eyes focus far off to ponder the best way to explain. "*If a shade touches a regular person, we connect with their actual soul. When we do, there is a brief disconnect between the being and the body. It is almost like they die or come fairly close to it. That is why they get a chill. When we move through them or touch them, we pull some of their life energy away from them for a moment. The human spirit is an enormous energy source. As we, the shades, grow weaker, we become kind of a vacuum, and when we touch someone we draw their power.*"

He looks at me to see if I understand. I wish G.J. were here, or I could take notes, because this sounds right up her alley. Me? Not so much. "Okay?" I say more in a confused question than true understanding. I hope I can remember all this to tell G.J.. "I don't get a chill though."

"Right. That is what makes you different. Your spirit stays whole. When I touch you and pull on your soul, it stays fully intact. So I can just bring you over. If I touched anyone else, I would only take the pieces I was able to 'Hoover up', as you would put it. Because you stay intact, you can go into this world or any other with all of your energy. Death drains energy.

"Like I told you before, slow or natural deaths gradually weaken the human spirit. Have you ever been to an old folk's home? It is always like eighty-five degrees in them. The elderly are getting colder because their spirits are waning. Same with the people with terminal illnesses, or people who are starving, they are perpetually cold. When people document slow deaths, they always mention how cold the dying claims to be. Their spirits are losing their energy. When those spirits make it here, they are already so dissipated they move past this plane almost immediately or by pass it altogether.

"When you're ripped from the human world, it's like I said before, you come here with too much energy to move on, and you have the ability to move between worlds, but only as a shade. A shadow of what you once had been. All death drains a certain amount of energy from everyone. You have nothing to contain your energy, and it slowly but surely disperses, eventually allowing you to move on. But you hold all of your energy or power so you're not weakened when moving between worlds."

"What about poltergeists or hauntings? I have heard of some pretty powerful ghosts."

"Humans have strong emotions that fuel our spirits, fear, anger, hate, love. This is why if you die holding onto anyone of those feelings, you tend to stay in the Shadow World longer. You can also use the energy those emotions have fed you to move

*back and forth between worlds. The spirit just won't be whole,
as you are."*

"Okay," I say, beginning to get it.

*"I can't pull a whole sprit out of anyone else. I can only pull
yours. And when I touch you and bring you here, I don't seem to
lose anything. You keep me whole too. Or at least as whole as I was."*

"That is what I need to be able to control. When you
touch me, I just leave my body. I can't get dragged here
whenever a ghost touches me. And I need to be able to get
back to my own skin whenever I want. I don't even know
how you did it the last time. I was just there. Can you help
me learn how to do it?"

*"Your body is your anchor. You will always be drawn back
to it. There is no chance of you getting stuck in this world. But
learning how to get here on your own? I don't know how you
would do that."* Hugo winces and shrugs at a loss for the
answer I need.

"I can go back to my body whenever I want?"

Hugo nods.

"Can you help me practice?"

"What do you mean?"

"Maybe if you bring me over enough times I can figure
out how to get here."

"Why would you want to come here?"

"To see what is happening. You know, make sure those
things you showed me aren't here hurting you."

"You care what happens to me?"

I'm not sure why it makes me uncomfortable, but his
reaction to my nod is off putting. He takes his free hand
and cups my cheek. His eyes are on mine and the moment
seems too intimate, like he's about to kiss me. I lean away,
pulling my face from his hand. I don't know about you, but
the idea of being smooched by a dead guy is rather icky.

He lets his hand fall away. *"I'm sorry."*

"Nothing to be sorry about."

"Can I ask you something?"

"Shoot."

"If I had asked you out, when I was alive, what would you have said?"

I look back at this boy, who lost all of his opportunities. He is never going to ask me or anyone else out. He is never going to wake up for school or get a job. He is never going to meet his friends at the mall or the movies. All of the possibilities of what his next day, or the rest of his life would hold, were all stolen from him. He could have been anything, and now he is just waiting here until he is nothing. I have no idea what I would've said if he had asked me out, while he was alive, but now I know he will never have the chance, my answer is clear. "Yes."

Chapter Twenty-Four

Hugo and I work out when we will meet again to start my Shadow World hoping. He seems more present with energy. He says we have to be careful. Since my physical being is my anchor, someone should keep watch over it when I leave it. I haven't given any thought to that so it's time to ask G.J. to body sit. When we separate, Hugo leans forward and brushes his lips on my cheek. This time I do get a chill, but I don't think it is because he took some of my energy.

When I come back to my body, I am in my room at the Wyfle house. Stanzi sits in the chair near the now boarded up window.

"Hey," I say, my voice a bit sleep slogged.

"Hey." Stanzi doesn't talk much.

"What happened with G.J.?"

"Jack thinks she was only upset by Adam and Hamilton fighting each other. They had fought through most of the Gammas who didn't immediately submit by the time she came down. Everyone except Lucas, so he called the match a draw." Stanzi shrugs. "G.J. is making all kinds of new rules." A hint of a smile twitches his mouth.

"I'd expect nothing less. They beat you?"

Stanzi shrugs again. "I don't really want to be too high on the food chain. I draw enough challenge fights just because of my size. I have no interest in spending all my time battling my pack members, just because someone feels the need to prove their manhood." He looks too tired for someone so young. Stanzi is only a few years older than we are. At the most, he is nineteen. Changing the subject, he moves on, "She wants me to go get her, as soon as you wake up. You gonna be okay?"

"I have no plans to cause trouble at the moment." I smile.

He nods before shaking his head, as he leaves the room.

While I wait, I try to call my parents again. I leave a voicemail for my mom. "Hey… it's me… I umm… I am trying to learn how this whole thing works so you don't have to be scared of me. Life has gotten a little more than crazy. I'm living at the Wyfle's with G.J. if you want to know where I am. If you care. The front door on our house is gone. I think Mr. Wyfle is having it fixed. It would be nice if you got a hold of him and took care of it. I didn't do it. Call me if you want to know what happened. I ummm… I love you. Bye."

I sit thinking how lame my message was. I should have told them to get their butts back here. 'If you care' how pathetic can I get. If they don't want to be my parents anymore, why should I care?

"Hey, world traveler, what did you find out?" G.J. disrupts my thoughts with her cheer and bad pun.

"A ton. I wish I could have taken your brain with me. Let me see if I can remember everything." I run through what Hugo had said.

"Huh?" is her response, as the distant look in her eyes tells me she is trying to assimilate the information.

"I also think Hugo was kind of hitting on me."

That snaps G.J.'s thoughts back to the here and now. "You have an amorous ghost? Lordy, we are a pair. Our numbers must have made it to a bathroom wall or something, if we find out where, I will bring the Mr. Clean eraser. We have enough to fool with, without boy troubles to boot."

Hamilton comes to the door and leans against the frame. He doesn't try to enter; he just stays in the door.

G.J. sighs. "Sorry, I forgot I was supposed to wait for my fierce protector to be done changing before I came to see you." She used air quotes when she said the word forgot so we were all aware she hadn't forgotten a thing. She focuses back on me. "So if other souls can't jump worlds without losing a piece of themselves, I wonder how the others can make it here without damage."

"Hugo said when he touches me, he didn't seem to lose anything when he made the jump," I offer.

"So if these other beings get a hold of you, they can come here with no damage," G.J. says.

"How would they get a hold of her?" Hamilton asks.

"Good question." G.J. wears a deep in thought mask.

"If I just stay out of the Shadow World, I wouldn't be anywhere close to them and they couldn't reach me. Just because I can do it doesn't mean I have to."

"If Hugo knows this, others will too," Hamilton says. "If you just go when a shade touches you, how can you avoid going back? What is to stop one of them?"

"He's right, Nat." G.J. gives a dramatic gulp. "Dear heavens that's almost painful to agree with Hamilton out loud. I'll do my best to avoid it in the future." She gives a joking smile. "If these souls are curious, and they want you, they can just come get you and there is nothing we can do about it. We need you to get a hold of this ability."

"I asked Hugo to come practice with me. But I need someone to keep an eye on my body while I am away from it." I regard G.J..

"Goodness, what a thing to have to worry about. I can put you in a Wiccan circle for protection. We're lucky nobody waltzed up and played puppeteer with your physical being before now. I'm gonna need…" She eyes me speculatively while making her mental list.

"What happens if you're not there to make a circle?" Hamilton asks, breaking her concentration.

"Looks like you found your missing gray matter today." G.J. smirks at Hamilton and considers me, like I am some kind of a puzzle. "Maybe… a talisman?" I think she is asking herself more than any of us present. She nods and hops up. "All righty, I am off to research what will work. I may need you in a bit. Are you gonna be good?"

"I'd be better if everyone stopped asking me that," I reply without responding.

G.J. pats my leg before adding, "Don't be so darn precious if you don't want us caring about your wellbeing."

As G.J. passes Hamilton, she reaches her hand toward him and runs it up his chest. She turns her face toward his neck and inhales deeply. She freezes and pulls it away, like she just realized she did something obscene.

""Bwahhh!" she screams in frustration and hustles off.

Adam asks her what is wrong from down the hall.

Hamilton has become almost a statue. He can't believe that just happened any more than I can. "Hamilton, don't push that subject. She is more spooked than that girl in the *Blair Witch Project.*"

"So am I, Nat. This is so screwed up." Hamilton looks truly conflicted. "Why couldn't we have met in a normal way? Why couldn't I have just asked her out on a date?" He bangs his head back against the doorframe. "I have made so many bad calls."

"I have to concur there."

Hamilton rolls his head to meet my eyes. He gives a sad smile. "You know I saw her once when we were younger?"

"No, I didn't."

"She was in the woods one day with her mom. I was just goofing off, learning to track on my own. Dad would have me shift and tell me to go stalk something. I was about eight or maybe nine at the time. I was sniffing around to see what I could hunt up when I caught this scent. It was like all things wild and the beauty of the earth. It was the most incredible thing I had or have ever smelled.

"Scents are different to us. Our human mind ties scents to emotions. Our wolf part untangles the complexity of it and leaves an impression of each smell as a permanent memory. We know what things are because they all have a category in our minds. This smell was unique. Its strangeness called to me. I stalked the aroma and found her. And she looked right at me. No fear. Here is this little girl and she sees a wolf in the woods and she is ready to meet me head on. I am a predator. I scare almost everyone on some level. Even other wolves get uncomfortable around me because I am an Alpha. But not her. It sounds corny, but it was like she saw me in wolf form as an equal." Hamilton stops, as if he can still see the moment he laid eyes on her.

"She told me she had seen a wolf when she was younger. That was you?"

Hamilton gives a wistful smile. "She remembers too."

"Hamilton, G.J. is open. Why do you keep her at arm's length? You could talk to her about this."

"Nat." He shakes his head in frustration. "Imagine from the age of eight to sixteen you have a dream girl. You have no

interest in any of the girls around you because you know…
you *know* there is just one person in the world you want to
be with. You tell yourself you can track her down when you
are older. It doesn't matter if she is missing a leg or dating
some other dude. You will find her and do whatever it takes
because there is something about the way she met your eyes
that you want to have happen every day for forever. You
convince yourself there is no reason to date anyone else. So
you kind of ignore them all. They aren't her. Then wham. One
day this totally hot girl slams into you at school. I mean this
girl is amazing looking. She is tall with these curves that…"

"You can skip those details. Thanks."

"Yeah…" Hamilton shakes his head, laughing to himself.
"Anyway. Wham there is this smokin' hot girl right in your arms
and you do what you always do. You start to dismiss her. Only
then, her scent hits you and as your brain hits on who this is.
She confirms it by meeting your eyes in that most amazing way.
And it's that strange perfume you remember of the wilderness
and the earth and it drowns out your ability to communicate."

"So you tell her she smells strange." I remember with him.

Hamilton's head falls and agrees. "Yep, you tell the girl of
your dreams she smells strange. Not some poetic crap about
wild things and nature. You live in stasis, waiting for the return
of a girl to your life, and when she comes back, she is so freaking beautiful every word you utter around her is ridiculous."

Hamilton sighs. "But it gets worse. When you realize
you need time to get it together, you ask your pack to keep
an eye on her so no one snags her before you get a chance
to figure out what would be your best approach. But these
are a whole group of male buddies, and you know damn
well what she does to a male libido. So you try to put the
fear of God in them to keep an eye out for her, but to keep
their distance.

"You then find her in the woods in your wolf form, and she shows you a vulnerable side she never would have if she had known you were some random from school. And that feeling of this is *the one* gets stronger. You understand her better. You get what kind of person she is and you are completely done for. You will do anything for this girl. Along with all her secrets, which your protective instincts make you want to lock her up in a tower somewhere, she tells you she is having trouble at school with some dude. So now, you tell your friends to keep an eye out for who was bugging her.

"The only guy anyone notices talking to her is one you would prefer not to mess with, but you are willing to take the heat if it means keeping her from hurting. So you think you have a plan. Only your best friend, who is supposed to be protecting her for *you,* discovers exactly how incredible she is too. Not only does she smell like heaven to us, but she is crazy smart … and funny … and caring. She can even freaking cook for God's sake."

Hamilton lets out a huff of utter frustration. "Now, in your head, this girl is yours. In your head, you think she must know on some level you are crazy about her and you two will be headed off into a sunset together someday in the future. So when the guy, who you thought was making her cry, touches her, you flip out and jump him. Your instincts want to protect her. Only in doing so, you knock her over and…"

Hamilton can't find the words so I help. "Injure her horribly and put her in the hospital?"

"Thanks, Nat." Hamilton seems ticked, but he knows that is an accurate recount. He rubs his chest, like his heart hurts.

"Yeah, you put this phenomenal girl in the hospital. And then she flipping moves into your best friend's house." Hamilton bangs his head back again. "So every night she is right next door with him, and all you can think about is what is she doing? Are they together? Why is her light still on? And you find out you are the guy she can't stand at school. She has no idea she is your soul mate. She thinks you freaking hate her. And every time you open your mouth, your protective nature has you saying something that, before it comes out, sounds like a gentle warning for her to take care of herself, but she doesn't ever get that. And that best friend of yours knows every right word to say. So as a human, he is her confidant and you only get her to open up when you have fur." He stares off in the distance. "To top off your incredibly f'd up relationship, your dad attacks her twice." Hamilton's eyes roll heavenward, as if seeking divine help.

"Then, you mate her against her will?" I ask, letting him know by my tone that won't help this situation.

"What did you want me to do, Nat?" In his defensiveness, he is tired of this situation.

"Maybe wait for Jack to think of something?"

"Adam couldn't see her like that anymore than I could have. G.J. in any kind of pain makes me insane. I was losing my mind, Nat. And my dad... Jesus, my dad... I had to be the one to make her better. I didn't care about anything other than making her better."

"And keeping her for yourself."

Hamilton shoots me a dirty glare. "She needed to heal."

"Yeah, she did, but you could have left her to Adam. But you didn't. You had to keep a piece of her for yourself. Sounds like you saw your needs were more important than hers to me."

"He could have backed off." Hamilton's eyes flare in true anger now. "Damn it, Nat. Don't you get it. She is it for me. Mark or no mark. If she had come back scarred or disfigured or had grown a third eye, I would have still wanted her. Even though the way she looks may seem like a bonus, it actually makes it harder. All kinds of men see her gorgeousness and want to possess her. They don't know her, though. They have no clue what she has been through or how brilliant she is. They don't care about what she wants or what interests her. They wouldn't watch to make sure she eats when she is focused on or upset about something. They probably couldn't care less if she was getting enough sleep or could get hurt when trying to climb a hill too steep for her. She is first on my mind all the time. If I had let Adam be the only one to mark her, that wouldn't have changed. My best friend would have been bound to *my* mate. Jack says we are too young but ..." Hamilton visibly tries to calm down. "... He doesn't get it. What I feel for her doesn't care how old we are. I felt this same thing when we were only eight, only every time I see her or learn more about her, it gets stronger." Hamilton rubs his temples with one hand. "God, I feel like a stalker."

"I was gonna say..." I tease him to lighten the tension. I am blown away by his feelings. I have read his mind a thousand times, but I never really understood until now what she means to him. "Sorry to be so harsh."

Hamilton gives a weak smile. "So now I have the girl of my dreams in a weird polygamist trio. I'm not sure how much more can go wrong."

"Well, there is that other guy she is supposed to be mated to."

"Gus is too late."

"Not Gus. The guy G.J.'s parents promised some Old King she would mate with in order to generate a new brood of Witches."

"Why the hell would Drake's dad make some deal with G.J.'s parents?"

Chapter Twenty-Five

"Drake's Dad?" I ask, sliding pieces into place.

Hamilton flinches realizing he just spilled some major beans. He glances out the door for escape "I should go check on G.J.."

"Freeze," I demand.

"Nat, Drake should talk to you about this. This isn't my business."

"Drake's dad has made some claim on G.J., and you are going to tell me you don't consider it your business?" I prod him.

"Drake's dad can claim whatever he wants. G.J. and I are bonded. There is no breaking that tie. I only have to worry about Adam and … well… her." Hamilton is utterly confident in this as fact until he gets to convincing G.J. there his voice peters out.

I try mining his brain for the info I want, but he is ready for me. All I get is a recap of all the emotions he just shared and a quick anatomy lesson using my bestie's body. *Gulp*. That is more explicit than a Nicki Minaj video. "Hamilton, no fair."

"You want to know what I am thinking, you are going to get a whole lot of that. Talk to Drake. This is his deal." Hamilton moves away.

"Talking to Drake isn't an option for me."

Hamilton turns back. "How's that? I thought you two were a thing."

I fall face first into the mattress and yell into it, "No. He walked out. He made it clear he thinks we are over."

Hamilton sits down on the bed next to me. "Nat, no way is that a possibility."

"He said good-bye. But it wasn't the words, but the way he said it. It was the big good-bye. As in see ya wouldn't want to be ya." I turn my head sideways, mashing my cheek against the mattress, and peer at Hamilton with one eye.

"Nat." Hamilton leans down, putting his hand gently on the small of my back. "Do you actually think Drake has hounded you for years only to want one date? I don't get how girls add two and two and get seven hundred and three."

I sit up a little. "What do you mean?"

Hamilton sighs. "Look, Drake and I don't have tea and discuss our feelings, but it seems to me he is into you. And unless you did something totally gross, like wiped boogers on his face, I can't see him just changing his mind." Hamilton gives me a grin and asks, "You didn't, did you?"

Fully upright now, I try to hit his chest, but he catches my hand.

"Okay let's try…" G.J. waltzes back in with her head down. When she takes us in, her statement dies on her lips. In a heartbeat, her eyes turn that extraordinary glowing gray.

As a growl low and deep resonates around the room, we sit stunned. Hamilton drops my hand but it is way too late. Just as she moves to launch herself at us, an arm snakes around her waist and holds her back. But this is G.J. so she doesn't need to actually touch us. Things fly around the room, smacking me in the head and arms. Hamilton throws himself over me, trying to prevent any permanent injury.

"G.J. stop!" Adam pulls her away.

I jump in her head to see what in the world she is freaking about.

"*He is mine. He wants her. Nat is my friend. Why would my friend take my mate? He protects her from me. She is so pretty and petite. Of course he wants her. He only mated me to heal me.*"

Her emotions are confused, made worse by these intense instincts she has no control over. And G.J. is jealous of me. Really, how can G.J. be jealous of me of all people? She sees me as better than her?

"G.J., it's not what you think," I try to yell, but Hamilton is heavy and pushes the air out of my lungs while squishing me into the mattress. "Hamilton get off! She thinks you want me."

Hamilton apparently absorbs what I've said and jumps off me. I cover my head, through the hollow of my protective arm, and watch Hamilton bat away everything G.J. throws at him.

He stalks toward her. Nothing distracts him from her. When he reaches her, with utmost care, he puts both of his hands on either side of her face. Debris smacks his back, but he stays undeterred. "Stop. G.J.. Just stop. Look at me."

G.J.'s eyes fill with tears. Adam is right over her shoulder, his arms still around her waist. Her chest shudders with a soundless sob until the smallest whimper escapes. The objects that had been dancing in the air fall to the floor.

"You never have to worry about me with anyone else." When G.J. lowers her eyes, Hamilton dips his head to catch her gaze again. "You are freaked right now. You've a lot to deal with. These are your new instincts and you have no control…"

G.J. winds up, as if starting to argue with him.

But he quickly adds, "Yet." He kisses her forehead.

G.J. struggles halfheartedly, but she isn't going anywhere with these two holding her.

"Easy, you will learn to handle them."

G.J.'s eyes are her normal color again as they lock on to Hamilton's. "Why do you believe that? How do you know what I feel?"

"Because I believe in you. And what you are feeling right now is how I feel when you are with other guys like Gus or Adam."

G.J. interrupts, "I haven't seen Gus since you and Adam spit bonded us."

"Right. It didn't take licking you for me to feel this way."

G.J.'s face screws up, her lip curling back in disgust. "I'm not sure if I should say aw or yuck."

Hamilton drops his head to rest his forehead on hers in defeat. "I am a true idiot. I can never say anything normal to you."

G.J. moves her hand to his cheek. "I'm glad you are finally able to admit that. Acknowledging you have a problem is one of the first steps to recovery." She smirks at him before kissing Hamilton on the cheek.

"Hey, if he gets one, I get one too," Adam half complains from behind her.

Pulling herself from between the two of them, she smooches her fingers and blows a kiss to Adam. "Go on and fetch it. I have some apologizing to do to Nat," and with that, the intense emotions of the last few minutes seem to be dusted away.

"I'm cool. Although you are helping me clean this place up." I survey the damage done by her temper tantrum.

Someone calls to Adam from down the hall, and he heads off. Hamilton starts to pick up books and clothes, as if it is no big deal that G.J. created a cyclone in my bedroom.

"This is my mess, I can clean it up." G.J. tries to take the things from his hands.

"Nah. This is my favorite mess ever. I am happy to take care of it."

How in the world does G.J. not get this guy digs her to the nth degree.

"What were you saying before you turned my room into a scene from *The Wizard of Oz*?" I ask.

"What?" G.J. shakes herself out of watching Hamilton methodically work his way around the room with a dumb grin on his face. "Oh, right. Okay, so I think there is a ritual we can use for protection and then we can channel whatever we call into a talisman. I think the best symbol is the Triquetra," she says, like I should know what she's talking about.

"The what?"

"The Triquetra. You would know it if you saw it. It is three eye shaped pieces made from one continuous line that overlap on one side of each in the shape of a triangle. It's the Celtic trinity knot?" She waits for me to nod. "While there are different theories of what it means, it pre-dates the time of Jesus so I'm not really sure it represents my favorite three, The Father, Son and Holy Spirit, I figure it can't hurt to have them onboard, though, if it does. Some say it represents the Goddess Maiden, the Mother, and the Crone..." She glances up and must read she lost me on my blank face so quickly moves on. "Anyway another theory is that it represents the mind, body, and spirit. If we connect a protection spell to a Triquetra charm, I think we can make it so your body will call your mind and spirit back, should it run into any trouble. What do you think?"

"I think this isn't my area of expertise."

"No. Of course not. Well, I think it will work. Can't hurt to try, right?"

"Do you think you know enough that it's safe?" Hamilton asks.

G.J. rolls her annoyed gaze to him. "I won't do anything dangerous. I'm not a moron. I will study up and run it past Ms. Stontz. I will need the coven to complete the ritual anyway. We will have to draw a circle in the woods."

"You aren't going in the woods," Hamilton commands.

"What is going to stop me?"

"I will," Hamilton dictates.

I mentally shake my head, poor stupid Hamilton.

"You and I need to just go ahead and get some things straight right now. You won't stop me from anything. So go set your bully guns blazing somewhere else."

"I …" Hamilton stops and tries to put his words together. "I would be uncomfortable if you went into the woods when we can't go with you. Your coven doesn't want us around. I know it is important to you that you keep their confidence and won't want us along. But there is something out there that you can't use your powers on that probably wants to finish what it started. G.J., seeing you after the attack made me crazy. Please understand, I need to keep you safe."

G.J. blinks back at him. "While I don't really care about your comfort level. I think that is the most articulate and well thought out thing you've ever said to me. It borders on rational discussion. Who knew you had that in you? Trying to keep this going may be a mistake, but let's give it a go anyway. Do you have a suggestion as to how I preform a ritual without at least some of my coven? I need at least three to work the rite."

"Are all of them unwilling to share who they are or is just a basic rule you all live by?"

Hamilton's ability to hold a well thought out discussion surprises G.J. again. "Ms. Stontz obviously told Jack who she was. I can put the question to the group. But I wouldn't be comfortable with you there."

"That's a good place to start. I have actually already seen them before if you recall. I was there the night Mrs. Ackers attacked you. Why don't you just ask the question and then we can see where things stand? But please, don't wander off unprotected. Even if you don't take me, make sure a pack member is with you so they can call for help."

"No, see I don't want any of y'all around."

"You have to take one of the pack, even if it's not me."

"Well that is gonna be awkward since this ritual is done in the buff."

Hamilton's face loses all muscle control. There went his ability to keep the conversation going. I know better than to pop in his head at the moment. I am sure he has G.J. starring in some kind of wood nymph fantasy. "You are a cruel woman, G.J.. Just plain old mean." I give my head a slow gentle shake.

"Well, besides me not particularly caring for the potential of one of the boys turning this innocent ritual into a blurry cell phone video they can share on Snapchat, I don't think the other ladies would want to be a screensaver either. So, the whole idea of an entourage, I think, is out."

"Yeah, it's definitely out. And you aren't going."

I guess his mental image of G.J. au naturel in nature fritzed his newfound ability for communication.

"Hamilton, you don't get to say what I can and can't do."

Hamilton's eyes are ready to burst from their sockets. His whole body is vibrating in frustration. "Can you find a ritual where clothes are included? You have something like seven million books. One of them has to include at least a towel or a toga. You cannot be seriously contemplating going out on your own, without a guard, a weapon, or a stitch on you. Please, G.J., be reasonable. I can go in wolf form. No one has to know."

"I will know. I will be breaking my promise to my coven, and what about you seeing me naked do you think works for me?"

Hamilton towers over her. "Well, nobody else is going to do it." His voice has that wild growl again.

"Thanks. I am sure you are right that nobody would want to see me and a bunch of middle-aged women stark naked. So we don't have to scar anybody. I can just go and come back real quick. Nobody has to know."

"G.J., you almost died."

Adam cuts off Hamilton coughing at the door. "Hey umm, G.J., that Megan girl is downstairs, she said you two had agreed to meet. The guys kind of hassled her and she seems a bit freaked out. You may want to go handle it." Adam seems very unsettled.

"Oh shoot. I totally forgot." G.J. turns to me. "We'll work on this in a bit. You want to come see what Megan and I are working on?"

"Might as well." Shrugging my consent, I get up to follow her out. I figure if I stay, I might have to help Hamilton on KP duty, and even G.J.'s math homework seems more interesting than that.

"We aren't done, G.J.. Don't think this is over," Hamilton slips in before we make our escape.

As we walk down the hall, G. J. grabs her backpack out of her room and grumbles, "Why that boy thinks he has any say over what I do is just beyond my comprehension."

"G., I don't want you out in the woods unprotected, either. I am all for having help, but I saw what happened to you. He's not wrong, and just because he is the one saying it in his usual not so eloquent way, doesn't mean you should ignore the point."

"What are you two talking about?" Adam asks, as he walks just ahead of us down the stairs.

"I need to go out in the woods to do a ritual by myself and your bossy best bud doesn't like the idea." G.J. informs Adam with her arms crossed in a great imitation of a petulant three year old.

"As much as I'd love to be on your side on this, I am going to have to go with him. G.J., you were wrecked. Nobody wants to see you like that again. As strong as you are, sometimes you need to lean on us. We are your pack. It is what we're here for." Adam is way better at convincing than Hamilton.

With a heavy sigh, G.J. looks about to concede, but throws out her last objection, "I see your point and it is a fair one but, Adam, I still don't know how to get past you all seeing me in the outfit the good Lord sent me in."

"Come again."

"The rite she is doing doesn't include clothes," I explain.

"I just don't know how I can live with you boys if you've seen me naked."

Adam barks out a laugh. "G.J.," he says in a tone that implies she is a silly girl, "Every time I close my eyes I see you naked. I'll just be comparing my imagination with the original." He grins and ducks as G.J. swats at him.

Waiting in the entry hall, Megan is rocking and her hands burst into a flapping motion until she seems to gather them back under her control.

G.J.'s voice changes to a soothing tone. "Hey there, Megan. Thanks for coming. Are you doin' okay?"

"You said we should meet here. The men at the gate said you didn't tell them, but you told me. You told me we should meet here. You said three o'clock. I was here at three o'clock. The men said you didn't tell them, but you told me." Megan's rocking pace increases, and she taps her temple with the heel of her palm. Megan's gaze darts, accusing G.J., before she stares through the floor.

"I am so sorry, Megan. I had a few things happen that made our get together slip my mind, but I am very happy you remembered. Let's go to the kitchen and we can work at the table. Is there anything I can get ya?" G.J.'s trying to normalize what is happening by ignoring Megan's behavior.

Megan makes me feel uncomfortable. I don't know what it is. She acts weird, yeah, but there is something that just feels off with her. I try to catch her eye to give her a smile. More for me than for her, but she won't look up from the floor.

Adam leads us all into the kitchen. As we walk, Megan keeps repeating, "You should have told them. They didn't know. You told me to come."

"Can I get you a drink?" G.J. asks Megan, as if the girl isn't ranting at her.

Megan continues, "The men at the gate didn't know I was coming."

Adam and I exchange a look, which holds a barely concealed eye roll.

"Megan," G.J. waits for the girl to look up at her, "Would you like something to drink?"

"I like milkshakes," Megan says with an earnest expression.

A laugh escapes me and G.J. shoots me an annoyed glare.

"I like them too. But that might be a bit much to get into right now. Would you like water, cranberry juice, club soda, or milk?" G.J. asks in her sweet, southern way.

"I would like half cranberry juice and half club soda," Megan replies.

G.J. nods. "That sounds nice. I'll have one too. Adam? Nat?"

"I'll just grab a water." I can't believe this girl wants G.J. to be her mixologist.

"I'll get myself a milk." Adam does so.

"Did you bring your notes from Friday?" G.J. asks.

"I brought my notes. The equation on the polarity is off. The magnet will only turn the mechanism part way past vertical, then it reverses direction. We need to find the angle the moment arm loses momentum on and set up a new magnetic field to drive the circuit to complete rotation." Megan digs in the swollen backpack she brought with her. Papers drift out and fall like mammoth snowflakes, as she draws out a notebook. Flopping the disheveled bound papers on the table, she flips through until she gets to her scribble, which I guess makes sense to her. Looks like gobbledygook to me.

While making drinks, G.J. says distractedly, "I think if we put the commutator in a tube shaped, like a donut, we can continue the circuit without needing a second magnetic field."

"G.J., what is it you are working on?" I have to ask since I'm not sure they're speaking English anymore.

"Megan and I are working on a magnetic engine. I think we're pretty close to getting it to work."

"It doesn't work yet. Why would we use a donut?" Megan goes back to their discussion, like I haven't spoken.

"If we use a bent tube, shaped like a donut with a channel cut out of the middle to deliver the current to the receptor, then the receptor can fall to the positive charge once it's past vertical." G.J. is back to gibberish. She walks over to the table, sitting down.

Megan practically sits on top of her and puts her notes under G.J.'s nose. "If the current is continuous, it will still reverse the direction and we won't be able to turn the wheel it will change directions," Megan argues.

"So maybe the answer is to find the angle the moment arm loses momentum and then set up a block of the current within the tube allowing the natural torque to switch the circuit to the positive flow of the current and therefore continuing the rotation," G.J. says the last part almost like a question.

Megan looks off into some mental chalkboard in her mind's eye, and I stare blankly at Adam. "Do you have any idea what these two are talking about?" I murmur to him.

"No clue, but they seem to be on the same page. And seeing her work that brain of hers adds a hot librarian aspect to the overall splendor that is G.J.." Adam almost leers at my BFF.

Shaking my head, I ask, "So what is her deal?" indicating Megan with a tilt of my chin.

"What do you mean?" Adam looks at me dubiously.

"She obviously has something going on. What is she? Aspy? Autistic? She's obviously not lacking in function if she is playing in G.J.'s league." I think I'm keeping my voice soft enough so the two in deep contemplation can't hear me

"I am high functioning autistic. My parents had me diagnosed when I was six, although they say they knew I had something going on from when I was young. If we use a wire fan-like connector that is long enough to curve I think the connection will me more durable." Megan answers me and continues her conversation with G.J. as if it were one stream of consciousness.

Apparently, my on the down low needs work.

G.J.'s eyes grow wide before her lids fall in accusation at me. "Nat didn't mean anything by that. She just is naturally curious. I consider it one of her faults." A pit bull strength bite enters her words by the end of her sentence.

Megan blinks up at G.J.. "Without curiosity, we would know nothing. Curiosity pushes humanity to the next great discovery. If we were not curious, we would be idle, and what would be the point." Megan bends her head back down to her work.

I wasn't trying to offend Megan. G.J.'s eyes are slitted and her scowl is one of the grumpier I have seen on her. I decide to pop in her head and see if she is really mad. As soon as I think about a mental perusal, the back of my neck starts to prickle in unease, like this is not something I really want to do. Shaking the feeling off, I begin again. Again, I seem to talk myself out of it. Now I am just freaked at my unintentional unwillingness to get inside Megan's head. I feel like I am discriminating against her by my aversion to snoop. I give it another go. This time, I am only able to brush up against her mind.

Megan's head pops up, and she spins to look directly at me. With her eyes fixed on mine, she tilts her head. Now I am obligated to get in and see what she is thinking. But it is like I am pushing against a plastic sheet. It's not like complete nothingness like with Drake. With Megan, I am forcing my way into her space, but I am still disconnected from her thoughts. There are just distorted images of what is going through her mind.

"Nat, what are you trying to do?" Megan asks.

Normally people don't know if I am there or not. Sometimes they guess, but they are never sure. "What do you mean?" I try for innocence, certain it isn't going to fly.

"You are pushing at my thoughts. What is it you want to know?"

If I thought Megan not making eye contact was unsettling, her penetrating focus is way worse. I give up, just to see her reaction. "I wanted to see if you were upset."

"About what?" Megan asks with no inflection.

"About me asking Adam what was wrong with you," I said.

As her gaze once again reverts to something below most people's knees, I lose contact with her eyes. She turns back to the table, rocking and gently banging the side of her head, this time tapping at her ear.

"Megan, honey, are you all right?" G.J. leans close to her, but seems unable to decide if she should touch her or not.

"She didn't ask Adam what was wrong with me. She asked if I was Asperger's or autistic. I answered her. She didn't ask what was wrong with me," Megan repeats again, her agitation growing.

"Excuse me for a minute, Megan. I'll be back in just a sec." G.J. gets up and points at me, then to the door.

Taking the hint we are about to have a pow-wow, I scuttle out the door before her. When we get to the entryway, I spin toward her for the confrontation. Defensively I ask, "What?"

"What is your problem? Why would you overtly offend Megan like that? She is a person, Nat. You don't get to talk to her like that."

"I don't get what the problem is. I asked the same question I had earlier, I just rephrased it and the girl goes nuts. How am I supposed to know what is going to set her off. She goes all wacky at the drop of a hat."

G.J. opens her mouth, but closes it again, unable to verbalize what she wants to communicate. If I know G.J., when she gets it out it is going to be a doozey. Taking a deep breath, G.J. says, "Nat, Megan is autistic. She takes things literally a good bit of the time. She may repeat herself on occasion. She has trouble with eye contact and can usually pick up many conversations at once. The lunchroom is hard for her because she can't focus with all the noise and different conversations. If you are within earshot of her, it is like you are talking to her all at once. That is why she could over hear your chat with Adam.

"Megan knows what right and wrong are. She knows better than most. She is a rule follower by nature because everything is black or white to her. So if you ask her if she is autistic, she thinks you want to know if she is autistic. If you ask her what is wrong with her, she now knows you think she is broken. That is not okay, Nat."

G.J. gives me a long stare, making sure what she is saying is sinking in.

"She is not broken, Nat. She is different, but so am I. So are you for heaven's sake. What is *normal?* Who gets to decide that? Megan is brilliant, funny, and yes caring. She has feelings. Autism does not mean robotic. Just 'cause she may express it in a way you don't get doesn't mean her feelings aren't real. When she starts rockin' and flappin', it means she is agitated. She is overwhelmed by something that is going on. She doesn't realize she is doing it, and even when she does, it is a release, like we roll our eyes or huff out a breath. I won't have you treat her like she is a thing and not a person. She's a nice girl. She is my friend and you need to quit."

I can't meet G.J.'s eyes for a minute. My stomach hits my toes with embarrassment and regret. I didn't mean to offend the girl; I just never dealt with anybody like her before. "I can't read her very well. That makes me uncomfortable. You know that. I will try to get past it. Maybe we can do something other than talk about subjects that I don't grasp."

"To quote one of my favorite little green fonts of wisdom '*Do or do not. There is no try.*'"

"Kermit the frog said that?" I grin, trying to ease the tension away.

"You and I need to have a George Lucas movie marathon." She gives me a half hug, and we walk back toward the kitchen.

Adam is sitting next to Megan, and she is explaining what all her scribbles mean. He says, "Wow, you and G.J. came up with all of this?"

"We are basing our work on the work of Nicola Tesla." Megan doesn't meet Adam's eyes as she speaks.

"Tesla was such a smarty pants. He had so many brilliant ideas. But we think we can refine what he was working on with magnetic currents to try to drive energy in a perpetual motion engine. This year the Governor's science award will be mine." G.J. realizing what she just said corrects herself, "I mean ours. Sorry, Megan."

"Principal Decker has given us time to work on this during school," Megan adds, glancing up she spots me and begins her rocking.

"I think he has some sort of side bet with the other school principles. We don't mind trying to help him out right, Megan?"

"We aren't helping him. We are working on an experiment. If he wins money, we should get some. It wouldn't be fair for him to make money off our work." Megan is matter-of-fact but is still unsettled if all her movements really are indicators.

"We already are signing over the rights to our experiment to the sponsors of the competition. I just hate that. Somebody will be making money off our brainpower and it sure won't be us. That is what's not fair. You try to get recognized for doing something cool as a kid, and somebody else reaps the financial benefit. I guess the youth of today has to forget all about the word fair." G.J.'s features pinch in disapproval.

"Hey, Megan," I glance at G.J. when Megan doesn't look up. "I'm sorry for what I said. I didn't mean to offend you."

"Nicola Tesla would not speak to a woman wearing pearls. He hated pearls," Megan responds.

My eyes flutter, blinking away the non sequitur. "Anyway, I hope you will accept my apology."

Megan changes the subject again. "Albert Einstein had delayed speech as a child."

"Okay…" I'm not sure what to say to that.

"Sir Isaac Newton had difficulty talking to people and would get completely focused on his work. Charles Darwin preferred to write letters than have a conversation, and *he* would get completely focused on his work," Megan said, still looking down, her body in constant motion.

I look to G.J., to see if she understands that I tried but Megan is impossible to communicate with, but she is smiling like Megan is brilliant.

"Do you think there is something wrong with them?" Megan quickly makes eye contact before looking down.

"What?" I ask, unsure of what she is talking about.

"There are indicators that Albert Einstein, Nicola Tesla, Sir Isaac Newton, and Charles Darwin were all on the autism spectrum."

"Ummm okay," is all I come up with to reply.

"I don't like you saying there is something wrong with me. And I don't like you trying to get into my mind. If you want in, it is only polite if you ask," Megan says.

Adam laughs. "That would be a first."

"How did you know I was trying to read your thoughts?" I am truly baffled.

"You didn't belong."

"What do you mean?" I am so curious.

"You mess up the way my thoughts move in my head. You don't belong," Megan repeats.

"You can feel Nat?" G.J. asks.

"She gets in the way," Megan explains.

"But I couldn't get all the way in. I could only see blurry thoughts," I object.

"You didn't ask."

"You mean if Nat were to ask, you would let her in," G.J. prompts Megan.

"It depends," Megan says.

"Depends on what?" I want to know.

With a sigh, Megan says, "It depends on if you say please." She grins and giggles a little. G.J. and Adam laugh with her.

"May I please, ahem, read your mind?" Well now I just feel ridiculous.

"Okay." Megan shrugs.

"Really?" Is that it?

"Yeah, it's okay. I will let you in," Megan says.

Let me in? She can let me in? I jump in her head.

This time there is not plastic sheet sensation. I still can't follow her thoughts, though. G.J.'s head moves at a mile a minute, but Megan's is like five hundred different miles being run at the same minute. Chaotic—she isn't thinking about one thing but several all at the same time. I try to pin down one of her thoughts, but that isn't how her head works. I feel like I'm standing in front of every major league baseball pitcher and they are all throwing at me at the same time.

The sound of the clock in the room and the smell of what was cooked last in here, her tag is poking her in the back of the neck, the table top is smooth, Adam is a muscular guy, the vein in his arm sticks out, if we use a cylinder bent round, how will we get the commutators inside.

I jump out. My hand clamps on my stomach to quell my nausea as I dizzily sway. Those were just the thoughts I caught. I missed so many more. My mind spins, confused. Megan's brain is disorienting. Shaking my head, I gain some equilibrium. My head literally hurts.

"You left," Megan says.

"Yeah, I was having a hard time following. How can you tell I am in there with all of that going on?"

"You slow down my head." Megan smirks at the ground.

"That was slow?" I sway a little again.

"How did you block her from getting in?" G.J. asks about my first attempt.

Megan shrugs. "It was more I had to let her in than I had kept her out on purpose. If she tries again, when I am not actively trying to let her in, I don't think she will be able to."

"Huh, I wonder why that is." G.J. is in deep ponder mode.

"To be honest, I didn't even want to try to begin with, but I thought I was just being weird. Maybe my natural aversion was because I shouldn't be trying to get in for some reason. I still feel ill and my head is killing me." Unsteadily, I take a seat in a barstool.

"You all right, Nat?" G.J. comes over to check on me.

"I'll be fine in a minute. I just…" I don't know if I finish my sentence or not.

Chapter Twenty-Six

Fluttering my eyes reflexively, I come to. The ceiling of my new room hovers, slowly orienting me to where I am. I move my hand to my head. The remnants of a serious headache is still drifting away.

"Hey kiddo," comes the gentle tone from Celia somewhere off to my left.

I roll my head to try to track where her voice came from.

"Hey," I manage to get out of my idle vocal chords.

"You had us worried. Here let me get you a wet cloth to wipe the blood off your face."

Well, that's about the worst thing you can hear when you wake up from an unsolicited nap. "Blood?"

"G.J. said your nose started bleeding, then you passed out. Adam grabbed you and brought you up here. Jack has the doctor downstairs. I'll have him come up now that you are awake. Do you remember what happened?" Celia hands me the damp cloth.

I dab at my nose. "I tried to read that girl Megan's mind, then I got a crazy headache. I felt like the lights were stabbing me and like I was going to throw up."

"Megan? Was she thinking something that awful?" Celia asks, her worry lines becoming more prevalent in her forehead.

"No… or not that I know of… it was hard to tell. I have never entered a mind like hers before. It was weird. I had a natural aversion of trying to read her mind. I had to force myself to do it and she had to let me in. I've never had that happen before." I sit up and retrace the experience in my mind. "It is so hard to explain. Her thoughts weren't negative or bad, there were just too many of them. And they ran in a way I couldn't follow. It was like they were extra intense. There were hundreds of thoughts, and each one was more vibrant… or… maybe I don't know… powerful?" I ask it as a question because the words don't seem to fit right.

"Do you think she meant to hurt you?" Celia asks.

"No," I say quickly. "When I go in someone's head, I get their emotions too. She wasn't being malicious. That is just how her mind works. I just don't think I am supposed to go in there. I think it is like a thing on one of those science shows. You know the berries are a certain color to warn off something from eating them. My instincts were telling me to back off, but I tried to do it anyway." I'm still a little foggy.

"Well, I suggest you listen to your instincts. G.J. did her best, but she isn't a brain surgeon…" Celia ponders for a second. "Yet." She grins with pride. "Let me go grab the doctor, just to be sure you are 100 percent and then we'll figure out dinner."

"What time is it?" I ask, eyeing the darkened sky outside.

"Just after six," Celia says, as she exits the room.

***

G.J. makes what, for her, is easy and what I call a gourmet dinner. She roasts several pork tenderloins with a tarragon rub, whips up some heavenly mashed potatoes, throws together a salad, and steams some asparagus. I think it is a ton of food, but when Adam, Jack, and Hamilton are done, there isn't a scrap left over. Those guys can pack it in. G.J. felt obligated to throw together a quick apple crumble because they were still hungry. Celia's theory is more like mine; if they want to eat, they need to cook. G.J., however, loves to do it, so she does for her own pleasure. They have quite a little routine down, and the mill of their family life makes me a little homesick.

After dinner, G.J., her two eternal bookends, and I head to her room. "Let me find the book with the ritual I was taking about…"

"Sweet, are there nudy pics?" This from Adam the Perpetual Love Machine.

"Adam, may we never go to a museum together. You'd plain mortify me if I found you fondling some statue's privates," G.J. replies, while she still searches through the tome she is balancing on her lap. The pages look like they will crack on the edges if she turns them too quickly.

"Is that even in English?" I ask.

"It's in Old English and some German, well, Old German, too, I guess. I'm getting better at translating it. Although really, I usually just need the gist. My will normally works just fine," G.J. explains.

"Then why do you need your coven to do whatever it is you need to do?" Hamilton asks.

"Because," G.J. says with an exhaustion born of many attempts to explain anything to Hamilton he doesn't like. "I need the four compass points to be lit at the same time and there are some other ritualistic things."

"We can light candles," Hamilton says.

"Who is we?" I ask. "I'm not ticking off Smokey the Bear, naked with you three.

"Nat, don't kill the dream." Adam holds his hand to his heart, like I've wounded him.

G.J. and I just shake our heads.

Hamilton pushes his point. "Shut up, Adam. I'm being serious. Why can't we be the ones to help G.J.? Then if something goes wrong, we will be there. Look, if it makes you feel better, I will close my eyes."

"I'll only commit to close one." Adam's grin says it all.

Hamilton slants his eyes at his friend in annoyance. "Not helping. We need to keep her safe. Turn it down or better yet, off."

"Why do you have to be naked anyway?" I ask.

"It says here the idea is to have the castors be the embodiment of the whole. Meaning the mind, body, and spirit. We are personifying the unity of the three. Clothes aren't part of that. Men aren't supposed to carry the same power as females according to Gus. I'm not sure if it would work," G.J. says, as if seriously contemplating this.

It is clear to me she is nuts.

"But we will need another person because Nat is going to be in the circle."

"Wait. What?" I am a little stunned. This idea of being the focal point of G.J.'s mojo is a little daunting.

"Well, yeah. You are the focus. We are binding the Triquetra to you, so you need to be inside the circle with it and nothing else."

"Is that your way of telling me I'm going to be nude too?" *She has got to be kidding.*

Tilting her head in confusion as to how I missed that, she says slowly, "Of course, Nat. That is the point."

She is *not* kidding.

"You need to find another ritual," I say.

"We are working with limited time here. Hugo could be back at any time and then what?"

"Fair is fair, Nat. You've seen us naked," Adam adds less than helpfully.

"I did not," I object. "Well, I didn't see you. I saw Hamilton."

"Well I can fix that," Adam says standing and pulling at the bottom of his shirt.

"You what?" G.J.'s eyes become that iridescent gray and her face loses a little bit of its humanity.

Hamilton puts his hand on Adam's arm, preventing him from removing his shirt, but his eyes connect with G.J.'s. "Easy," he draws out the word in a soothing tone. "I had shifted to track Gus. When we found him, I needed to talk. I shifted back to human, but my clothes were back at the car. That was all."

"He's right, G.J., it was for convenience only. I did my best to keep my gaze at eye level." I hope what I am saying helps. I have no interest in playing fifty-two pick up with all of G.J.'s books. Those suckers are heavy.

Hamilton moves close to G.J. and Adam follows his lead. Once again, they make a G.J. sandwich. *Enough with the P.D.A. people.* If they ever start kissing, I'm going to have to draw the line.

Whatever is happening among the three of them finally settles G.J. down. From between the two muscular chests, G.J. whines, "This has to stop. If I can't handle Nat, how in the world am I gonna make it through Sara and her nonstop lust-filled stares. You eat up all her oozings, like it was your favorite syrup at IHOP."

G.J. shoves at Hamilton's chest, bringing her point home by pushing him away. "That isn't going to go over very well. I can see it now, she does her normal 'Oh my! What big muscles you have Hamilton,'" G.J.'s normal twang goes to a ridiculous level, drops back, and finishes, "and I pretend she is a paper airplane and fly her to somewhere around Topeka… Kansas. None of this is fair to you, me, or her. I have to get control over this territorial jealousy. I don't like my instincts ruling my mind."

G.J. scrubs her face with her hands. "Bwhaw, how did this get so messed up? I really appreciate you trying to save me and all, but I don't want to stop you from being with Sara or anybody else you or Adam are in love with. But whatever it is that has a hold on me is in the driver's seat and apparently intends to run you down if you even try being with someone you actually care about."

"I don't care about Sara like that. She had a screwed up Mom and made some bad choices. I can see how things like that would happen so I don't want to be a dick to her. But, G.J., for God's sake, what is your major malfunction?" Here he goes, that smooth talker. "How is it you don't get how I feel about you? I don't know how a two year old could miss it. How the hell you are doesn't make any sense at all. What does it freaking take to get through your thick head?" Hamilton holds G.J. by the upper arms grimaces down at her.

"Ease up, Hamilton," Adam warns.

"I wish you wouldn't do that." G.J.'s eyes won't meet Hamilton's; she fixes on his chin.

"Do what?" Hamilton growls.

"Say God like that," G.J. responds.

"That's all you've got to say?" Hamilton asks dumbfounded.

"What do you want? You think I don't know? You tell me all the time. I'm thick. I jiggle. I'm big. It takes a lot of food to run a body my size. Nobody else can carry me but you, one of the strongest people on Earth. I'm sorry this happened, but I didn't ask to be this big, and I while I appreciate your pack meaning so much to you that you wanted to help me, I didn't ask to be mated to either of you, needless to say both of you." G.J. is rolling now. "I will figure out how to un-mate us and you can go find your petite princess. And the two of you can run off and plan your future of attractive offspring."

Hamilton in return gets quiet. "None of those things I said would be offensive if you saw yourself through my eyes. I think all of those things make you insanely beautiful. Nobody else can carry you because I don't want to let them. You in someone else's arms is my personal nightmare. G.J., you are so freaking smart. Facts are your thing. Where is the empirical evidence that I think you are unattractive? What are you basing your theory of what I find beautiful?"

"Everyone knows what is beautiful and I don't fit that bill. I will never grace the cover of a magazine, and you should have a freaking marble statue created to help America bump up its cultural tourism." G.J. still won't meet his eyes.

Hamilton gently grabs the sides of her face and tilts her chin up, lowering his head to grab her gaze. "I'm not a magazine editor. I don't have to or want to sell your beauty to anyone else. I guarantee you some dude in the fashion industry has no clue as to what I think is hot." He shakes his head and glances at the ceiling before dropping back down to connect with hers. "I am and have been borderline obsessed with you since the first time I saw you when we were eight. Yeah, that was me. Eight. Half of my life. Your eyes, your smile, and then you show back up and instead of a fearless little girl, I get a brilliant, beautiful, yes beautiful, funny, courageous woman. What is it you think is there for me not to find amazing, 'cause honestly I don't see it. And even if you weren't wrapped up in gorgeous, the best parts of you have nothing to do with your looks. You and I are so good together when I am wolf. I want that all the time. I want you to be comfortable with me and talk to me like you do when I am in that form. I want you to laugh and play around. Because that is who *we* are. G.J., why do you think I am around here all the time? Do you really think Jack would make me if I hated you? Do you think Adam is what keeps me by your side? I'm sorry we were mated the *way* we were." An unspoken part of that sentence hangs in the air. Hamilton takes in a deep breath. "G.J., would you like to go to the movies with me."

G.J. doesn't say anything.

"Or dinner?" Hamilton tries.

Her frozen face still doesn't move.

"A walk? Can we try a walk when I am human?" Hamilton's voice gets weaker with each option.

"A walk." G.J. finally gives a response.

"Yeah? Really? Okay. A walk it is." Under the caution in Hamilton's reply is the tenuous hope, like he might have just won tickets to Disney.

G.J.'s phone rings and she fumbles to get it; she seems relieved by the distraction. "Hey Drake," she answers, after glancing at the display.

All of my senses fire at once. My face grows warm and my ears do their best to compete with a sub's sonar equipment to hear Drake's half of the conversation.

"Ummmm." G.J.'s eyes land on me, then pop over to Hamilton who has started growling. "Just a sec," she says into the phone, and she hustles out of the room holding her hand up so no one follows her.

I pop in Hamilton's head.

"She will not meet him for dinner. I just got her to go out with me. Drake will not date her."

Hamilton follows G.J. into the hall, and my heart shatters all over again at the same time. My eyes fall on the only other person left in the room. Adam has the same look of lost hurt I am feeling.

"So that didn't take long. What twenty four hours and Drake is onto the next girl? Why are you glum? Were you hoping he'd call you?" I try really hard to mask the way my insides feel. God, he called G.J. for a date. My best friend, not even a day after whatever the hell happened between us. Is this a joke? Why did he even ask me out? I am such an idiot. I knew I hated that boy. Why did I let myself give a crap?

Adam manages a sad smile. "I know how Hamilton feels about G.J., but *she* never knew before. It was bound to happen eventually. He was going to stop being such a jackass and figure out how to form a non-offensive statement. But it's tough... he's my best friend. I want the best for the guy." Adam rubs the top of his head mussing his sandy-blonde hair.

"But the best is G.J.," I help. with a sour jealous tone I can almost taste.

"Yep, the best thing to him is the best thing I have ever seen too." Adam voice is tired.

"Seems to be the best for everyone. Well you are all still mated so you should ask her out too. With how these instincts seem to go, I don't see how you couldn't. In fact, it looks like it is hard for anyone not to ask her out. Take a number." Wow, bitter much. Jesus, I wish I would stop it, but I am so pissed I can't help myself.

"It isn't all the mating thing."

"What do you mean?" Is he about to tell me G.J. is irresistible to all men? I bet he is. I bet he is about to sing the praises of her. I have to get out of here. No way can I handle one more G.J. is wonderful sonata when she is going out on a date with Drake.

"I'm just as crazy about her as Hamilton. I might not have seen her when she was eight but, man, she has me by something right around here. He rubs at his chest. But I don't think she feels the same way. I thought she might, but the mate bond has proven she doesn't."

"What?" My brain makes one of those record scratch-ing stops. I feel my eyebrow raise in that way that lets him know I think he is nuts. I sigh and shut down my internal pity party for a minute. Adam hasn't done anything wrong. Drake is who deserves my fury. Taking a second to calm down, I pull my mouth to the side, twisting my lips, when it relaxes back, I say, "You need to understand G.J.'s head isn't in girly flirty mode at all. Sure, she isn't blind, but G.J. is really sort of oblivious when it comes to men of any kind. From what she's told me, she really has almost zero experience with boys with the exception of one back in Louisiana. And from the sound of it, that guy had as much luck with her, getting he liked her as you two do."

"No. I know. It isn't that she prefers either one of us. I mean she is comfortable with me, but she doesn't flip out over me. Just him."

"How's that?"

"Watch her. A girl gets near him and she turns Sci-Fi fantasy chick. I flirt with you or Megan, and she doesn't bat an eye. I don't think she means to do it. I seriously don't think she can even admit how she really feels about Hamilton to herself. But it's pretty clear to me." Adam lowers his head. "It might just be her emerging wolf. Everyone assumes Hamilton is the more dominate of the two of us, just because I joke around. Strong wolves are drawn to strength in others. If I prove to her and everyone I'm more Alpha than he is, maybe this will change." Adam takes a little mental trip to map out a plan.

"How will you do that when she won't let you two fight each other? Isn't that how you guys prove dominance?"

"I don't know but I'm not giving up. She is worth fighting for." Adam gives a small snort. "Literally."

"That's great but what about Drake. You gonna take him on too?" And… bitter slides back in my tone. I quickly add, "And if Hamilton thinks he is obsessed, he's got nothing on Gus," to disguise it.

"Gus will need to worry about the whole pack. Even if Hamilton and I are out of the picture, there is not a wolf that has met G.J. that will let a vein chugger have her. As for Drake? Nat, I don't know what the whole dinner thing is about, but that guy only has eyes for you. He doesn't scare me." Wolves have good ears and I guess he's heard her conversation too. "The question is do you think *he* is worth fighting for?"

"I'm not fighting G.J. for dominance."

Adam laughs. "Yeah, I wouldn't if I were you. But I don't think it will be an issue. I mean are you just going to give up? Roll over and play dead? If you like Drake, then you need to work at it. If you don't think he is worth even trying, then it's probably best you just let him go."

Damn it Adam. You aren't supposed to be the contemplative one.

Chapter Twenty-Seven

The inevitable happens and Monday rears its ugly head. Oh the joys of high school. G.J. spends the bus ride trying to convince me she is only going out with Drake to figure out what is happening. This might be her motives, but I don't think they are Drake's.

Ms. Stontz proves narrators matter by having some poor boy, with zero confidence and remedial reading abilities, muddle through the profound words of Emerson. "Is it so… bad then… to be… misunderstood? Pie…Pyth…" The butchering is so bad I have to tune out. G.J.'s mouth silently shapes the words for the kid in an attempt to coach him along. She has a day off from her experiment with Megan and is always mentally involved in class time. Me, not so much, I spend my time drawing the cutest doodle dog with huge sad eyes.

"Hey, I'll see you at lunch," G.J. says, as the bell rings to release the masses into the cattle shoot of the hallway.

"Yeah, I'll catch you later," I agree, as we move out into to hallway.

G.J.'s face registers awkward with a false smile and widening eyes, her gaze sliding from me to someone behind me. I dart away without looking back. I just can't face Drake. As

I move away, a sea of letter jackets swarm in the direction of G.J.. The pack is in protection mode. What surprises me is now two of the boys break off and follow me to my next class. How sweet. Overbearing but sweet.

My day moseys toward lunch. Our little midday meal group has grown exponentially since last year. Now most of the pack crowds our table. To be fair, it only takes a few of those guy's shoulders to make a person feel cramped. Green and white letter jackets mark every potential entrance and exit. It amazes me how the rest of the pimpled population of this school is so self-involved they miss the fact that the majority of the jocks have begun acting like the secret service. Boys known for rough housing and raucous laughter now scrutinize the turtle kids—you know the kids hunched forward, trying to balance the weight of every book they may or may not need crammed in their backpack in an attempt to not have to use their lockers. But the wolf pack on high alert seems a bit overkill. I can't see anyone getting to G.J. in school, but what do I know.

"Hey." I drop my lunch back on the table next to G.J. and glare at Adam trying to get him to move over. I can't tell if staring down a wolf is a lost cause or if Adam is just obtuse.

G.J. shoves his shoulder to give me room to sit. "Adam, honey, you wouldn't last two seconds in the south. It is only polite to offer your seat to a lady. Go on and scoot down."

"I have to count Nat as a lady? What kind of standards are those?" Smirking, he slides over, giving me room.

Dismissing Adam's comment, G.J. flips topic channels, "Have you seen Gus today?"

Speaking over the low rumble that sounds from virile igloo that surrounds us, I shake my head and say, "Not a glimpse. Pretty sure he isn't interested in trying to chat with me anyway. You are his prime objective."

Waving her hand in dismissal, G.J. finishes the bite before responding, leaving time for Hamilton to chime in, "Gus is toast if he shows his face."

G.J. whips her head to face Hamilton on her other side. After her swallow, she sucks in a deep breath. "I need to talk to him, you dolt. I need to understand who is here and why. We all need to stop the attacks that have been happening. Our little group has already been among the top ten list of suspects. If this continues, it will draw scrutiny to this area I am fairly certain none of us need or want. If there are others like Gus in the area, he can be an ally in finding and stopping them. People are dying. We need to prevent more deaths. If you can't muster up compassion for the people who are dying and their loved ones, how about the warnings Hugo gave Nat being your motivation?"

"You almost died two days ago, remember? How about you leave dealing with anything that can do that to you again to people who are more equipped to handle it?" Hamilton holds her eye contact and doesn't bat an eye at her indignant huff, which is the prelude to her next rant.

Mind reading has nothing to do with knowing if you tell G.J. she isn't prepared for something, she is going to blow a gasket.

"*Nat,*" Hugo appears just behind Hamilton, "*I need you to come with me now.*"

"Now?" I grab G.J.'s arm.

"May I join you?" Drake's familiar voice asks from behind me.

Before I can tell G.J. what is happening, Hugo rushes forward and I flash away from the cafeteria and into the Shadow World.

"Hugo, I need to get my body to a safe place before you waltz my being away from it. What are school officials going to think if my body is left slumped in the cafeteria? You are setting me up for an unneeded MRI." Indignant that I have been swiped from my world much less my sandwich. By the time, I get back Adam will definitely have scarfed it down.

"There are more coming than even before. You need to see them."

"What?" My focus is only half on him trying to adjust to the swift change in environment.

"There are so many more coming. You have to see them. They are … You must see."

"Is this gonna be gross." Maybe I'm better off I didn't get to my sandwich.

We dart swiftly through the mist. The blurring of our speed gives an impression traveling through cotton candy, just less sticky.

When we stop, the thinner mist encircles a group of shadows the same consistency or denser than Hugo. The group's furtive glances give the shades the impression of cornered animals. Thin shades circle the group of what I suspect are the newbie dead. It kind of looks like a tornado but of ghosts. When I finally look, I mean really look at the shades captivated in the vortex of the departed, I realize they are all female. They are all girls about my age. They are all tall. They all have short bobbed hair. They are all rough copies of my bestie. I gasp. "Oh my God! Someone is killing G.J. lookalikes."

"I thought you would want to know. All of these girls have been sent here this weekend. So far there are nine of them. When the last one arrived, I decided I needed to come get you. They were all attacked, like I was. Nat, we are trying to contain them, but we really have no control over them. Anytime, they can move through the shades trying to contain them. It is a visual boundary only. It has to stop."

"Ya think?" I am dumbfounded he thinks I need that to be explained for so many reasons. "Get me back to my body right now!" urgent demand evident in the last two words.

Hugo's concerned expression turns slightly annoyed. Without another word, he moves us through the mists. Abruptly, he stops. Looking down at me, there seems to be a personal debate moment happening. I would normally pop in his head and watch what was happening, like I had front row seats at the US Open, but after my last attempt at perusing his thoughts, I think better of it. Besides, at this point I am in a bit of a rush.

When he reaches some kind of resolution, he leans forward and plants one right on my kisser. Really? He shows me a strong indication pictures of my BFF are most likely the wall-paper collage of a serial killer and then thinks I want to smooch. The sensation is not unlike wearing peppermint Chapstick. His lips really apply no pressure, and create a cool, tingling sensation. Since he's not stopping, I decide to kiss back, just to see what happens and how it feels. Closing my eyes, I pucker to press my lips against his chilly touch.

"Nat? Are you back? Why are you puckered up like Kissing Gouramis?" G.J.'s voice makes my eyes pop open, almost as fast as I can feel blood rush into my cheeks.

"Hugo was kissin… Ummm, nevermind. What in the hell is a Gouramis?" Anytime G.J. talks, she'll usually refer to something that will help you change topics.

"A kissing fish found in Thailand. We are putting a Post–it–Note on what you started to say. So glad you are back. No more putting it off, we are doing that ritual pronto."

"How long was I out?" I sit up, trying to get my bearings. If the infirmary bed and low lighting are any indication, it looks like I am in the school nurse's domain. Three people hover near the doorway. Adam, Hamilton, and Drake all stand there watching the interaction between G.J. and me. And while three of them might be there, my eyes connect with Drake's and everything else recedes.

After a moment or a millennium, Drake inhales deeply and looks away mumbling, "I'll catch you guys later."

Then he's gone. Did he know I was going to kiss Hugo? My emotions need some Xanax. My heart flutters, like I am having a panic attack. My chest seems to collapse under the weight of that betrayal, and, in the same instance, I am gleeful after what he made me feel. What the hell is wrong me? G.J. touches my arm and other sights and sounds return.

G.J. pulls up one eyebrow and half her lip. "That was less than awesome."

"Why was he even here?" I swing my legs over the side of the bed.

"Because he brought you here." G.J. squints, as if she can't believe I would ask such a stupid question.

"Why would he do that? Now we have to explain things to the nurse."

"Oh right, leaving you on the cafeteria floor was a much better option. Then we would only have to explain to the custodian why you were stuck in the nubs of their oversized dry mop." G.J. tilts her head glaring at me.

"That's not what I meant," I grumble.

"Look, Nat," Adam explains." I would have brought you, but the guy wouldn't have it. The only reason why he was that far away from you was because G.J. was going to try to see if she could bring you back and we weren't sure what would happen,"

"How were you going to bring me back?" My forehead wrinkles in skepticism.

"Well… I wasn't right sure how, but the nurse was acting like you were in a coma and went to track down your parents, so we thought if we were going to do something, now was the time."

"Crap. She is calling my parents?"

"Honey, did you miss the part where you passed out on school property? What do you think emergency medical forms are for? To weed out the kids whose parents don't give a damn so teachers know who will be at the lower end of the grading curve without a fuss? An unconscious student is a hot potato in the eyes of any academic institution. Settle down, I tried a little mind control and I called Aunt Celia. She said she would handle the fact that your parents are M.I.A. I am new to the Jedi mind tricks so I could only stop her from calling an ambulance."

Hamilton gave a cough letting us know our conversation was about to be interrupted. *What a good little watch dog.*

"Oh good, you are awake. You three, I know you are concerned for Nat, but I need to speak to her alone for a few moments. Please return to your classes. If you need a note, get one from the front office." Shooing G.J. out to join the boys, Mrs. Pitner, the school nurse, turns to me with a serious expression. "You gave us quite a scare young lady. Have you had any episodes like that before?"

"Like what?" I play dumb and don't answer.

"Where you have lost consciousness?"

I examine how my fingers twine together. Mrs. Pitner believes if she doesn't say anything, eventually I will. If I were G.J., she would be right, but silence isn't a prompt for me. We sit quietly for a long time. Finally, Mrs. Pitner turns her chair, opens her desk drawer, and riffles through it slapping small pamphlets on her desk top creating a little angry stack. Spinning back to face me as fast as her well-oiled 1950's office chair will allow, she hands me the first in her series of trifold reading materials, this gem titled, "No is your friend."

"I'm not on drugs," I say in the voice I attribute to the Angry Cat when reading its posts.

"Admitting you have a problem is difficult, but it is the first step to a brighter future."

"Oh, I have lots of problems. But drugs aren't one of them."

"I know it can seem like they make life better for the short time you are high, but they are a problem for you."

"Still not on drugs. So…"

"I know there is a good bit of controversy over pot these days. Some places saying it's okay, some saying it isn't. And most of us have tried… well never mind that…. But to take any substance to the point where you lose consciousness is when you are talking about addiction. It is important that you admit your usage or I will have to call in the authorities."

"But I am not using. Why do you just suppose I am? What if this was an undiagnosed blood sugar issue. Or some other medical problem. Why suspect cartel connections right off the bat?"

"Nat, really, you have always been a bit of a loner until recently and look at how you dress."

I glance down at my outfit and slowly raise my eyes to her. "So, you assume I am a drug addict because of a fashion profile?"

Before she can make her many jaw movements form an actual pronounceable word there comes a quick, sharp knock and the door pops open. Principal Decker's eyes roll wildly behind him in a warning to Nurse Pitner that he is not coming in alone. Celia comes in the room, like a force of nature. Mr. Decker narrowly misses being shoved out of the way for her to get to me.

"Nat, honey, are you okay?" Even if Celia knows why I took a trip to the land of unconsciousness, her concern is real.

"I'm fine."

Celia runs her hand gently over my head. Mrs. Pitner makes a phlegmy low hum interrupting Celia's caring ministrations. "I know you aren't Nat's legal guardian, but I must address her substance abuse concerns prior to releasing her to anyone."

Principal Decker's pasty complexion transforms to a whole other level of gaunt. Celia slowly faces Mrs. Pitner, whose expression melts from determined to uh-oh as she takes in the visage of Celia's fury.

"For what reason do you presume Nat has a substance abuse problem?" Celia's voice is as sharp as a razor blade.

"I… Well… People don't normally pass out without reason," Mrs. Pitner defends.

"No, that is true. But Nat has an undiagnosed, as of yet, condition. A doctor saw her yesterday at our home. It is unclear what's causing her to blackout, but it has happened four times, that I know of, in just the last few days. Since her parents are on sabbatical and unreachable, we are having some trouble dealing with the situation, but drugs have nothing to do with it. I was personally there when one episode occurred. And I can assure you no illegal substances were in use. I suggest we all take a step back and address this situation with the new information provided. We should have sent in a note to bring you up to speed, and for that, I personally apologize. However, I hope going forward your first assumption when dealing with any child is not the worst case scenario." Man, Celia does adult really well.

Mr. Decker steps forward. "Thank you, Mrs. Wyfle, for updating us on what is happening with Nat. Is Nat staying with you at this point?"

"Yes, and for the foreseeable future. I should be listed on her emergency card. If anything else concerning Nat occurs, please contact Jack or me."

Nurse Pitner sits quietly watching the interaction.

"Why don't you grab your stuff and I will go ahead and take you home?" Celia directs me.

I leave the three of them and head to my locker, sorting out what I need. Slamming the door, I find Gus leaning on the wall beside me. After my startled hop, I ask, "Come to hold me hostage again?"

"I see G.J. is up and around. How did that happen? I thought she wasn't healing." Gus is rubbing his arms, like an addict in a bad movie.

His junkie appearance unsettles me. Nobody wants to be near a strung out vampire. Glowing unnaturally, his angry eyes have a lost sense of focus.

He glances at me, but his gaze slowly wanders into the distance until he sweeps it back to my face. "What did they do?"

"What did who do?" Taken off guard, I pull my chin back and shake my head trying to follow while my mind flashes to all the G.J. clones with their necks ripped apart.

"The pack, Nat, what did they do to heal her?"

"Adam and Hamilton took care of it."

"What?" He moved his livid face maybe an inch away from mine. Very quietly, he asks, "How? You told them."

"Not exactly. They overheard me tell Jack how they could fix it, then took it upon themselves."

Gus paces away but spins back. "You have to help me get her alone."

As alarmed as I am by Gus at this moment, my facial muscles reflexively move to my are-you-nuts expression. "Uhhh, why would I do that?"

"I can still stop the mating if I bite her again."

I roll my eyes sideways, seeing if there is anyone else hearing this or possibly a hidden camera. Inadvertently, my head gives a little shake.

Gus grabs my shoulders. "She will not be theirs." He shakes me. "It will not happen."

"Gus. Stop it, you are hurting me."

Gus drops his hands quickly. I pop in his head to see his plans.

"G.J. cannot be mated. She is too precious. Must get to her."
Images of G.J. and of biting G.J. fill my mind. Coveting and lust are so powerful. His mind moves, and I see one after the other of the G.J. doppelgängers lying dead.

"Oh God, Gus!" I cover my mouth with my hand in horror.

Shaken, Gus reaches out to grab me, but I pull back.

"Nat, no I…" Whatever he is about to say is cut off by the bell ringing. The hallway fills with the oblivious masses. I duck into the crowd and hustle to the office as fast as my terrified legs will carry me.

Chapter Twenty-Eight

Celia has already handled the office side of my dismissal and waits for me in the school entrance. Mr. Decker and Mrs. Pitner are not so discretely watching us go and murmuring to each other. It isn't hard to see why misunderstood is the most common portrayal of teens. I have three more years at this school and the staff now thinks I'm a druggie. Nice.

Buckling up, Celia says, "Don't worry about them. If you are confronted fairly often with disappointments by other people, you can become jaded. I am sure Mrs. Pitner has just been told one too many lies not to suspect everyone. Just be yourself and they will come around. Or better yet, stay out of the nurse's office."

"I'll do my best."

"You okay, really?" Celia is back to her concerned voice and makes it hard for me to swallow past the squeezing in my throat.

"Celia, there are so many not okay things happening right now I don't know where to start." I stare out the front windshield at the familiar scenery.

"You're right, Nat. There is a whole lot of unbelievable happening to you... well, to all of us right now. Take a deep breath and we will try to tackle one thing at a time. But

I meant we when I said we, Nat. You are not alone, even though it may feel that way. I am not particularly fond of your parent's choices. But just because they aren't here doesn't mean you don't have support. Jack, G.J., Adam, and I are ready, willing, and able to help you work through whatever you face. Sometimes the strongest bonds are family by choice. We choose you, Nat. You are one of our own now. Remember that when you get overwhelmed. But the rest of us aren't mind readers, so you will have to tell us what is going on with you. Got it?"

The juggernaut in my throat tightens, and it's as if the additional pressure pushes water out my tear ducts. Somehow, I gulp easing the strain and blow out a breath, trying desperately not to let the water gathering in my eyes spill down my cheeks. I nod, turning to the passenger window. "Is Jack at the house?" I ask, my voice not as controlled, as I like.

"He was in a meeting downtown today. He should be back around five-thirty. Something up he needs to know about?"

"Yeah, definitely."

Celia pushes a button on her steering wheel and over articulates, "Call Jack." The sound of a phone ringing fills the car.

Jack's voice follows. "Ceily? You left the house without Stanzi."

"I have Nat with me. Her ghost took her out while she was at school."

"Is she okay?"

Wow. He really cares. And now I am fighting tears again. Super.

"She seems fine, but she wanted to talk to you. Go ahead, Nat, but speak up a little the phone mic is one my side of the car."

"So Hugo took me to see the nine G.J. lookalikes that were killed over the weekend in this area. And then, I ran into Gus. He wants to bite G.J. and I saw the dead girls in his head too."

"Oh my God." Celia looks ill.

"I'll be home in a half hour. Celia where are you now?" Even not in the car with us, Jack is commanding.

"I'm almost to the house. I'll go back and grab G.J."

"The boys are with her. It is almost time for school to get out. I'll text the kids they are to skip anything after school today and come straight home. Nat, take care, kiddo. Be careful, Ceily, I love you."

"You too. Love you." Celia's thumb hits a button, and the disconnect tones beep through the speakers.

We pull up to the gates swinging wide to let us in. Stanzi opens the front door of the house as we pull in. He comes down to the car and gets the door for Celia.

"Sorry I ran out on you. I got the call about Nat and just left. I forget I have a babysitter."

Stanzi moves his massive shoulders in an attempt at a nonchalant shrug, but his heart isn't really in it by his agitation. "I should have been ready to go when you said you were leaving. I will be next time."

As he ushers us into the house, Celia pats his arm. Once inside, Stanzi locks up the front door behind us. I head up to my temporary room.

"I need to wrap up a few things I left hanging when I ran to get you. But if you need anything, let me know. I meant what I said, Nat."

I nod, not looking back down at her.

****

Jack, as promised, is home a half an hour later beating G.J. and her wingmen by maybe twenty minutes. When the others arrive home, he calls me down. Time for the pow-wow. Reluctantly, I trudge down the steps.

G.J. has her worried face in full concerned mode. "You okay?"

"Sure, I got out of school early. That always makes for a good day. Even if the faculty apparently has me on the she-who-should-pee-in-a-cup-list."

"Ew. You know I love science and all, but people peeing in cups always has me concerned somebody is gonna think it's just warm apple juice and take a regrettable swig." G.J.'s eyebrow scrunches and her lip does an Elvis curl in her disgust. "In other news, I talked with Ms. Stontz, she came up with another option for the ritual where we don't have to be naked. I figured that would make you a touch less squeamish. But I am gonna have to teach you what to do. If we go that route, I won't be the one in control of the power. It will be all up to you. I can give direction and feed power to you, but you have to handle the ritual in its entirety alone. Are you up for that?"

"Do I get to keep my clothes on?"

G.J. nods.

"Option B it is then."

"Dream killer," Adam grumbles.

Rolling my eyes in dismissal, I add, "Hugo says I can get back all by myself, though."

"Good, but you may not be aware you need to head back. The binding to the object will alert you to the fact that something is happening to your physical form. You had no clue what was happening today to your body while you were off smooching your shadow man." G.J. smirks.

"Nice, BFF. Way to have a friend's back there." My tone drips my annoyance.

"I told you we were getting back to that. Did you think I would forget?" she asks.

"I thought you would be a little more discrete."

"Discrete? This is G.J.," Adam says, throwing his arm around her shoulders. "She has trouble with discrete."

"Let's head to the living room," Jack beckons from that direction, saving me from embarrassing moment number 10,236.

We all settle on the oversized furniture in the living room. While the men look like it was made for them, I feel like a doll propped against the cushions. My legs stretch out; the edge of the sofa hits my calf more than halfway to my ankle. Celia is the only person here even close to my height, and she has me by a couple inches. I forget how big these people are until confronted with the everyday minutia of having to climb to sit on furniture they just plop on.

"Nat, why don't you tell everyone what you saw today with Hugo," Jack prompts.

I run through the disturbing news of the nine new victims. Then add, "I ran into Gus. He wants to get G.J. alone. He says he can un-mate her from you guys. Then, I went in his head and I saw the nine dead girls. Or their bodies because they were not alive in his head."

"He can un-mate us? Thank heavens!" G.J. says.

"Nine… Dead… Girls," I repeat.

"We aren't getting unmated," Hamilton rumbles, his eyes glowing.

I look to Adam and he is shaking his head. His eyes are lighting up too.

"Settle," Jack commands. "How can Gus reverse a mating?"

"By biting her. But I think he has to do it quick."

"Oh, phooey. I really didn't like the first bite. But if that's what it takes, I guess I can suck it up." G.J. waits a beat. "Or … umm… I didn't mean to say suck…"

"Nine Dead girls, G.J.. Nine. They all look like you, and Gus had the image of their corpses in his head. He isn't right,

G.J.. I mean the guy looks like an emaciated Keith Richards wannabe. Strung out might be the kindest way to describe him. And I cannot stress enough, he is colossally fixated on having you in every sense of the word."

The chorus of growls that comment makes the whole room shake.

"Boys, calm down." Celia tries to no avail.

"Did you see Gus harm those girls?" G.J. asks.

"What?"

"In his head. Did you see him attacking those girls or did you just see them after it had happened?" G.J. asks.

"They were dead. All of them." Man, what is it going to take for her to understand?

"If Gus… wants me." G.J. flips her hand in a circle almost generating the words. "Then he won't hurt me. And he could have just happened upon all those girls, like he did when I was attacked. You said he was tracking this killer. So maybe he has seen all of these girls, but he didn't kill them. I can't be mated to two people. I'm losing my mind. If Gus can stop it, I need him to do it."

"Gus could kill you. And even if he doesn't, we have no idea what his bite will do to you. G.J., is it worth dying to break the mate bond." Hamilton's voice is quiet and wounded.

"Hamilton, I am not sure what you are feeling on your end, but I can skip the X-rated dreams and the inability to be away from you two for any amount of time. I like being able to use my brain for other things than wondering what it would feel like to … Well…" Her cheeks flush, and she closes her eyes and shakes off her mental image. "Never mind, and then last night. Bwah! I can't keep this up."

"What happened last night?" Jack asks, his gaze flipping between Adam and Hamilton.

Both boys shoot their attention to the floor.

Jack turns back to G.J.. "What happened last night?"

Poor G.J., her mortification is painful to watch. "I attacked them." She puts her face in her hands.

"You what?" everyone including Adam and Hamilton chime in surprise.

Celia moves over to sit next to G.J. gently rubbing her back. Jack turns furious eyes on the two stunned boys.

"Dad, nothing happened. Seriously, it was no big deal."

G.J.'s head shoots up. "No big deal?" Her eyes wide in disbelief.

"Well, I didn't mean…" Adam can't find his next word.

"We handled it," is Hamilton's fabulous input.

"What did you handle?" Jack's voice lowers by the second.

"G.J. got a little, ummm, aroused?" Adam shrugs his shoulders and winces not happy with his word choice but guessing it's the best he's got.

"I was a maniac. If the two of them hadn't worked together to stop me, I could have ended up a cautionary tale at sex addict retreats." G.J. puts her face back in her hands. "That was night one. I can't go through that every night. At least I know now seduction is not in my skill sets. But the embarrassment might kill me, even if the rejection doesn't."

"Rejection!" Hamilton and Adam's faces are now horrified, sounding synchronized.

"You think we rejected you? You are unbelievable. It was all I could do not to respond last night. But Jack said it would be better for you if we didn't, so we didn't. Jesus, G.J., we stopped you from doing something you would regret. We didn't reject you for Christ's sake." Hamilton is beside himself.

"Stop cursing!" G.J. yells. "Color it any way you want, but I served myself up to you. Heaven help me, both of you, and neither of you took me up on it. Why am I the only one who is having trouble keeping my hands to myself?"

"We have been wolves our whole lives. We have battled our instincts since birth. It is something we have struggled with and know how to cope with. You calmed down after a while. It will get easier with time," Adam says hopefully.

G.J. rubs her face. "The point is I don't want get used to this. I want this to stop. Gus can stop it. I need him to try."

"All right," Jack calls focus back to him. "Nat, can you get a hold of Gus?"

"What?" Hamilton and Adam seem to be forming a boy band with all their harmonizing reactions today.

"You would separate mates?" Hamilton's disbelief is palpable.

"That is against pack law, Dad," Adam chimes in.

"This situation is untenable. This falls outside pack law. You can't mate three people together. It won't work," Jack explains.

"What about Gus? I told you he is nuts. He possibly killed those other girls. You can't count on him in this scenario not to hurt you. His emotions are out of control. Please, listen to me when I say his obsession is psychotic. And even in his own mind, he isn't sure he can stop once he actually bites you." I push my genuine worry through my eyes so G.J. gets how serious I am.

"Nat, I have to try. I can't feel like this all the time. It has been two days and I can't handle it. This will break me. I can't stand not being near those two. Right now, I want to curl up between them. Nat, I am hurting them too. They say they are okay with it being the three of us, but have you seen how they treat each other right now? They barely speak. They are best friends and I am destroying that bond. It is breaking my heart that I am hurting them. I can't do it. Jack is right, this is untenable. If Gus can make it stop, we have to let him try." G.J. is trying to get me to understand. "Look in my head."

I take her up on the offer. Along with her shame of her poorly attempted seduction, her real pain is tearing apart the friendship between Hamilton and Adam. It physically hurts her heart to do this to them. I see her confusion and stress over the whole ordeal. She is on the verge of tears constantly and wants to lash out. I see the amazing amount of will power she is exerting not to wreak havoc.

I pull out and move my gaze to Jack. "You have to protect her. Gus can't be alone with her."

"Nat, what the hell? You are supposed to be on our side." Hamilton's knuckles are white with the intense balling of his fists. His glowing eyes relaying his fury.

"Hamilton, if you realized what she is going through right now, you would be the first to go get Gus. This is killing her. And if it doesn't stop soon, she could blow like an oil rig," I shoot back.

Hamilton throws his hands up, seething.

Adam moves toward G.J. and kneels in front of her. "If this is what you need, I'll go get him."

G.J. puts her hand on his cheek. "I can't do this. I care about you too much for it to be like this." Her eyes are wretched and her voice shakes with emotion.

"All right," Adam swivels to face his father, "How do you want to handle this?"

"Go get Gus and bring him here. I will talk to him. Nat, if we can borrow your skills, you can help us understand the ramifications of what might happen to G.J. if he is allowed to bite her. As long as there are no other side effects that we can't live with, we will undo this mating and move on." Jack focuses his attention back to G.J.. "However, if there is anything that puts you into further danger, we will look for another option. I need your agreement here, G.J."

"Gus won't hurt me." G.J. is emphatic.

Jack, alpha stares her down.

"What if there are no other options?" G.J. challenges his glare.

"What if this option makes you like him?" Hamilton quietly slips in the horrific thought.

G.J. looks at him thoughtfully. "Then, all my options suck."

Chapter Twenty-Nine

Adam leaves to find Gus, and G.J. begins to walk me through the binding ritual. As much as I appreciate her efforts, I can't seem to care enough about this to pay attention. The guilt about the whole Drake and Hugo mess is eating me up inside. Up in her room, she draws a diagram of what will happen. There will be a circle with four elemental points equidistance apart on the circle. I am to concentrate on the triquetra and send my energy into it while repeating, "My spirit be bound, my soul be tied, should my body require, return swift spirit and mind. This symbol protect, this knot stay sure, keep tied, mind, body and spirit secure." I will stand inside the circle and say this toward each point on the circle. G.J. says she will stand nearby and see if she feels any power movement. That way she will know if it works. Yeah, corny and totally not in my realm of giving a crap.

"This sounds absurd you know," I grumble.

"Really, you kiss dead people and you think this is bizzare?" G.J. shoots back.

"You make it sound like I'm a necrophiliac."

"No, you weren't making out with his corpse. But the guy is dead. Do you see a long-term relationship happening? I thought you liked Drake. You have been giving your smoocher a workout over the last few days."

"Drake seems to have moved on to you. Or have you forgotten about your date." Green claws of jealousy rake me inside. I examine her extensive book collection in order to avert my gaze.

"Nat, it is not a date." G.J. shoves my shoulder in order to get my attention, to give me a dirty look. "I wanted to find out what was up *for* you. The boy is cute, don't get me wrong, but I would never date somebody you were interested in. There are lines you just don't cross. Shoot, if I can't mac on two perfectly good boys who were asleep in my bedroom, why on earth would you think I would want to branch out. Back to your spiritual Romeo. What was that all about?"

"It wasn't like that. He is…" I try to find the right way to describe it. While I feel guilty for some bizarre reason about Drake, I don't feel guilt about kissing Hugo. My head is a wonderland of contradictions. "He just kissed me and since it was happening, I kissed him back. I don't know why he did it. There was no discussion. I think he liked me when he was alive. He kind of said so. The guy will never be able to go out with anyone. I don't know. It makes me sad that he never had a chance to ask me out. You know. I mean, let's be honest, if he had, I probably would have read his mind, found a flaw, and abruptly rejected him. Or maybe I would've ended up dating him and missed the Drake fiasco. But we will never know. So I kissed him. There is no future in it. He is already fading. He is mistier than when he first started coming around. I think it takes a lot out of him to come get me like he does. He is a good guy, G.J.. It is sickening that this happened to him."

"It is sickening that it happened to any of them. Hopefully, Gus will have even more answers than just the un-mating one."

"How do you feel about that? I mean are you scared about the bite. It didn't seem like something you would want to repeat." I find it easier to move the topic away from my confused emotions.

"No, not particularly, but what I really don't want to repeat is the humiliation of last night. If I ever have to admit I writhed again in my lifetime, I will simply expire of mortification. You know how boys are just supposed to fall at the feet of a willing woman? Not so much. It seems if the girl in question is so utterly bad at it, she causes laughter to burst forth, they *can* find the ability to restrain themselves."

"They laughed?" My jaw muscle control flies out the window and it hangs in shock. I know how much each one of those guys wants her. Never in a million years would I have thought laughter could have happened if they were given the opportunity to sample the merchandise.

G.J.'s cheeks turn pink, and when she confesses, her face screws up, "I may have used the term, 'Come here, you little love puppies,' while squirming around on my bed like an idiot."

I cover my mouth holding back the burble of my first giggle, but when the tide is unstoppable, I hold my sides and bend over laughing. G.J. covers her face with her hands.

Wiping tears from my eyes, I calm down. "Let me get this straight. You have probably memorized the poetry of the masters of romance and, you, the girl who uses more words than humanly necessary on a regular basis come up with love puppies." I erupt with more laughter.

She half-heartedly whacks me with her hand. "You could be a little more understanding. I mean I went from primal need to primary school verbiage. I could have done a monumental deed, but instead, I made a giant idiot out of myself. It is all I can do not to crawl under something and die today."

"Isn't it better if nothing happened? You didn't want to have a different story today, do you?" I remind her see the bright side.

"Oh, sure, today I'm glad they lost their senses to laughter so much so I got mad. But if we are talking wants, last night *want* was redefied for me. I can't feel like that all the time. All day long I have had to hold myself back from rubbing up against them, like a bear with an itchy back does up against a tree. I need my self-control back."

"Adam laughed first." Hamilton makes us both jump with his appearance at the doorway.

G.J. closes her eyes and shakes her head. "It is official, it cannot be possible to die of embarrassment. If it were, I would be a goner for sure."

"Dude, you really shouldn't have listened in," I admonish Hamilton.

"It isn't as big of deal as she is making it out to be. It was just..." Hamilton stops really trying to find the words. "I mean... Come on, G.J., love puppies? In all my wildest dreams, and trust me there have been many and varied versions of them, Adam nor love puppies were with us in the scene. Both of them... made it so laughter was the only option."

"Is there something you wanted, I mean besides trying to make me even more humiliated?" G.J. asks not looking at him.

"Jack wants Nat out of sight. He thinks if Gus knows she is there, he will clam up. So he wants to put her out of sight in his office. Adam is on his way back with Gus now," Hamilton explains.

G.J. blows out a breath. "I know I want this to happen, but I am a bit scared."

Hamilton crosses over to her chair and squats in front of her. "You don't have to do this. We can find another solution." He cups her cheek.

She meets his touch and draws her jaw across his palm. When her lips find its center, she closes her eyes and kisses it. I don't know what she was doing wrong last night, but it looks to me, from this little display, her seduction skills are just dandy. She catches herself, squawks and flaps her way out of the chair and across the room away from Hamilton.

"See! This has to stop. It has to stop right now." G.J. flies out of the room.

Hamilton who had been knocked back onto his butt, with G.J.'s lunatic departure, slowly finds his feet.

I slap him of the back with two swift pats. "Breathe deep, big guy. You will be on a better track when there aren't three of you." I wish someone felt about me the way any of these guys feel about G.J..

"She is my mate, Nat, I don't think you get what losing her is going to do to me. I don't think she knows what she will go through by losing us." Hamilton's tone sounds defeated.

"Won't it be better? If there aren't three of you involved."

"Have you ever seen a wolf lose his mate? It tears them apart. I don't want her to go through that. I definitely don't want to lose her."

"Just because you un-mate now doesn't mean you can't re-mate in the future. Let her undo this now and then go on that walk with her. You can't go from the first step to the last in one big leap. Go back to the beginning. Try dating and move on from there. Slow and steady…" I don't finish the phrase.

"I hear you. As hard as it is to admit, I know you are right. Jack just said basically the same thing. I just want her so badly. And as screwed up as it is right now, she is mine. Letting her go is unimaginable to me. But I have to do it. I know I have to. I just don't have to be happy about it." Hamilton sighs and walks out of the room with what seems the physical weight of all that his happening settled on his broad shoulders.

I follow him down to Jack's office. While he obviously runs through his own mess, my mind flashes to Drake's smile, our dinner together, his helping me pack up my parentally abandoned house. Bwahh! I hate this. It was easier when I hated the guy. I try to get my heart back to the whole hate thing, but it won't budge. How did that happen? How could my own heart prove to be such a traitor? It seems set on clinging to Drake. Maybe it is because he was there when my parents deserted me. If I hadn't had been on the outs with G.J. at the time, I wonder if it would be easier to let go?

Shaken from my thoughts, as we enter Jack's office, it is decided I will hide under his enormous desk. This space is big enough they could use it as their nursery. The doorbell rings as I wiggle into some assemblance of comfort. In mere seconds, I hear people entering the room.

"Jack, so nice of you to invite me over." Gus' voice drips with irritation. "G.J., you are looking well."

"We need to understand a few things." Jack is all business. "Why don't you tell us what's been happening?"

Showtime. I slip into Gus' mind and monitor his thoughts.

Gus sighs. "What exactly do you what to know?" *Are they really going to let me drink from her? Will she allow this? So sweet. I know she will taste so sweet.* Images of biting G.J. flash through my mind.

Blech. *I only can imagine how she tastes* means he isn't remembering it.

"Gus!" Jack commands his attention. "Walk us through what's happening."

Images of finding corpses and hiding bodies floats through his mind. Sadness at the waste of the humans. Anger over the invasion of his territory. Starvation in order to track better. Rage over G.J. being mated. The urge to protect her. To steal her away is strong.

Gus explains about the other vampires who are in a frenzy, "They believe they are facilitating a great change. We have long missed the existence of the witches. We blame the wolves for their loss. If you recall, we have not always been on the best of terms with your kind. When we were most at odds, it was discovered the witches were who helped you reproduce. We are created by biting humans to make them our offspring. Your species moves more along the lines of mammals in nature. Witch blood is a delicacy."

Ew, ew, ew.

"Turning a witch vampire takes special care. We cannot simply turn one. They have to be of age and willing. The turning takes years. To the vampire turning the witch it is torture. Small sips are all you are allowed of the most decadent thing you have ever tasted, for years. It makes us protective of them, even more than a human-turned child.

"One of our elders attempted to turn a witch woman named Estrild several centuries ago. He only wanted her, but she had a sister. This was a remote part of the world even for the time. A pack of *weres* were in the area. The sister had already been mated to one of the wolves. Our elder bit Estrild's sister and undid the mating. They ran but the sister was pregnant with the wolf's child. She had not wished to leave her mate. She died in childbirth.

"Estrild mourned her sister and cursed wolf-kind that they all would feel the loss she felt. She believed it was the wolves that killed her sister. So she cursed all the beloved mothers of their offspring so they would be lost in the birthing. She was eventually turned vampire. Sometime later, the wolves learned a witch had the ability to bring their mates through the birth process. From then, witches were coveted by the wolves and protected. Estrild found out and began killing all witches. She used compulsion and turned humans against witch-kind. She created vampire children and set them to the task of being certain no witch lived to help wolves survive.

"Eventually she was killed. But her legacy lives on. They are like a plague we have to hunt down and kill off when they enter our territory. They don't live within vampirism law. I was in the process, ridding the area, when one scented G.J.. They laid in wait for her and when she was in the woods unprotected, attacked. It has been so long since witch blood has been tasted." Gus makes a gross slurping noise, like he just had too much saliva in his mouth.

Blech.

"Now there are many of their kind here trying to get to her." *The power the witch vampire and her maker had was incredible. G.J. is even more powerful than Estrild. She is my future.*

Get in line Gussy boy.

"How do the witches help with the birth process?" G.J. asks.

"I do not know. Are you willing to have me bite you?" Gus asks back. *Say you are willing. Say it. Say it.*

From under the desk, I say, "She needs you to bite her, she is not willing." Wriggling out, I confront Gus' angry stare.

"Oh, I get it, you are trying to get me to be willing." G.J. is quick on the uptake. "How about you just go ahead and bite me so I am not mated, and we can call it done right there."

The room vibrates with all the growling.

"For Pete's sake, it's why he's here. Let's just get it done," G.J. grumbles, walking toward Gus.

Gus flashes images of all the things he wants to do with, and to, G.J. through his head. I jump out, unwilling to be quite so well versed in her anatomy.

"You will not harm her and you will seal the wound," Jack commands.

Tension pulsing through the room is oppressive. Gus moves slowly but eagerly to G.J.. Hamilton and Adam stand right next to her. Gus draws his nose down the side of her neck.

"Gus, honey, this isn't a make out session. There is just nothing sexy about this moment at all. I mean having your parental units present really does nothing to help the ole libido giddy up and go."

"I wanted this to be so different," Gus says softly in her ear.

"There are so many things I want different right now. Could we just get this over with?" G.J. has a pleading note in her voice.

Gus licks her neck. Hamilton shoves Gus halfway across the room. Adam stands in front of G.J. as Jack pulls Hamilton away.

"Calm down!" Jack uses his Alpha power and cows Hamilton.

"If I don't lick her it will hurt. I don't want to put her though any more than she has already been through." Gus stares down Adam.

G.J. taps Adam on the arm. "Let's just assume this is going to be icky and let it be what it is. Come on, Gus, let'er rip." G.J. turns her head to the side.

Hamilton looks away. Adam stays right by G.J.. Gus repeats the lollipop moment before rearing back like a snake and strikes. G.J. lets out a squeak that turns into a smut-novel-audiobook moan. The girl has a calling if her super crazy smart brain doesn't get her very far.

Gus, however, pulls away, his face screwing up in disgust. Crimson blood staining his teeth and lips. G.J. is still bleeding from her neck. Rousing himself, he forces his mouth back on G.J. and licks her neck again. Almost instantly, the blood stops flowing from her wound.

"Is that it?" Celia asks.

Gus nods and says, "What have you done?"

"What do you mean?" G.J. says, rather dazed and holding her neck.

Gus glares at Adam, who is closest. He shoves him so hard Adam flies back across the desk landing next to Celia. Gus is suddenly attacking Hamilton. Only the aftermath of each blow an indicator of movement, Gus is so speedy. Somehow, Jack gets a hold of Gus. Hamilton, while battered, attempts to contain him.

Time for me to mind surf again. *She is in transition. She could die. They turned her. She is mine.*

"Jack, he is freaking out because G.J. might get furry," I explain.

Gus' eyes are an electric blue displaying his rage.

"Gus, I cannot fault you for your anger. The boys didn't understand what they had done. We are waiting to see what happens with G.J.. Our hope is that she will make it through the change because she has the ability to heal herself. I, too, would have preferred a different outcome, but this cannot be changed at this point. Thank you for helping us with the—"

A keening cry from G.J cuts off Jack. She falls to the ground. Adam who had just gotten back to his feet crumples as well and finally Hamilton. All three lay in the fetal position, shivering. The boys whimper while G.J. takes large, gaping breaths and rubs above her heart.

"What is happening?" Celia asks, soothingly patting Adam the closest fallen to her.

Stanzi pulls G.J. into is lap and curls his big body around her.

Jack's face seems to lengthen with the concern lines etching deep. "The mating bond is broken. It is like having your heart ripped from your chest. I was hoping since death wasn't involved it wouldn't be so bad. There are no records of un-mating like this. The only way we knew a mating could break was by death. Once again, we are on uncharted ground." He studies the three on the floor.

"How long does it last?" Celia asks her tone shrill in concern.

"With death comes grief. I can't tell you when the pain changes from loss of the bond to loss of the person. I simply don't know what to expect. Gus, do you have any ideas?"

Gus' contemptuous glare and locked jaw make it hard for him to spit out, "No, the only time we have un-mated anyone, they have been witch or human. No one was *Were* or in transition. I have no idea what we have just done." Gus pointedly stares at Jack's hands on him. "Let me go, I can't do any more damage than what they are already feeling."

Jack hesitantly frees Gus.

Gus squats next to G.J. gently pushing the hair away from her pain-contorted face. "I am so sorry. I did not know what they had done. I'm not giving up on you. We will be together."

Hamilton convulses making a weak lunge toward them. Stanzi pulls G.J. away from Gus. Jack barks out a command, and within moments, two men who had been standing guard come in, gather up Hamilton and Adam, and carry them away.

"Before you go, is there anything we need to know before we track down these murderers and take care of them?" Jack asks Gus, distracting him from his attempt to stay with G.J..

"I need to handle this. Unless you wish to start a major conflict." Gus keeps his gaze on G.J., as Stanzi lifts her up and takes her out of the room.

"They started a conflict when they attacked one of the pack. We would never let that stand. And your leaders know that. The fire breed is on our side as well. These feral creatures need to be put down." Jack's confident in his words.

"These feral creatures, as you put it, have the backing of at least two of the old ones. They tend to dismiss their horrific behavior as an overindulgent parent does a spoiled child. They laugh at the antics. Long lived ones tend to dismiss human value."

I can't tell if Gus is bored or disgusted.

"This is different," I chime in. "The murders are wreaking havoc in the Shadow World. Hugo told me it has to stop. The ones being murdered by supernatural means have too much energy to be held in the Shadow World. They are exploring beyond it and …" the image of the soul being devoured stops me. "It's got to stop."

"What is it they are exploring?" Gus focuses on me.

"They could bring Fae through the Shadow World and back here. The Fae I saw should never come back here. They *are* destruction. If you believe your kind has no value for human life, you have no idea. These guys think souls make a delightful afternoon snack," I plead with Gus to understand.

"Soul eaters are old myths." Gus scoffs.

"I am telling you, I saw one gobble up a soul that escaped the Shadow World like it was a hot fudge sundae. If people are killed with a truckload of energy left in them, and the idea that there are strange things to be explored than their bland little lives, they go in search of the other natural and expose themselves to these creatures. The more that happens, the more likely it is the Fae will find their way back to our world. Your kind has to stop exposing themselves to people and/or killing them. As it is, this weekend alone, there are nine G.J. doppelgangers, all of which have a ton of energy and died knowing about other kind predators. The shades are doing what they can to hold them but can't contain them forever."

Gus stares me down, as if that will get me to change what I meant.

"How can you know all of this?" Gus tilts his head slightly.

"My mom said I'm a bridge. Hugo's been taking me to the Shadow World. I have witnessed this firsthand. One of the Fae connected with my mind, I can't explain how creepy that was." I shiver remembering.

Gus looks surprised for a moment, but his gaze wanders around the room, unseeing, as if searching for an elusive thought. "I am not so old that I remember the Fae. There are only a handful of vampire-kind that are. We did not fair very well when they were among us. The Fae relegated us to darkness and we lived off scraps. Humans were their cattle. They tended them like over protective shepherds. From what I understand many of my kind lived like rats. Stealing what they could and starving for long periods of time. That is why some of our elders are keen on gluttony. They really don't like feeling as though they cannot have whatever they want. Most of us see the value in leaving our food alive to draw from again. The old ones are not fond of any restrictions on us. They speak of the time of darkness with loathing."

"So the Fae protected humans from vampires." Celia's voice rings with her discomfort over our subject matter.

"They kept you for themselves as slaves. Not all were soul eaters but none cared for you," Gus explains.

"It's okay to die, just not have your soul taken?" Celia challenges.

"Celia, that was one of the worst things I've ever seen. Something comes after death, but nothing comes after what that thing did. Not that either is on my top ten list." I close my eyes and shake my head, trying in vain to lose the image.

"The actions of these feral vampires can bring back those times for your kind. We don't expose ourselves to the humans. Our history says it can cause the Shadow World to fall. As Nat said, if humans truly believe we exist, their spirits don't rest as easy. If they die with enough energy, they push into other worlds. It's possible the beings in those worlds can follow them back, eventually," Jack tries to persuade Gus to let the wolves help.

"I am not saying I could not use your help. Jack, you have your own problems to address. I am aware that some of your wolves don't particularly like your management style." Gus levels a hard stare at Jack.

"They've been addressed. You and Lucas were close. You'll be glad to hear he's on the mend. As of an hour ago, when I checked on him, he almost had all of his skin back. Young Mr. Aldrich did quite a job on him. But he's patching up. Can't say he is enjoying the healing process, but I don't really care." Jack keeps a cool stare on Gus.

Gus juts his lower lip out in consideration. "Knowing your kind, I would have thought ending him would have been your reaction. Some will say that is a sign of weakness. Some say you have been getting fat and happy after marrying Celia. That you are so focused on your new wife that you have lost sight of your duties as Alpha. And G.J. isn't a true Beta. She isn't even a wolf," Gus taunts.

"G.J. isn't a wolf… yet. People say all kinds of things, it doesn't mean I have to give a damn. Keep your lowlife, vein-chugging machinations to yourself, Sanzor. The wolves don't need your input." Jack's tone is low and flat.

Gus puts his hands up in defense. "How do you think the vampire found G.J.? This is my territory. It has been for over a century. I do not share. Someone informed the feral of my kind about G.J.. Who would do such a thing?" Gus lets silence leave room for thoughts to progress forward. "I would not. Like I said, I do not share. G.J. is mine."

While none of us agrees with him, we don't focus on disabusing him now. Gus surveys the office collection of bric-a-brac before posing, "If someone knew about her and wanted her gone, what better way than to get one of my kind to do it. We have lived comfortably in this territory together for years, Jack. You have not gotten in my way, and I have respected your habits. That is rare as you may be aware. Our kinds don't always live in such close proximity without some issues. I would have even gone as far as to call us friends. I have years before I can take G.J.. Where else would I consider her safe but with you? When she displaced Lucas, he was not pleased. There have not been strong wolf females in generations. Estrild must have added that to her curse, it cannot be coincidence. That can lead to a rather sexist attitude among those who don't see women as their equals. To have a teen *girl* take you down when you were planning on challenging for Alpha?"

With that, Jack's eyes no longer focus on Gus. Last year, Jack had found out Lucas had planned on challenging him, so this isn't anything new to him, or me since I'd read his mind then too.

Gus continues, "Well that might be more than you can accept. It might urge you to enlist the help of some you had never before considered an ally."

"You and Lucas were close, closer than you and I. Why didn't he come to you?" Jack tilts his head and questions.

"Ahhh, the magic that is G.J.. Lucas had asked for my support before she came into our lives. I try to stay out of your, what would be a good phrase? How about we call it lowlife canine machinations? All I agreed to was to not get involved. But she breezed in. Lucas would not be a protector of G.J.. He would leave her on the side of the road like so much carrion. But you have Celia, which makes G.J. important to you. It was in my best interest to help keep you in your current position.

"Now, forgive me if I am wrong, but Lucas cannot challenge you until G.J. is out of the way. He isn't overly fond of the way you boss him around, and his son follows you, as if you are his favorite Avengers character. You have Celia, who Lucas desires, and then your ward humiliates him. Jack, I don't have to be an HR consultant to know you have a disgruntled employee issues."

Gus' smug smirk is hard to look at. How could I have been so wrong about him? Our whole friendship seems creepy now. For a mind reader, I am a horrible judge of character.

Gus shakes his head. "I didn't realize he would go so far as to harm G.J.. That was my error and I will have to live with that. Honestly, if you don't take care of Lucas, I will have to. He has caused me more trouble than our friendship would permit. He invited other vampires into my territory, after I told him I would not help in his coup. Because of his egocentric desires, I am going to have to defend my territory. Not to mention his threat to G.J.. His hubris is his death sentence. You can do it or I will."

"We have called the pack. You won't involve yourself in pack matters." Jack's flat visage challenges Gus to disagree.

Gus shrugs. "Like I said, as long as you rid us of Lucas, I won't need to be involved."

"Do you know how many vampires we need to take out?" Jack asks.

Gus sighs. "As far as I am aware, there are five in the area now. But they are not loners. They report back and should they not, we will have even more visitors. G.J. cannot protect herself against my kind. I hope you will take more care with her. She is precious."

My mind flashes to the creepy dude from Lord of the Rings when he says that.

"We will start to hunt tonight." Jack's tone bodes no argument.

"So be it," Gus replies, "Oh, and Natalia, you have betrayed me. For the sake of our old friendship, I will give you this warning. If it becomes known to the vampire world you and your family are fae, there will be no place you can hide. Be prepared to die." And in a blink, he is gone.

Chapter Thirty

Holy crap, it is shocking to receive a real death threat. I would seek comfort from G.J., but she is an utter mess. She sits, with her arms wrapped around her knees, at her desk chair staring off into space most of the time. She doesn't want to eat or sleep. She has no interest in schoolwork, and the scariest part is she doesn't want to talk. And damn it I need to talk. Adam and Hamilton haven't been much better. They've kept busy hunting the vampires with the other wolves, but their tempers are set on eleven. Stanzi has gotten a workout pulling them off each other over the most inane conflicts. They've come to blows for simply trying to decide who will go through a door first.

Jack had thought it would help if we put them all in a room together. G.J. had curled into a ball unable to stop crying, and the boys had nearly killed each other trying to comfort her. After that, Celia had refused to let them anywhere near G.J..

When I come down for breakfast, Celia faces off with Jack in the kitchen. "Jack, we need to give this time. Until everyone gets a grip, I don't want them around each other."

"Celia, I have lost one mate. If I could have been close to her again, I'm sure it would have soothed me. The boys aren't going to calm down knowing she's here and they can't see her," Jack argues.

"Too bad. Let them sulk. What is to stop them from hurting her in some ridiculous attempt to get her to mate one of them? I'm going to take up a tray and see if I can get her to eat. I mean it, Jack, you and I will have a major problem if you let them anywhere near her. We tried it your way, not again." Celia heads out of the room carrying the tray. "Nat, please get G.J.'s work from her teachers when you are at school today. I really don't think she can make it in."

"Megan called her cell when I was up there. She wants to come over. What do you want me to tell her?" I ask, as I sling my backpack onto one of the bar stools at the island.

"Have her come by after school. Maybe it will help get her mind out of this funk," Celia calls over her shoulder, as she exits.

With a scowl on his face, Jack watches Celia leave.

"She's right, Jack. Space is what they all need. They won't get past this if they stay in each other's faces. G.J. is a wreck. Think about it. If something you've been physically attached to was taken from you but waived under your nose all the time, I don't think it would help. I wouldn't deal well. Not to mention she whimpers like a puppy, which freaks her out too. Thank God, I have faith in my bestie's brainpower. Otherwise, I'm not sure her psyche could handle all this. She lost her mom less than nine months ago. She's tough but let her at least get through the first full moon before she has to deal with anything else."

Jack blows out a breath. "You are a fairly smart young lady. I guess I'll go tell my wife she's right… again. This gets old after a while."

"Jack, you married Celia, you have many, many more of these moments ahead of you."

Jack grins. "I am one lucky man."

I shake my head as he leaves. Sadly, with G.J. out of commission, I have to hunt around to pack my own lunch. My head is inside the fridge. Adam scares the crap out of me by reaching for the juice above my head. "Bwahh! Damn it, Adam. Wait your turn."

"I have to get to school too," Adam grumbles back.

I grab my lunch items and place them on the island. "Yeah, I know but I wasn't in your way that long."

"Are you fixing me lunch too?" Adam asks.

"What about me would make you even ask? No. You have two hands, fix it yourself," I grumble right back. Not even sympathy will make me a domestic goddess.

Adam starts slamming things around and grabs the lunch-meat right out of my hand. "Adam, being a jerk isn't endearing."

Adam doesn't say anything, just keeps pulverizing what he intends to eat for lunch.

I finish my lunch and move around to put it in my backpack. Hamilton comes in and the tension level makes me squint; my gaze darts from one gigantic boy to the other. I don't see this ending well.

"Are we making our own lunches?" Hamilton asks.

Now, I heard a simple question, but Adam must have heard something else entirely. "I'm not your slave. Fix your own damn lunch."

"I wouldn't trust you to make it. I don't consider spit a condiment," Hamilton says coolly, but his shoulder slams Adam's on his way past him.

Adam drops his already abused lunch and shoves Hamilton. *Here we go.* The shoving match escalates into verbal insults and while I never met either of their mothers, I am certain the terms they're using are slanderous. I try to interject some sanity, but I feel a bit like a swatted fly.

"Enough!" Jack roars from the doorway. "Clean up this mess and get to school. The bus gets here in ten minutes."

I slink out of the room. Not my mess. Not my problem.

****

At school, it continues and the boys' sullen mood seems to be infectious. All the letter jacket crew are extra edgy. *Super* just what all the socially awkward school goers dream of, the simple joy of a day when the muscle bound squad has a hair trigger. It is almost comical to see kids literally try to scoot along the wall past these boys without getting their back belt loop hung up on the locker handles as they slink by. More than one turn and face the wall until the big guys pass.

Other than that, the day goes rather quickly. I let Megan know she should come home with me, and I sit with her and her lack-of-verbal-skills pals at lunch. No way do I want to hang out with the wolves today. Not to mention Drake might sit there.

I am so into my own thoughts it is kind of nice not to even be tempted to mind read. When you aren't paying any attention to a teacher drone on, it is amazing how quickly the minute hand turns. Thoughts fill my head, like QVC items do a house on an episode of *Hoarders*.

Drake keeps showing up so I have to dart around other kids, making them my human shields. I manage to duck him repeatedly. I almost make it through the day, but at the final bell, he catches me as I shut my locker.

"I guess this is your way of telling me you're done." Drake glares down at me.

"You're the one who moved on. I hope you have a nice dinner with G.J. when she gets out of the fetal position." I will not be taking any crap from him.

Shock, then true concern flashes across his face. "What is wrong with G.J.?"

"Why don't you call her? You have her number." Well this is a regrettable moment, but I just can't seem to shut up. I turn around, escaping my snide mouth from embarrassing me further.

"Nat, what the hell? You are the one kissing dead guys."

"At least Hugo isn't your best friend."

"It ... I... Look I'm sorry there are things I just *can't* tell you. My dad would freak if I did. I know I promised you I would tell you anything you asked but I can't. I'm trying to get it sorted out. With G.J. being mated I think I can ..." Drake blows out a breath in what looks like an attempt at editing what he might reveal.

The inability to read this guy is beyond frustrating. "Well, she's not anymore, so have at."

"Wait... what?" Drake's handsome face screws up in confusion.

"Gus bit G.J. and she is no longer mated. Hence her bedridden status."

"Gus did what?" Fire leaps in Drake's eyes.

Someone should really create an early warning system for my response to this little display; four emotions hit me at once, like a tsunami. Hurt, fear, rage, and jealousy draw and quarter me. On my exhale, my chin raises letting fury gain control. My voice becomes a staccato whisper, as I fire, "She couldn't be mated to two guys so Gus came and undid it. Apparently, that is possible. So get in line, she is back on the market."

"Christ!"

"You are going to have to work on that, she isn't a fan of the whole Lord's name in vain thing." With that, I slide in between kids heading down the hall and don't look back. When I get back to the house, I am curling up in a ball too. I'm almost to the promise of sunlight at the doors, but Principal Decker flags me down. And the thrills keep coming.

"Nat, is G.J. alright? It is not like her to shirk responsibility and Megan is very upset."

"I'm sure she will be fine. Megan is coming home with me to see if there is anything they can work on."

"Excellent, I will come by later to see how the girls are getting along. It is very important to the school to have such a prestigious award. I know, if they stay focused, this idea of theirs has a real chance."

Unsure what to say, I just nod and head to the bus line. I think about going back to my own house, but Megan is waiting to ride back to the Wyfle's. Honestly, it's easier not to find an excuse and go with her. Luckily, Megan is never overly chatty, so we are both content to ride in silence.

G.J. is out of bed when we get home. So… progress. Unbathed and in her pajamas but out of bed.

"You look awful." Megan beats me to the statement.

"I've been better. I don't know why they asked you to come, Megan, I am not feeling well. Maybe we can work on this later."

"Our final draft of the proof of concept is due to the committee tomorrow. Are you contagious?" Megan asks.

"It's not that. I just don't think I am going to be very helpful." G.J. is always nice, even when trying to dissuade someone.

"That's dumb. I need you, if you aren't contagious than we need to do this. Can you take medicine?" Megan won't let her go so easily.

G.J. has no fight in her so with a sigh she concedes. "Fine, we can work for a little while."

"We have to work until it's done."

At that, the doorbell rings. I bet I know who that is. Sighing, I allow Mr. Decker in. G.J. appears to really feel like vomiting at the sight of him. Nothing like a deadline when you have zero motivation to even be vertical. With all the enthusiasm of a sloth on Ambien, we greet our beloved principal.

"G.J., I was just making sure we are all on the same page about the importance of the project." Mr. Decker, may not be aware. Extra stressors are not really motivators for the students who already take initiative.

Suddenly, Hugo poofs in next to me.

"Ahh, Hugo?" I'll have to admit this is not my most suave moment.

"Nat?" G.J. spins her worried glance searching the room.

"*They have taken over shadows*," Hugo panics.

"What do you mean, 'They have taken over the shadows?'" I ask, while letting G.J. hear what is happening.

"*Instead of eating the soul, somehow they entered it. Now there are Fae in shadows loose in the Shadow World.*"

"Holy crap." My eyes sting with how wide they have gotten.

"Pardon?" Mr. Decker asks in a shocked tone.

"What?" G.J. is on high alert now.

"The Fae have possessed shades," I explain.

"*You must come see.*" Hugo grabs my arm, and we are off.

The atmosphere in the Shadow World is different somehow. All of the mist seems to shudder fear through me. Unease creeps up my spine, like a sack of baby spiders hatched and they head toward my scalp. A breeze of mist sluggishly passes us.

Hugo turns to me, terror having taken over his face. Wind picks up to torrent level when he says, "*They are here.*"

Three shades stand before me, their gaze so direct it seems to draw me in. It is terrifyingly familiar.

"*You have come,*" the voice arrogant and compelling, "*We so hoped we would find you here. You will bring us across to where humans reign.*"

"I vote no, on that suggestion. How about you go back to where you reign and we call this field trip a bust?" Still holding Hugo, I back up. My subconscious must want the distance because I'm not aware until it happens.

All three shades tilt their heads. One of them speaks in my mind: *"There is no suggestion, there is only a command. You are ignorant of our ways, but there is no excuse for disobedience. We are of the court. All Fae must follow our will. It is as it always has been. Take us now."*

"It may be the way you have always done things but not me. Change is good. Try to embrace it. I am not Uber so I've no intention on conveying you anywhere." As I step away, they follow so the distance between us stays the same, until the three begin to moving apart, forming a triangle. My gaze arcs from one to another of them, measuring the distance.

"Nat, you need to get outta here." Hugo turns to me. Goodbye is all over his face. *"I am so sorry I brought you, she said I needed to bring you. This is my mistake. I will try to fix it. Go now, and…goodbye, Nat."* Hugo leans forward and kisses my cheek.

The understanding of what Hugo is saying clenches my heart. I take a deep breath to ease the aching. If I go, they will do to Hugo what they had done to the shade that entered their world. They will devour him and he will simply be no more. His life was already taken from him too early. I can't comprehend this happening to him twice. No more of this sweet boy, who tried to find a way to prevent this from coming to fruition.

"I'm not leaving you here to do this alone." But just as I object, Hugo lets go at the same time two of the Fae reach for us.

Chapter Thirty-One

It is really quite disorienting to go from one reality to another. Particularly when you aren't prepared for the leap. Back in the Wyfle foyer, G.J. kneels over me, along with Megan and Mr. Decker. Mr. Decker is slapping my face.

"Is that really necessary?" I ask, cringing away from his next blow.

"Nat! Good lord, you scared the pee out of us." G.J. is as eloquent as ever.

Mr. Decker sits back on his heels and looks around the room.

"You fell down," Megan sums up what happened on their end.

"Thanks for the info. I couldn't tell by my being on the floor or anything. Would you like to tell me the sky is blue or any other pertinent information?"

"The sky isn't blue, it appears blue due to sunlight hitting Nitrogen and Oxygen molecules, which scatters the light. The blue wavelength is affected more than other colors making the predominant color appear to be blue," Megan informs us.

I just shake my head and glare at G.J..

"Thank you, Megan," G.J. says, "I think Nat now knows more about our atmosphere. Let's try to get her upright and we can find out what is going on. Mr. Decker, I am sure you have better places to be. Megan and I promise to have all our work done for tomorrow. It'll all be fine. You just leave it to me." If that is G.J. subtly giving someone the boot, I'm not sure what direct would be.

Mr. Decker's face is void of all emotion. He slowly turns his head, as if investigating the house.

My chest tightens with unease. While I never considered my principal a guy I would like to wrap up in a big bear hug, his demeanor is ultra-cold. When his disdainful eyes settle on mine, my Oh-crap-o-meter hits new heights. "Uh G.J.…. I think I came back with a stowaway. And it isn't Casper."

With a lightning fast strike, Mr. Decker grabs G.J.'s arm. Pulling her toward him, he places his mouth over hers. By the way, the image of your Principal lip locked with your best friend is one of those take-a-gallon-of-bleach-to-your-brain sights. G.J., unable to break his hold with her physical strength, sends him flying across the entry hall with her power. She collapses to the floor, breathing heavy. Her eyes are deeply shadowed, like she hasn't slept in a month. And I thought she looked pathetic before.

"You are almost the most delicious thing I have ever tasted. But you have… an undertone of a beast. If it were not for that, I would want to taste you for eternity. That is… disappointing," Mr. Decker says in a voice so smooth his words almost don't come across as super creepy. *Almost.*

"Ew," is all my loquacious friend can come up with.

"Do all human's taste like that?" Mr. Decker's gaze moves to Megan.

"I would think that would be improbable. Every human would most likely have their own flavor profile as they would scent based on their genetics and environmental changes. I think the school board would object to your trying to find out," Megan states flatly. To her, our principal is trying to neck with her lab partner.

I am certain she has no idea Mr. Decker has had his mental controls carjacked by a Fae.

The door opens and Adam and Hamilton enter the chaotic scene. Instantly Hamilton rushes to G.J. on the floor. Adam starts as well, but Principal Decker grabs Megan and plays sucky face with her too. As Adam rushes to stop the bizarre make out session, Principal Decker rears back from Megan making an ice pick to the eardrum kind of noise. He is bleeding from his nose, eyes, and ears.

Adam shoves him away from Megan and touches her face, looking for damage. "Are you alright?"

Megan is hitting her head with her palm repeatedly, but she nods. Adam pulls her stiff form under his arm, cautiously protective. Hamilton and Adam turn and stare down Mr. Decker.

In pain and weakened by his encounter with Megan, Mr. Decker backs up slowly.

"No!" I scream, as he vanishes out the door.

"What the hell was that?" Adam asks.

"Mr. Decker kissed G.J., then me," Megan states.

Adam and Hamilton Growl.

Struggling to my feet, I race toward the door. "That wasn't Principal Decker. That was a Fae." When I get outside, I search for where he might have gone, but I have no idea where he went. I race back into the house and command the two boys, "Go find him!"

G.J. is weakly getting to her feet with Hamilton's help. "How about we start with what on Earth is happening and move on from there. I need a second. It's not every day your principal lays one on you and sucks your energy, like you were a chocolate milkshake."

"Oh God! Hugo." My heart is firing like a machine gun at the thought of what happened to Hugo and what that thing might be doing to someone else.

"Hugo? Is he here?" Hamilton searches the room for the unseen boy.

"No." I take a deep breath and slowly let it out, figuring out where I need to start. "Hugo came and got me. There are Fae in the Shadow World. When we were there, they attacked us. I think when I came back, one of them came with me. Mr. Decker was touching me, and I think the Fae jumped into him."

"Then, he grabbed me and tried to suck my soul out of my mouth. I couldn't get him off. I had to zap him with my will to get him away from me. Kissing your principal is just as awful as one might expect. Then, he went after Megan," G.J. said leaning on Hamilton heavily.

Everyone turns to Megan. Adam is rubbing her back gently trying to calm her down. It doesn't seem like our unwavering attention is making her more comfortable.

"I don't think that was a kiss. I think that was something like what Nat tried to do when she was attempting to read my mind. How did you get him off you? He just flew back?" Megan says, her face angled, as if she is talking to the floor, but her words address G.J..

Ignoring her interest in her abilities, G.J. asks, "How do you figure? When Nat reads my mind, I don't hardly notice."

"It felt like it was blocked by the same thing," Megan tells the floor again.

"Well, whatever you did, worked. He was a mess."

"We have to go after him. He is going to try to do that to more people. What happens if he jumps to someone new? There will be a Fae loose in this world. What if he brings over more of them?" a stream of stressors fly out of my mouth.

"Slow down. We need a plan. What are we going to do with him when we find him? Hopefully, Megan bought us some time. With any luck, he will be unwilling to suck face with just anybody. Self-preservation should deter him for a little bit," G.J. says.

"The Fae are mythical creatures originating in Celtic lore. They are not supposed to exist. Why would you think they exist? Mr. Decker should be reported to the school district. That isn't okay. He should be reported. I'm sure that has to be illegal. The Fae are just stories. Aren't the Fae just stories? What Mr. Decker did wasn't okay." Megan tries hard to come to grips with the reality bomb that just went off in her mind.

"Megan," I say sharply to get her attention, "I am Fae. I do exist. I promise not to put you in a lip lock. Mr. Decker is … Well… he is kind of possessed. So he wasn't the one who really did that to you or G.J., either. I just hope our favorite school administrator is still in there somewhere. If that Fae took him over, I don't know what he did with the soul that was there to begin with."

"Mr. Decker kissed you?" Disbelieving Hamilton searches G.J.'s face. Really? Out of everything we just said, Hamilton is only concerned that someone kissed G.J.?

"Not really. He more tried to pull my very being out of my mouth like a Dyson." G.J. waves off Hamilton's question. "Why do you think he can body hop? And why do you think he can do anything without you? You are the bridge. Isn't that what your mama said? You are who can bring those folks over. So I think as long as you don't go back, more of those fellas won't be able to come here." G.J.'s always works the logic. "So how do we get that one out of Mr. Decker?"

We all look from one of us to another thinking the next face might have the ah-ha on the tip of their tongue.

"Nat, try to get a hold of your parents again. I know you haven't had much luck but leave them a message and let them know where things stand now. They might be willing to break radio silence if it means stopping this dude," G.J. attempts persuasion.

"The boys should go after him. And then we should see what we can do from there," I object.

"Who is to say he can't take over the boys? And one of them controlled by a Fae is a whole lot different than our wimpy Mr. Decker." G.J. over exaggerates her facial features so I pick up the werewolf hint without including Megan in the info.

"Megan, are you alright?" Adam asks her.

Megan shakes her head, then nods.

"Why don't we get you home?" Adam asks.

"We have our proof of concept due tomorrow. G.J. and I need to work on it." Megan's still stuck on her primary objective.

"Megan, honey, I think we have bigger fish to fry at the moment. I'll shoot you an email with the changes I had and trust you to handle any issues."

Again, Megan shakes her head and then nods. She repeats this two or three times before walking toward the door. "Please, email me soon."

"I'll make sure she gets home safe." Adam follows Megan out.

After they leave, I whisper loudly to G.J., "I don't think he will go after wolves. He didn't like your aftertaste."

"What is that supposed to mean?" she asks almost hurt.

"I think that your soon to be wolf status might have just saved you from being his favorite flavor Slurpee." I'm still in my dramatic whisper mode.

"Well, at least there is something good to come out of it. Does that mean I smell like a dog now?" G.J. asks, while discretely sniffing herself.

"You smell better than before."

Dear lord, please help Hamilton not sound like a jackass someday. G.J. glares at him.

"You are soooo smooth, Hamilton. Really." If he catches the sarcasm in my tone, he ignores it.

Hamilton flips out his phone, calls someone, and turns his back on us.

"I am going to go check on my books and see if I can figure out a spell that might help us. Using the principles of the triquetra casting, I may be able to bind that Fae's essences to an object. After that, who knows but it might work."

"Do me a favor. Make it a solid object. The last thing we need is to have it break open and out pops a soul-devouring Faery."

"Good thought." G.J.'s replies distractedly, while heading up to her study cave also known as her bedroom.

Hamilton turns back and says, "I've told Jack what's up. He is sending all available pack members to look for Mr. Decker. I also called Gus and Drake."

I wince at the mention of Drake's name.

Hamilton comes over and puts an arm around my shoulders. "He cares a lot about you."

"Don't start," I grumble.

"Hey I'm not cupid by any stretch, but I think there has been a significant miscommunication between you and Drake. You were there for me when I needed to talk about G.J.. Just know I'm here for you too. Sometimes it takes an outside eye to help us see things that are too close."

Well look at that. When not conversing with G.J., the boy can make sense.

Chapter Thirty-Two

Almost every time I think about my parents these days, I get so angry I tear up. They abandoned me. And now I have to beg for help from the ether or their voicemail? So obnoxious. I'll do it. Because I have to do it. I just hope when I call I don't sound as pathetic as I feel. I am just about to dial, when my phone rings in my hand. Awesome. What does he want? A picture of Drake fills the screen in my palm. I put off one torture for another and answer.

"What?" No need to pretend.

"Are you all right?" Drake asks.

"Fine."

A big sigh fills my ear. "Nat… please talk to me. Hamilton called and said you were attacked. I just… I just want to know you are all right."

I reply with my own sigh. "I wasn't really hurt, just scared. I'm more worried about Hugo. He jumped in front of me, trying to stop the Fae from getting to me. I don't know what happened to him. I need to get back in there and see if he's okay."

"You can't go back in there." Drake's voice has command to it.

I don't do well with empirical decrees. "You don't get a say in my can and can'ts."

Another sigh. "It isn't safe. Think about it. What happens if you go in again and more Fae come back with you. Is that dead guy worth it?"

My cheeks flame, like I have been slapped. "Yeah, that dead guy *is* worth it. Hugo *is* worth it to me. He didn't just save me, he knew protecting me would cost him his afterlife. The last part of him existing at all. He was willing to give that up for my sake. I have to know what happened to him because he does matter to me. And if you don't get why, you don't know me at all."

"Nat, don't you get how dangerous it is for you to go back?" Drake switches tactics to persuasive.

I'm not buying that either. "I understand better than anyone. I've lost my parents and seen my principal try to suck the soul out of my best friend. So I get it. But I have to know. I will be careful. I just need to find a way in."

"And what if something happens to you in there?" Drake asks.

"What do you care?" I snipe back.

"God, Nat. Really? You don't think I care?" Anger rides on the edge of his voice. "Listen, you asked me to just be honest with you. And I promised you if you asked a question, I would answer it. I had no idea about the G.J. thing at the time. I still can't talk about it. I really want to. But I can't. So instead of lying to you, I walked away. I need to get it straightened out. I can promise you this though, I don't want G.J.. Sure, she is great, but I don't want to be with her. I only want to be with you. But you need me to be honest with you and I can't be right now. It isn't that I don't want to be, I really can't."

"So you dumped me for my own good? Thanks... I guess. Remind me in the future your idea of a favor sucks. I have to go."

"Wait, Nat... please..."

"Please what?" I don't even attempt to hide my annoyance.

"Please just … don't go."

"Good-bye, Drake." There is a good deal of spite in my disconnect.

I make the call to my parents. It is weird to feel so estranged from people I love so much. I give them the basics on the message. When they find out I did bring to fruition their greatest fears, it occurs to me I may never see them again.

Sick of mulling it over, I track down G.J. in her room. Of course, she is nose deep in a book.

"Hey, I gotta find out what happened to Hugo. I still don't know how to world jump on my own. Do you have any ideas?" I ask.

G.J. blinks up at me, bringing her considerable mental powers to my topic and not the one she had been pondering. "Tell me again how it works according to Hugo."

I run back through the energy explanation.

"Huh. I will have to think on that. If you need to go quickly are there any other ghosts you can communicate with?"

"Well, Mrs. Ackers, but I would prefer not to. There have been a few more, but I don't even know their names, so I'm not sure how to call them or where to start looking for them." I try to think back to when I had seen shades. "Hey, there was that first guy. Remember of the field trip. I wonder if he is still around."

"The old timey one?"

"Yeah, do you want to go down there with me?" I ask.

"I want to find a way to contain this Fae and get him out of Mr. Decker. Besides the boys would be super jumpy if I even fainted toward the front door. But take somebody with you."

"Me and my shadow…" I sing, as I leave her to her mental musings.

****

Stanzi must have drawn the short straw because he plays my bodyguard. He drives us down to where I had seen the first ghost. People mill about everywhere. It lightly rains, making the whole adventure that much less pleasant. As I walk back and forth around the old rail yard, we dodge the poking of errant umbrella points.

Stanzi's large, quiet presence somewhat comforts me. He isn't one for small talk. But as I get frustrated, he says little things to help calm me down, "Relax. It is a nice day for a stroll," or, "We could hold hands and skip," making me shake my head and giggle. It is such an odd sensation to find a lighthearted moment in the middle of all of this dark chaos.

After almost a half an hour, I spot the old miner. He wanders with a lost look on his face. He is far more transparent than he had been before.

"Hey." I dart toward him.

"Nat?" Stanzi calls.

Reaching the shade, I blurt out, "Can you take me to the Shadow World?"

"*It is not safe. They are there. We must help the workers here. Do you know when the next rally is?*"

Super, I get the ghost with Alzheimer's.

"I need to find a Ghost named Hugo. He is from my time. Looks like he had his neck mauled. Can you take me to him?" I push.

"*I can go look for him. You cannot go with me. They are there.*"

"One of them is here. I need to know how to send them back. Hugo was helping me. Please, help me find him. I have been to the Shadow World before."

At that little tidbit, the old guy looks sharply up at me. "*You have?*"

"Yeah, a few times. Please, I need to make sure Hugo is all right."

"It is not safe. I will go find your friend."

As he fades out, I reach forward and touch his arm. I focus on the sensation of my consciousness leaving my body. I split from my physical form, like pulling taffy. My consciousness stretches and releases my frame. I concentrate and assist in the disconnection.

Arriving in the Shadow World, the old timer's eyes verge on falling out with the shock widening them at the fact I am there. *"You should not have done that."*

"Well, I did. So, let's go find Hugo."

"I'm afraid that won't be possible. But, you may be happy to know he was delicious," a melodic voice chimes from behind me.

Spinning, I come face-to-face with one of the creatures. Before he can reach out and touch me, I yell to the old timer to run, as I let go of his arm, mentally seeking out my body.

Stanzi cradles me in his arms and carries me back to the car. Tears fill my eyes. Hugo is gone. Permanently gone. Even though I can walk, I wrap my arms around Stanzi's neck and sob into his shoulder. When we get to the car, he rearranges me to get his keys out and open the door. He puts me in the seat and buckles me in.

After sliding into the driver's seat, he gently runs his big hand over the top of my wet hair. "You want to talk about what just happened?"

I shake my head.

"I take it your friend didn't make it."

A loud aching sound of grief explodes from my throat. Instinctively, I suck in hard. My gutted chest retrieves air back in my weakened lungs, but the emptiness doesn't dissipate.

Stanzi pulls me toward him and wraps me in his huge arms. We are both soaked, but he is warm, and I take the comfort he offers. I'm not sure how long we stay like this, but eventually I pull away and Stanzi drives the car to Jack's house.

Celia is in the entry. After taking one look at me, she grabs me in a fierce hug. "Whatever it is, kiddo. I'm sorry."

"We grieve death because we see it as a permanent loss. But it isn't really. The souls are still there. They still give us energy and their consciousness is still connected to ours. Hugo's actual soul is gone. The finality of it is incomprehensible. These soul eaters cannot exist. They are an abomination." My mouth finds words that I can't really get my head around.

Celia rubs my back. "Loss is hard. And you may have been able to see and understand there is an afterlife, but the rest of us have to take that on faith. So, the only advice I can give you is what we all are given when we lose someone we love. You have your memories of Hugo. Cherish them and don't let his loss mean nothing. Use it to find the best way to honor him."

I pull away nodding slightly. "I need to go talk to G.J.."

"She's in her room."

I find G.J. scribbling notes as she references back to an enormous book sitting on her desk. When I come in, she glances up. Dropping her pen, she gets up and pulls me into a fierce hug too. I might be the mind reader, but G.J. doesn't even have to ask what happened. I'm not normally a touchy-feely sort, but I'm incredibly grateful for the cuddle therapy this crowd so willingly offers.

"Wow, I leave for a little while and fantasies erupt in my absence."

We both turn and look at Adam.

"Whoops. Not the time for that." His joviality slides away and concern replaces it. "You okay, Nat?"

"Hugo is gone. Those stupid Fae …" I can't finish.

"Oh, Nat, I'm so sorry," Adam says.

I can only wobble my head in a semblance of a nod.

"All right. Let's figure out how to get the little bugger back where he came from. Any news on Mr. Decker and his alter ego?"

"They think he's hiding out in the locker room at school. But we aren't sure how to contain him. If he can body jump, we need to work fast. Drake has him contained, for now, but he can't keep it up forever."

"Contained how?" G.J. asks.

Adam screws up his face in search of the best description to use. "The term vortex of fire is the most accurate I can come up with."

Chapter Thirty-Three

Sure enough, when we open the door to the boy's locker room, it's as if we are entering a blast furnace. The heat is staggering. Waves of hot air catch our hair and make it dance around our heads. When we turn the corner toward the communal shower area, a small cyclone of fire circles Mr. Decker's form standing within its eye.

"Are you sure that isn't gonna bake him like an Ore Ida?" G.J. asks Drake.

Drake's flame filled eyes focus on his column of fire. His hands, which seem to be shaping the cone from a distance, have a slight tremor as I study him more closely "I am controlling the temp for now. Any chance you know how to get the fae out of Mr. Decker? This isn't as easy as I make it look."

"Let me in there and I will see what I can do." I'm not as confident as my voice indicates.

"Absolutely not." Drake takes his eyes away from his handy work and shoots me an annoyed glare. My breath catches at the extraordinary inferno burning in his eyes

"Drake, Nat is our only chance at this. While my books talk about possession, I don't think they address the Fae," G.J. persuades Drake.

"What do they say about possession?" Drake asks,

Taking a deep lung full of the hot air, G.J. explains, "Possession can happen a few different ways. A strong spirit pushes aside a weaker soul. A person can willingly invite a spirit in and finally, there are demonic possessions."

"How do those work?" Hamilton asks.

"Those are more complicated. A demon can be directed into another being through ritual. Or, the summoner can accept them, but that usually entails a bargain of some kind. By the way, never bargain with a demon. They are old and crafty. They end up taking your soul nine bets out of ten. Finally, there's the release of a demon from a ritual object that contained them. As Nat pointed out earlier, breakable items are a dumb place to contain any kind of entity."

The Fae in a Mr. Decker suit laughs. "This world is so amusing. You don't even know your real history."

"Thank you for your valuable input," G.J. dismisses the Fae.

"Demons. Ha! That is wonderfully delicious. He will love that."

"Who will love what?" G.J. is now actually interested in what the creature has to say.

"Daimhin. It sounds similar of course, so I can see where it sprang from, but it is funny."

"What are you talking about?"

"Your demons are a race of my kind. But the word is D A I M H I N. They are servants. We are their masters. You honestly believe you can control one of us?" The evil music of his laughter echoes off the industrial tile.

"Looks like Drake has you under control." G.J. lets that knowledge bleed the arrogance from the fae.

"I am limited by this pathetic, physical form. Humans could never control one of us. They summon our kind and we send our servants. Our servant does as you bid, and we reap the rewards as their masters. Do you honestly think we would put ourselves under the power of such a weak race? Humans are so pitiful. They call on us to give them power for so many ludicrous, selfish excuses. Their requests are so short sighted. And we… we get their souls. Their eternities for that one moment of vengeance, or greed, or gluttony, or lust. It really is delightfully easy. A human lifetime seems so short, but a human soul, ahhh, you never can truly comprehend eternity."

"What does eternity have to do with it? You eat souls. There is no forever. They are just gone."

The Fae's evil smile distorts Mr. Decker's face. "We need fuel to continue our existence. Souls are the embers within us that keep us living for eons. When we 'eat' a soul, it burns within us for eternity. That is the true definition of your Hell. Burning for all eternity within one of us. Being a part of all that we are. Consciously forever incinerated and aware of everything we chose to do. My race can be quite unkind. And your spirits are along for the ride. Some enjoy what we do, others suffer with the idea they are a party to how we go on. The more turmoil within the soul, the more power we reap."

I can't breathe. Hugo is somewhere burning for the rest of eternity. That sweet caring boy is now part of an evil being forever doing awful things.

"So, you are some kind of powerful being, huh?" G.J. asks but her mind is running a mile a minute. "What stops you from coming over and just taking over here?"

"We were sent back a long time ago. A traitorous race wanted this place all to themselves and tricked us back to our world, then slaughtered all the bridges. We had no way back. Until now." The Fae moves his gaze to me, and the corners of Mr. Decker's mouth turn up.

"What about this summoning thing? How can these Daimhin's come over but not you?"

"Like I said, we would never come if we were under the control of another being. The ones we send are our minions."

"Huh, but when you come, you have to take over a body?"

Really, G.J., now is the time for your knowledge hunger pang to strike?

"Our physical form remains in our world. It would take a rift to connect our worlds so our physical form could crossover. That has happened on a rare occasion. The last time was thousands of years ago. So long the creatures are only legends to your kind."

"I'll be right back," G.J. says, as she runs over to Adam and does what looks like grabbing his butt, before she darts out of the room.

"Drake, look, I'm not an expert at this world hopping thing, but I am the only one who can do it. Let me in your towering inferno and let me try to take that guy back. It is our only shot."

"No." He doesn't even raise his voice.

"What is your plan then? Offer free roasted marshmallows to the P.E. classes?"

Drake glowers at me and I scowl right back. This goes on for a few minutes until G.J. pops back in with one of her tomes. Plopping it and herself on the floor, she flips through the decrepit pages, scanning each one until the look of eureka takes over her face, and she thwaps her finger down non verbally declaring ah-ha!

Wriggling off the unnoticed backpack from her shoulders, she opens it and pulls out items. "We are going to exorcise him. Quickly and carefully draw a salt circle. Drake is your fire-nado based on centrifugal force?"

"I guess so."

"Well, it won't be perfect, but it will have to do. Use the fire as a guide." Pulling out some candles and a compass from a backpack, she follows me around the salt circle, setting the candles down when she gets to certain points. Just before I close the circle, she stops me by putting a hand on my arm and puts an open, small Tupperware container just inside and motions for me to finish closing it up.

"Drake, can you light the candles all at the same time for me?"

"Sure…"

"Try not to melt the candles before you do," G.J. instructs, "As soon as the candles are lit, you can drop the fire. The salt circle should hold him now. Nat, when I get to the part about water, spray this three times toward him. Don't let your arm cross over the salt. But hold it just over the candles. Move onto the next each time I repeat."

Kneeling back in front of her book, she pulls a generic spray bottle from her bag. She hands it over. Giving me an are-you-ready look, I confirm with a nod of agreement. She then begins to chant, "The body strong, tie the soul that belongs, the being unwanted now to be gone. Elements be true to what should be. Cast out the intruder, set this human free. I call fire to burn the tainted bond. Earth to strengthen the true soul." There is a rhythm to her words and her drawl smoothing out the cadence. G.J., with a flick of her hand, sends some dirt from a container inside the circle and toward Mr. Decker. "Wind drive away the unwanted." A breeze sweeps the room, flickering the candles. "Water to leave only this form's true spirit."

Quickly I realize that is my cue and pump the handle three times. After she chants, the first time through, the fake Mr. Decker looks a little less arrogant.

The second time around, Mr. Decker's face distorts. It kind of looks like pulling taffy between two images. By the third go round, he is lying on the floor, shaking.

When we finish the fourth candle, G.J. stands up and comes to me. "Okay, Nat, time to take him back. I'm going to open the circle real quick and you go grab that Fae fella and pop him back over to the Shadow World. I'd say take him back to his own, but we haven't played with that yet. So, the Shadow World will have to do."

"Huh?" is all the articulation I've got at the moment.

"What the hell, G.J.? No way. You don't know what can happen to her." Drake is all up in G.J.'s space prompting Hamilton and Adam to start their inevitable shoving match to protect her.

"Nat, you're all we've got. That Fae dude isn't connected to anything really right now. You have to get him out of here, or he will be loose, sucking souls and doing heaven only knows what else. I believe in you, Nat. Now go on." She swipes her foot on the floor opening up the circle and shoves me in. She quickly closes it.

Dumfounded, I stare at my bestie. Or should I say former bestie. This has to break the friend rules.

Drake goes nuts. He runs for the circle only to get slammed back by the world's most aggressive mime box. G.J. shoos me with her hands to get going. Nausea of fear squeezes my stomach hard. Turning, I take a deep breath, trying to inhale some courage. I mentally go over how I think going to the Shadow World should work. Peripherally the scuffle of the three boys continues in the room, but I shove away everything outside the circle. As soon as I feel ready, I suck in another huge breath and reach out for the Fae.

Chapter Thirty-Four

My first thought is holy crap it worked! My second is the same but with less enthusiasm. I let go of the Fae as soon as I remember I have a hold of him. Luckily, his buddies are nowhere to be seen. If I were to categorize the expression on his face, I would say hostile.

"Your friend holds an enormous amount of power. In all my time, I have never felt its equal in a human. She will be quite an acquisition to my own. I will have her."

"Yeah, she gets that a lot."

The Fae tilts his head. "You do not believe I can make it so."

"I believe there is a long line of Supernats and regular ole people who are in line ahead of you. So, add her to your Christmas list, too, and let me know how that works out."

"Her energy could give me the ability to change the hierarchy in my world. I could overthrow the court."

I can't really tell if he is thinking out loud or talking to me. "What is with you people? She is not your personal energizer bunny. First Mrs. Ackers, and now you nut jobs. At least the others just want her for well…"

"Leslie Ackers knew of your friend?" the Fae asks.

"You know Mrs. Ackers?" This is only mildly surprising.

"She helped us locate you. In exchange, we are to spare her daughter when we cross."

Even dead, that woman is trouble. "You know, I think she is playing both sides of the fence. She has been trying to get me to tell her daughter all kinds of stuff. None of which do I think you want her to know."

"She is who brought you to us. Leslie Ackers said she could make you bring us over. She told us if we were to stay near Hugo, you would appear."

"What does she get out of it? I doubt she gives a damn about Sara. That chick is out for numero uno."

"I get G.J.," says a voice I know way too well.

I turn. Mrs. Ackers is in her spooky form.

"G.J.? Lady, you have literally taken fixation to another dimension." Shaking my head, I try to express how crazy I think she is.

"G.J.? This is your friend with the power?" the Fae asks.

I nod.

Mrs. Ackers' eyes squint in annoyance, like I spilled the beans. *"She is who I will possess when I get back to the human world. No need to concern yourself with her. Just use Nat as the bridge as you had intended. I will take care of G.J.."*

"This G.J. changes our agreement. I will take her when we cross. I am not pleased you failed to mention one such as her. She will be mine."

"That wasn't part of the deal." Mrs. Ackers does a great impression of a spoiled three year old.

"You are correct. G.J. was never mentioned in our deal. Therefore she falls outside of its parameters." The Fae's eyes are as flat as a professional poker player's.

Mrs. Ackers' expression gives away the fact that her mind is desperately seeking a retort to help her win. From the looks of it, she is coming up short.

I offer my helpful input. "You know… the Fae are kind of known for their negotiating skills. They usually win. It's best not to try."

"I have worked too hard to just let him have her. That girl!" Mrs. Ackers takes a second to bring her tone down from a shriek. *"First that wolf sends me here. That was all her fault."*

"Or yours for being a selfish psycho," I interject.

"It should have been dead, but she healed it. Who knew she could do such a thing? They needed to pay. I watched and waited. Jack doesn't have the control over his pack that he believes. And G.J. isn't the best at making friends in her new position as beta. It was easy to persuade Lucas to get rid of her. If weakened, with the help of my coven, they could help me possess her. I would have all of that power."

Mrs. Ackers' eyes roll up in her head, like she is enjoying a private moment of pleasure just thinking about the idea. *"But Lucas feared Jack enough he didn't want to do it himself. So he called in a favor from an old friend. I had no objection to the use of the Vampires at the time. They were to drain her down and stay with her until Sara could bring the coven and perform the ritual allowing me to take control of her. She would be weak and it would've been easy. But Gus intervened. He chased away the vampire, and the wolves found her before the coven could get there. The stupid vampire became obsessed with G.J., and in a ravenous rage has been killing girls repeatedly who even remotely look like her."*

"But the killings have been going on from before G.J. was attacked. Hugo was killed by a vampire." I am trying to piece everything together.

"Lucas's friend came to town and of course, they had to feed while they were there." Mrs. Ackers simply dismisses the murder of several people.

Sociopathic much?

"But I discovered you can come here. I followed you the day that boy brought you to where the Fae world meets the Shadow World. I heard what he told you. And I thought if they can cross over, maybe I can too. So, I started sending all the newly dead their way. That helped the Fae get here. Then I told them if they followed Hugo, he would lead them to you. Hugo was so gullible. Anytime I mentioned you might want to know something, off he scampered. Ahh, young love, how pliable it can make you. Ha! What did he think was going to happen between the two of you? He was truly pathetic."

My hatred of this woman seems limitless. Rage boils the blood in my veins.

"Little bridge. I feel as though you and I can strike a bargain." The Fae moves right behind me and leans down in my ear. "It is a simple one and only requires you to visit the Shadow World again."

The two other fae appear out of nowhere. My neck tingles with apprehension. I know better than this. I know, I know better than this. "Why would I bargain with you?"

"We can remove this trouble you have… permanently." The two Fae surround Mrs. Ackers.

"I can't have someone killed."

"She is dead. There is no killing necessary. She will be gone in a way where she can never again cause you or the ones you care for any harm. It is a simple solution to your problem."

"And what about you? Will you harm the people I care for?"

"I will not. The one I crave is on her way to becoming what I cannot have. The transition is not complete yet, but before long, I suspect she will be lost to the way of the wolf."

Mrs. Ackers is completely still and I realize the Fae have her in some kind of spell. She isn't reacting at all to our conversation of her removal from existence. "What do you want from me?"

He smiles and it almost seems friendly… almost. "You will visit me here. Every three human months. You will tell me of what goes on in your world. It has been so very long and I do miss those humans."

"That is it? Just come tell you about my world. Nothing else?"

"I would be very interested in knowing about your friend's family. That is all."

"She doesn't have any. She's an orphan. She lives with her Aunt, but her Aunt isn't gifted."

"Well, then, you can tell me of yours."

"Mine left as soon as they knew what I was."

"You have been abandoned by your line?"

"I'm not sure."

The Fae turns me to face him. "When you are sure, please, know I will take you in hand."

I may not have G.J.'s brain, but even I can tell that is more a threat than a kindness. "I will not take you to my world. And I will only come three times."

"You will come for ten years."

"One year."

"Five years."

"Two years."

"Rather than debating this, I will tell you three years is as few times as I will allow. Or I will release Leslie Ackers and she will continue to try to obtain your friend."

Protect G.J., just protect G.J.. She would do this for you.

"Three years but I won't take anyone back with me."

"Was that so hard?" The Fae runs his finger down my cheek. "What a treasure I have found." His face is pleased, my stomach not so much.

One of his buddies beings to end Mrs. Ackers for the last time. I let go of the Shadow World and head back to my own.

Chapter Thirty-Five

When my eyes open, they are maybe eight inches from Drake's. He holds me against him, the corners of his eyes crinkled in concern. Flicking my gaze away, I note we are still in the locker room shower area.

"Nat? Are you okay?" Drake's fingers gently run through my hair, leaving warm tracks on my scalp.

I sit up, moving away from the intimacy as I do.

"Hey what happened? Why did it take you so long to get back?" G.J. gives me her hand to help me up.

Shaking my head, I try to sort out where to begin. Should I tell my friends I bargained to end Mrs. Ackers. What does that make me? Am I now a murderer? I grab G.J.'s hand and get to my feet. For having recently been the scene of an inferno, the locker room looks good.

"Nat?" A note in G.J.'s voice rings with concern.

"There is a lot to go over. Let's get back to the house. I'll tell you all at once."

****

Back at the house, Jack has some big news. He set up a video conference with my parents. When they come on the screen, I can barely make them out through the tears in my eyes.

"Oh, Nat, honey. We are so sorry it has to be this way. We love you so much."

"You love me? You just left. You didn't even return a phone call."

"We weren't sure what it would take to cross back over. There has never been a bridge while technology has been in existence. I am so sorry, baby." My mother tries desperately to explain her unexplainable actions.

An arm wraps around my shoulder and I realize Drake is attached to it.

"Is this the young man you mentioned in your voicemail? I will set up an appointment with my gynecologist as soon as possible."

"You what?" Both Jack and my dad yell at the same time.

"Really, Mom? You have been gone for weeks and within two minutes of talking to me you go there in front of every-one." I can't tell who is more uncomfortable Drake or me.

Half-sentences fall out of Drake's mouth. All are some assemblance of, "Jack, I haven't… I mean we haven't… Not that I don't … I mean…" He only stops when I use my elbow to knock the air out of him.

"Ever since your call, I have been so worried. None of us have ever dated outside the race. We have no idea what it will take to get you pregnant or what disease you can catch."

Oy, mother, please stop talking.

"Let's move on shall we." G.J. proves she should have the BFF title by getting me out of that awful awkward.

"Why don't you tell us what you know?" Jack thankfully allows the subject change.

Taking a deep breath, my mom says, "We are Fae. We have been here since the time before. That is what we call the time when the worlds connected by bridges. Bridges didn't just connect this world to the Fae world but could connect all worlds. The human world was desirable for many reasons. Humans are such interesting creatures. The passion, pain, joy, the love are fascinating to our kind and many others as well. The regency of our kind discovered if they obtained the souls of humans, they increased their power. The more powerful they became, the more they wanted. It soon became clear they wouldn't stop until the humans were annihilated. The stronger the emotion the human died with, the more power they conveyed to the Fae who consumed them. It was horrible to watch humans be manipulated into extremes and murdered. So, some of us decided to end the connection between the worlds." My mom's voice breaks, and her eyes plead with me to understand.

My dad picks up the informational session lead. "We tricked the Fae who were the worst of the offenders and sent them back. Then all the bridges were eliminated as were any Fae who remained and crossed the line."

"Killed you mean," I interrupt.

My dad gives me his annoyed face. "Yes, Nat, killed." He sighs and continues, "We never considered we could create a bridge by reproducing. Our conference decided it was time to allow select couples to have offspring again. Nat was one of the first Fae children in a few thousand years."

"Wait. What?"

"You are one of the first. We shouldn't have created a bridge. Our conference believes there must be a reason you were created, but since we have no desire to repeat the past, we will halt our conception allowances until the humans are ready."

"What do you mean until the humans are ready?" Celia asks.

"Humanity is amazing. They adapt so quickly. A few centuries ago, some of our kind had the idea of preparing for the worst. The Fae returning. They noticed that the humans they spent the most time with, well their children became harder to read. We decided to try to enhance that, and we spread out around the globe. We used to stay close together in clusters. The idea was to expose as many humans to us as possible and see if they built up an immunity. It seems to be working."

"In what way?" Celia asks.

"Many humans are building up a resistance to our kind. The humans call the ones most resistant autistic. There is also ADHD. Some humans have seen it as a problem, but it is what we are hoping will help. As with any evolution, nature has kinks to work out, but we are progressing toward a humanity the Fae cannot consume or control."

"That is why you couldn't read Megan." G.J. loves any kind of science stuff her eyes glow in fascination.

"You tried to read an autistic? Nat, you could have been killed."

"Well, would've saved you some trouble?" I snipe at my mother.

"Nat, don't say such things to your mom. We don't want to hurt you. We just can't be near you. Jack and Celia have agreed you could stay with them until... Why would you have tried to read this Megan person? You should have had a natural aversion." My dad acts like he is mad at me.

"I did. But I thought I was being a jerk by treating her differently." I can't believe I have to defend myself to a parent, who walked away from me.

"You don't have to be rude to them. They are just people, but please, follow your instincts about reading them. It is a wonder you survived," my mother says.

"Thanks for the tip, it would've been great if you had mentioned any of this before you abandoned me."

My mother starts in a pleading tone, "Nat—"

Celia steps in, "There are a good deal of legitimate hurt feelings that aren't going to get resolved right now. G.J., why don't you bring them up to speed with what we know."

I'm betting she doesn't call on me in order to give me time to calm down. I love Celia.

When G.J. is done, I tell everyone about Mrs. Ackers. Jack is fuming. I omit the part about me having to visit the Fae for the next three years. I'm sure that won't go over well, and I can't stand the idea of freaking my parents out even more. It would be like me proving them right.

"So Leslie was eaten by one of those things?" Celia asks rather horrified.

I nod, unable to muster up a verbal response.

"Nat, we do love you. Please believe that. We will try to remain in contact now you seem to have more control and this seems to be a safe way to communicate. The others are very concerned, but we will handle them. Just stay away from the Shades if you can. We will see you soon." And with a flicker of the screen, my parents are gone again.

"Okay, at least one threat is gone, G.J.." Jack moves to his assessing the sitch mode. "Gus was apparently not the main issue but could still be a threat. This other Vampire or Vampires are a problem for not only G.J. and Nat, but the humans around here as well. That has to be resolved. Lucas will be brought up on charges at the next pack meeting. Once that is done, things should settle down and get back to normal."

G.J. starts to laugh. "Normal. Ha! Good one, Jack."

"What about G.J. being a wolf?" Celia asks.

"We should know more about that in the next few weeks. Until then, we are in wait and see mode. We can't really predict that outcome yet," Jack says. "We need to keep working on how to keep you and our little one in there safe." Jack enfolds Celia in his arms, placing one hand on her belly.

Dude, watching them makes you want to be in love.

"I think we need to keep an eye on Mr. Decker. He was really shaken up after his possession. He seemed kind of aware of what was happening. He was very apologetic to G.J.. He believes he kissed her. He talked about turning himself in." I add to the list.

"Great. Just what I want. To be the Lolita that tempted Principal Decker. No. Thank you so much for the offer, but I would prefer to be not linked to him. I can't even imagine our celebrity name combo." G.J. is in her ranting finest.

Someone grabs my hand and tugs. Drake seems unwilling to let go. "Can I talk to you?" He tries to be discrete, but that isn't possible when you live with werewolves.

"Why not?" I shrug. I feel Jack's gaze as Drake leads me into the hallway.

"Nat, here are some truths. I want to date you. I want to be honest with you. I want to be able to tell you anything you ask. I just can't. Not the date part. We can do that. If you want. But we will just have to keep it low key. And as long as it doesn't involve my dad, I can be honest and tell you anything you ask. I will sort out this crap about G.J.. I really can't talk about it, but I don't want to go out with her. I want to go out with you. Can you give me a chance? Even if it means I can't tell you that stuff?"

Damn his beautiful stupid eyes. He looks so stinking sincere. "Dumbass, why didn't you just say so."

"Wait. What?"

"You could have just said that, and we could have skipped all the other nonsense. Seriously, Drake, I understand the way of the secret. There is a difference between withholding things from me and keeping someone else's confidence. I am not completely unreasonable. You should trust me in the future to know the difference."

"I did try to tell you. A few times even. Wait... in the future?"

"Yeah, when this comes up again in our relationship."

"Relationship?— So you're my girlfriend?" Drake tugs on my hand he is still holding, pulling me closer.

"I don't know how I am going to feel about sneaking around. It could be fun." My cheeks lift with my impish grin.

Drake pulls me even closer the corners of his mouth matching mine.

"Settle down, tiger. I only said that stuff to my mom to get a reaction out of her." I turn so I can poke him in the chest.

"Oh sure. I wouldn't presume..." I have no idea what he was going to say next because I shut him up with a kiss.

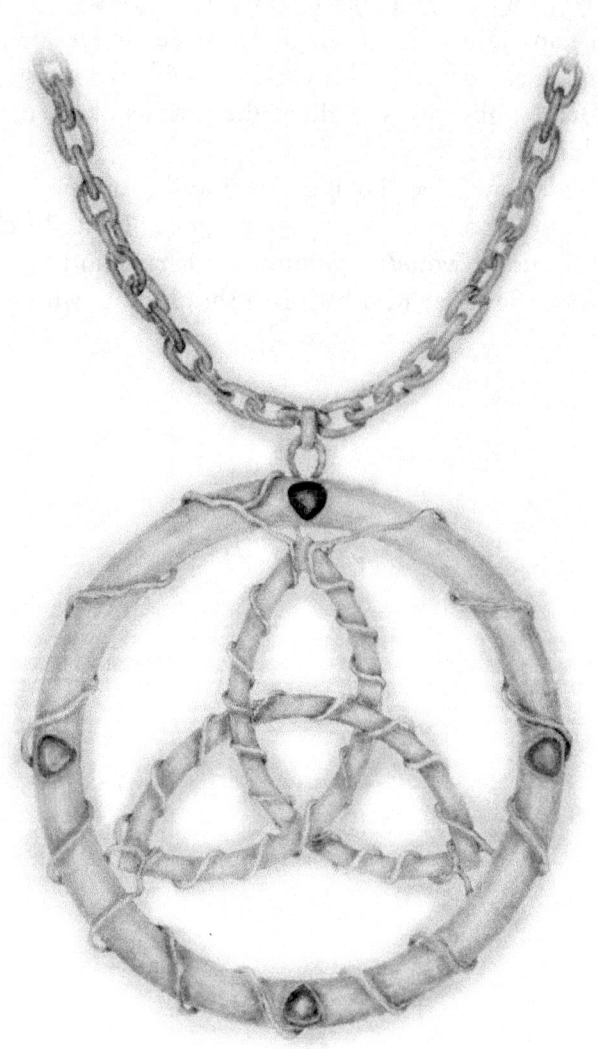

Epilogue

When G.J. brings Drake up to speed on her plan to keep my mind, body, and spirit as a collector's set things get weird again. We are in the Wyfle great room. G.J. as far away from Hamilton and Adam as she can get. She is curled up in a chair sipping a glass of water while she fills him in. Drake and I are on the sofa close together. Adam is on the far side of the sofa slouched down with his legs out stretched, and Hamilton is leaning on the wall by the entry.

"What is it you need from the coven?" Drake asks thoughtfully stroking his chin.

"I need to light the four compass points at the same time. And it wouldn't hurt to have a little magical boost and focus." G.J. responds but in her thinking two steps further kind of way.

"I might be able to help," Drake says a little too casually.

"How can you help?" Now her focus is squarely on Drake.

Immediately all the candles in the room light as well as a blazing fire in the hearth. Drake's arrogant smile I am growing to love creeps across his face.

"Well, I can do that." G.J. huffs. "I need to focus on binding Nat though."

"Try to do something and see if I can't help you focus," Drake prompts.

"Why would you be able to help me focus?"

"Just try it," Drake urges again.

"What do you want me to try?"

"Whatever you want." He grabs my hand.

"All right." G.J. survey's the room and then nods deciding on something. The sofa we are on lifts in the air. Adam, who was not fully seated, slides to the ground. His reflexes have him landing in a crouch. She swaps out the sofa and the love seat and settles everything back into place in the precise spot as before. The dents in the rug perfectly lined up.

"Are you finished?" Drake asked.

"Wow. Yeah. That was awesome. I mean, I normally can do stuff sure, but the control was spot on. Why did that work so well?" G.J.'s eyes are wide and a bright smile changes her normally pretty to totally stunning.

One or both of the wolves in the room let out a little whimper.

Drake shifts and then shrugs. "You and I work well together because of genetics. It's a long story."

"Is that why your daddy wants us to shack up?" G.J. pulls no punches and asks basically what I wanted to know.

Another shrug, this one seeming to usher all the blood that can get there into Drake's cheeks. The wolves of course make the room rumble in synchronized lupine disapproval.

G.J. squints her eyes in speculation and just says, "Huh."

"You don't feel the need to elaborate." I nudge Drake with an elbow to the ribs.

Dropping my hand, he puts an arm around my shoulders and whispers in my ear, "This is one of those I want to but I can't deals."

I sigh in annoyance.

"He's not gonna spill is he?" G.J. asks.

"Nope." The "p" popping a little as the sound leaves my mouth.

"Anyway, I'm just pointing out you may not need the coven."

"You aren't going out there with her." Hamilton the persuasive snarls from the far side of the room.

"Why not?" Drake is way more relaxed than Hamilton.

"Because the ritual is done in the nude." It has to be hard for Hamilton to form words without his jaw being able to move.

"Nooooo, I found another one. So you can stop with all that over bearing nonsense. Geez, you'd think traipsing around in what the good Lord gave you was against one of the commandments. Meanwhile I can't tell you the number of fannies I have seen living in this house. Why is my naked so off putting, but these boys drop their drawers every hot second?"

"Trust me, G.J., you naked is NOT off-putting," Adam assures her.

"Shut up, Adam!" Hamilton starts toward Adam who had stayed on the floor and just rested his back against the sofa when it had returned. Three steps toward him and his begins to float.

"Boy, I have told you, I won't put up with that. Why do you refuse to believe me?" G.J. doesn't even seem to be paying attention to Hamilton dangling in the air. "Anyway, I have been working on a pendant design give me a second. G.J. jogs out of the room. A second later, Hamilton drops to the ground, and she yells from somewhere in the house, "Sorry."

When she comes back, she hands Drake a rough drawing of the triquetra surrounded by a circle. At the top bottom and both sides there are spots on the circle. "So my thought was the triquetra representing her, mind, body, and spirit surrounded by a protection circle that calls on the four compass points to help give her direction should she need it to get back in her own skin."

"Wow, G.J., this is really powerful." Drake's hand has a tremor when he takes the picture. "Can I borrow this for a few days?"

Shrugging, G.J. says, "Sure."

****

When Drake returns to the Wyfle's a few days later, he has a box with him. Handing it to me, he says, "We need G.J. to juice it up, but I made this for you."

I sit on the sofa in the great room and open the box. The lid creaks a little as I lift it. Inside is a real life version of the drawing G.J. had made. It is absolutely stunning. In the four spots on the outside of the circle there are the most beautiful stones. The pearlescent green unlike anything I have ever seen before. I look up at him speechless.

"If you don't like it, you don't have to use it." Drake is rubbing his hands down his legs in an uncharacteristically nervous gesture.

I grab his hand. "Drake, I–love it." This is the most beautiful thing I have ever seen, and I am so overwhelmed that he made it for me.

A gigantic grin takes over his whole face.

"What are you smiling at?" Adam comes in sourly ruining the moment.

"What's wrong with him?" Drake is taken aback at Adam's demeanor.

"Hamilton and G.J. are on their walk." I use air quotes around the last word. I had told Drake about Hamilton's confession and request in one of our late night phone conversations. It is hard to get off the phone with this boy.

His mouth makes a soundless oh. "It'll be all right man. You should take her for a walk too. The girl loves the woods. I'm sure she would go."

"Yeah, I know. I just don't like them alone together. The dude might care about her, but he and his dad have both done bodily harm to her. I don't care what the intentions are it makes my hackles rise to leave her in his care."

"Where is his dad?" Drake asks sitting on the arm of the sofa next to me.

Adam looks away. "He's locked up until the pack meeting. Dad has an old friend coming in to be an impartial judge so everything will be on the up and up."

"Is Jack around? I was hoping Nat and I could go out tonight, and I know he wants me to run it past him."

"What about running it past me?" I nudge Drake with my arm.

"No point in getting your hopes up if Jack says no." Drake nudges me right back.

"God, you guys are so cute." Adam draws out the last two words. Then, he mimes barfing into his hands.

"Adam," Jack calls sharply from the foyer. "They are here."

"Time to go be charming." Adam stands with a rather evident lack of enthusiasm in his slow movements.

Curious, we follow Adam out the front door. Two very tall men are standing on the drive, unloading luggage from the back of the biggest pick-up truck I have ever seen. The blue paint gleams in the afternoon sun. Jack who has to be six foot-six or six foot-seven is shorter than both these guys by at least a couple inches, but Jack has them in muscle mass. Coming down the front steps, Jack says in a low but friendly voice, "L.J. it's good to see you. Thank you for coming all this way."

"Jack, now how could I pass up dis opportunity to come roun' here an' meet cho new woman." This L.J. has a thicker southern accent than G.J.. L.J. looks around, as if trying to find Celia.

"Settle, old man. She will be home soon. She had some appointments today," Jack says, wrapping the other man in a bear hug.

The other man turned and put two large duffle bags on the ground. L.J. coming out of the embrace puts his hand on the obviously younger man's shoulder and says, "Dis here is ma boy, lil' Louie."

Louie, rubs his right hand down his worn jeans, then reaches for Jack's to shake. "Pleasure to me cho, Mr. Wyfle." His accent as rich as his fathers.

Holy Cannoli, this boy is stunning. He has his father's almost blue-black hair but his has more curl to it. Although L.J's is graying at the temples in the wings that add to a man's appearance. Louie's cocoa golden skin emphasizes the muscles on his arms. And his eyes are that caramel color so common to the wolves I know. He flashes a grin toward us and I remember Drake is standing right next to me. God, I hope I'm not actually drooling.

"Nat, Drake, these are my friends the Garots." The last name has a French sound to it as Jack says it. "Nat is under my protection."

L.J. examines me for a minute, then eyes Jack. "Zat right."

Jack nods once.

"And you boy, you don't belong to dis here pack. Who you people?"

"I'm an Aldrich," Drake answers in a cool tone.

L.J. rocks back on his heels and spins his attention to Jack. "Whew boy, Jack, I say we gots to do some catchin' up right quick." Smiling L.J. shakes his head like he can't believe what he is hearing. "What is goin' on round here?" The way his says the last sentence reminds me of a train chugging up hill. When he gets to the end, it is almost a shout.

Louie begins to bend to pick up the luggage, then freezes half way down. His posture seems alert and his head comes up scenting the air. Straightening up with the bags forgotten, he turns his whole body toward the woods. Seconds later, G.J. stomps out of the woods with Hamilton right behind her.

Of course they are bickering; I expected nothing less, but I fear this is not going to end well. I pop in Louie's head: "*She. Mine. It is She. She is wolf? She IS wolf!*" Uh-Oh.

Louie lets out an ear splitting noise that sounds like, "Eeewww- weee"

At that, G.J.'s head comes up. Whatever Hamilton was saying is left in the air behind her as she races toward us. Reaching Louie, she jumps on his torso like a flying Koala. He grabs her and spins her in a circle, burying his face in her neck and inhaling, like his lungs have no bottom.

Hamilton jogs up seething at the two unable to find words.

All of our reactions are completely dumbfounded. After a really long hug, G.J. slides down, but Louie keeps her in the circle of his arms only allowing her to pull far enough away to look up at him.

"Wha—How—Why are you here?" G.J. starts and stops three times before landing on her first question.

L.J. says, through a smile that reaches from one ear to the other, "Now dis here is lagniappe. Dat boy been missin' her fierce."

"Louie, it has been a minute." G.J. squeezes this incredibly hot boy again.

"Where y'at?" Louie says.

"Been good. Missin' mama. But can't complain," G.J. responds.

It is like they are speaking English, but the words don't mean the same thing.

Louie takes his hand and slides it over G.J.'s head, "Aw, Cher, I have been missin' you boo coo."

Well, maybe not exactly English.

G.J. laughs and slides her arm around his waist turning to face the rest of us. "Y'all this is my friend from Louisiana." She gives him a side squeeze.

"I didn't realize you knew each other." Jack eyes the distance between his boys and this new one.

"Are y'all stayin' here?" G.J. practically sings through her smile.

"Hell, no!" Hamilton objects.

Drake pulls me behind him a little as everyone's eyes light up with the telltale amber of wolfie ire.

Oh Hamilton, you poor, poor stupid boy.

www.ingramcontent.com/pod-product-compliance
Lightning Source LLC
Chambersburg PA
CBHW062025170626
46813CB00001B/298